# MAGNIFICENT FAREWELL

# Karen J. Hasley

This is a work of fiction. The characters described herein are imaginary and are not intended to refer to living persons.

ISBN-13: 978-1517796464
ISBN-10: 1517796466

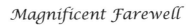
*Magnificent Farewell*

To commemorate the anniversary of the end of World War One — November 11, 1918 — and to honor the valiant men and women who served and suffered in so many ways during *The Great War*

Cover: Helen Johns Kirtland in trench during World War I, Women Photojournalists Collection, Library of Congress, LC-USZ62-115862

3

# Prologue

From the very start—although for a long time I didn't know or care or even understand that it was important—what set Lucy Rose March and me as far apart as earth and stars was that I always ran from and Lucy always ran toward. We were two young women caught up in the same war on the same continent at the same time. But Lucy March, with her unruly hair and clear, serious gaze seemed always to be looking out at a bright horizon that only she could see. And I—well, I was a hunted thing and so had to keep a watchful eye on the shadows behind me to be certain they did not conceal my pursuers. Running toward. Running from. Looking ahead. Looking behind. A small distinction, one might think, and hardly significant enough to make a difference in the midst of a war that devastated a continent, laid waste thousands of towns and villages, and annihilated an entire generation of young men. But it would be wrong to underrate the contrast between looking ahead and looking back because in the end it made all the difference in the world. In our worlds, anyway, Lucy's and mine. And Mac's world, too, of course. Perhaps his most of all.

War broke: and now the Winter of the world
With perishing great darkness closes in.
For after Spring had bloomed in early Greece,
And summer blazed her glory out with Rome,
An Autumn softly fell, a harvest home,
A slow grand age, and rich with wild increase.
But now, for us, wild Winter, and the need
Of sowing for new Spring, and blood for seed.

*Wilfred Owen*

# Part One – 1917

# *"~summer blazed her glory~"*

# Chapter 1

Lucille Rose March and I crossed the Atlantic on the *Ausonia*, strangers then, our only bond the ability to maintain an appetite during rough seas. Had the crossing been calmer or had either of us been prone to sea sickness, I doubt we'd have made an acquaintance. I was traveling alone and she was with a cadre of Red Cross nurses, all of us en route from New York to Southampton, England, and as I would later discover sharing the same final destination of Calais, France. The *Ausonia*, originally called the *Tortona* before it was sold and renamed, could carry over a thousand passengers, but by 1917 people were not as eager as they'd once been to travel to England or to the European continent. The fates of the passenger ships *Lusitania* in 1915 and the *Britannic* the following year had dampened the American public's enthusiasm for Atlantic travel, even if one was a citizen of a country that had remained ostensibly neutral in the great conflict rampaging its way through France and Belgium. Now with war between Germany and the United States official and public, the American flag our ship displayed no doubt had the same effect as a brightly painted target of concentric rings painted on the prow. My fellow passengers and I were reminded daily of our vulnerability through regular mandatory fire and boat drills during which I wondered with vague curiosity if I would have the coordination needed to climb down the slippery rope ladder that led to the life boats. I was afraid of very little in those days but couldn't quite see myself in the role of an acrobat.

It was during the first boat drill that I first noticed Lucy Rose March. I didn't know her name then, of course, and she was a nondescript figure at first sight, but once she volunteered to climb down the rope ladder she was impossible to ignore. A slight young woman, she wore a heavy cape that slid to the deck as she straightened her thin shoulders. After a hasty tug with both hands to her hat, the unlikely volunteer swung herself over the edge and onto the ladder with quick grace and disappeared from view. I heard a smattering of applause from some of the passengers and crew when her head—and eventually the rest of her—reappeared above the rail. Someone stepped forward to help her back onto the deck and another person scooped up her cloak and threw it around her shoulders again. Before my eyes, the valiant, lithe little monkey disappeared and became once more the unexceptional woman I'd first seen, young and somewhat gawky with a thin face that ended in a firm, pointed chin, a light sprinkle of freckles across both cheeks, and dark eyes. A likeable little thing, I thought at the time, but peculiar. Why would any woman volunteer for such a grandstanding task? I had seen and heard enough to know that only a torpedo would send me over the railing on a rope ladder. Anything less than that and I'd take my chances with both feet firmly planted on deck.

We both appeared for breakfast at exactly the same time the next morning and under normal circumstances doing so would probably not have necessitated our exchanging any kind of greeting. Even with the *Ausonia* carrying only half her maximum number of travelers, there would have been no reason for me to acknowledge Miss March. One person can be easily ignored, even lost, among a few hundred strangers, and because I both desired and cultivated anonymity, I was prepared to pass people by without word or eye contact. As it was that particular morning, however, even with the firmest resolution to maintain my privacy, I could see that the two of us standing there staring into the sparsely populated dining room would have to interact in some way. The few passengers already breakfasting were seated in multiples, and there was no one else anywhere in our vicinity. No waiting line ahead of us. No one to whom I could turn as if we were acquaintances and so bypass the plain woman that stood beside me. No one coming up behind us. No one else anywhere at all.

"Apparently my companions are not the only ones made miserable by the choppy seas," the young woman by my side observed. I recognized her as the volunteer ladder climber from yesterday's boat drill.

After a silence that bordered on the rude, I finally responded, "Apparently not."

She smiled at me. "How do you do? I'm Lucy Rose March. Please forgive any presumption but would you care to share a breakfast table?"

It was something I most certainly did not care to do but with no way out of the invitation, I responded, "It's no presumption, Miss March. With so few passengers possessed of sea legs, it makes sense that we should share one table. I'm Meg Pritchard." We did not bother to attempt a handshake but followed the steward to a nearby table and sat across from one another.

"All the members of my traveling party are incapacitated, though I think the worst is over and they're on the way to recovery. I feel guilty for being so hungry, but I can't help it." She smoothed the napkin across her lap and raised her gaze to mine. "I saw you yesterday at the boat drill. You're very kind not to remind me of the part I played in it."

"You displayed admirable balance," I murmured.

She gave an audible chuckle. "No doubt I displayed more than balance," she admitted in a rueful tone. "My father always says face your fears and get them behind you. That's what I believe and that's what I was trying to do during that drill, but I'm afraid that even he would never have allowed that behavior. He has such high hopes that I will one day learn to comport myself like a lady."

I smiled at her words but didn't speak. Timed to her comment, a steward appeared at our table, announced the morning's menu, and took our requests. Lucy March, possessed of an appetite as unladylike as her forthright behavior, ordered a large, hearty platter of breakfast and allowed a beatific smile to curve her features.

"I fear the ocean air has made me hungry."

"It would seem so." I had the grace to soften my words with a small smile, but her expression remained completely unabashed.

"You're traveling alone, Miss Pritchard? Or is it Mrs. Pritchard?"

"Miss, and yes, I'm traveling alone."

"How brave of you—" I did not detect anything mocking in her words but knew a moment of suspicion, nevertheless "— to travel into a continent at war. There's every reason to expect a perilous journey."

"I anticipate it being something of a lark," I replied, annoyed at her placid observation that hinted I might not be literate enough to read newspapers. Tired of trite conversation, I thought, let's see what kind of reaction I can poke from this self-composed young woman.

"A lark," she repeated. For all her calm, I could tell my blasé words had jarred her. Presenting myself as coolly avant-garde—a new French term I'd recently come across—would be just the thing to ensure that my companion did not try to further this chance breakfast encounter with future interactions. I did not travel across oceans and continents for the purpose of making social contacts. Just the opposite.

Except for repeating my final two words, Miss March said nothing. Her dark gaze, however, rested on my face with enough grave thoughtfulness that I could almost have been made to feel uncomfortable except that the *Ausonia* chose that moment to lurch and rattle the silverware on all the tables and immediately after the ship settled, the steward appeared with the cart carrying our breakfasts. Miss March dropped her attention to her meal, I did the same, and neither of us spoke for quite a while.

After I had finished my meal, I lit a cigarette and waited for Miss March to place a dollop of marmalade on her last morsel of toast and pop it into her mouth. She caught me watching her and grinned.

"My duty as a nurse compels me to eat on behalf of all my traveling companions presently unable to participate in a meal. A sacrifice, of course, but the Red Cross counts no cost too great to maintain our solidarity of purpose."

Despite myself, I smiled in return. The grin and the sparkle in her eyes made her thin, lightly-freckled face suddenly engaging, even charming.

"Nursing demands a certain nobility of character I've been told."

"You're not in the medical profession, are you?" Lucy March surprised me by asking. "I could somehow see you as a doctor."

"I in a medical profession?" The incredulity and horror in my tone made her smile again.

"Is the idea so very preposterous?"

"I haven't the slightest desire to care for the sick," I answered, making no attempt to mask the aversion I felt for the idea. "I'm impatient and spoiled and I possess none of the tender emotions necessary for the vocation."

"Of course, I should have realized the obvious. I'm sorry for my impertinence." Her few words, spoken with fervent agreement and the hint of a smile, carried the tone of an apology but were not apologetic in the least. Instead, they gave the distinct impression of something not complimentary, something even mocking. I realized with quick clarity that Miss Lucy March had just put me in my place and had done so quite neatly, every word perfectly tuned and on the surface acceptable, even humble.

I shrugged, accepting her disapproval. "I'm sure I deserved that, Miss March. Now if you'll excuse me—" I gathered my bag and gloves and stood. "Thank you for the breakfast company. I hope your companions feel better soon."

She nodded, looking up at me from her breakfast chair. "I'll pass your good wishes along to them. I'm sure they'll be up to a meal soon, but if not—"

"I know. Solidarity of purpose. Hopefully, your keen sacrifice will be noticed and rewarded." I stepped past her through the dining room and out onto the deck.

Much of my life had been spent on the water lounging on fine yachts and sleek sailboats, and as a child I had learned to swim with the natural fluidity of a fish. I'd never been sea sick a day in my life and had no sympathy for the malady. Another reason—if I needed one—for avoiding anything to do with a medical profession. At the time I believed that illness had the power to incapacitate a person only if she chose to allow it to do so. With the arrogance of a woman of strong constitution and even stronger will, I hardly believed in illness at all, only that it was a weakness to be overcome by strength of will and mind. But I was young and arrogant and foolish then and had not experienced war firsthand, had not yet seen how a mortar shell could shatter the human body or what mustard gas could do to human lungs. All that still lay in the future.

The next morning Lucy March appeared with three other young women in the dining room and stopped by the table where I sat long enough to greet me and make introductions. In appearance she was the slightest of the four nurses of her party, and I would have guessed the least vivacious of them, as well, but for all her wallflower potential, neither her smile nor that steady, dark gaze could be ignored. I had the suspicion that opposing Miss March over anything about which she felt passionate would be a risky venture.

"I'm glad to see you're all up and about," I said. "Fully recovered, I hope."

A short, plump girl introduced herself before answering, "I won't be fully recovered until I'm standing on solid ground, but I think I can keep something down and I'm hungry enough to try." The others nodded agreement and the four of them moved away from my table to take seats on the other side of the room. As I ate my breakfast, I was able to hear their laughter and chatter, and after a few minutes I felt, more than saw, someone's presence next to me. I looked up again at Miss March.

"Would you like to join us?" she asked without preamble. "I should have thought to ask you. I'm sorry. There's no reason you should have to be all alone."

Suspicious of kindness, I was more brusque than I needed to be. "No, thank you. I'm quite content with my own company."

She nodded. "I am, too, actually, but sometimes there's comfort to be found with others."

"Not in my experience." The words came out abrupt and disdainful.

She considered my comment before nodding and saying slowly, "Yes, well, perhaps it depends on who the others are."

"Perhaps." I was not interested in continuing the conversation.

A bright woman despite her nondescript air, Miss March read my tone accurately and concluded with, "Well, I wanted you to know we would enjoy your company." I gave a shrug and a slight smile of acknowledgement and she returned to her companions.

The next few days of the trip passed uneventfully. Once recovered from seasickness, other people materialized on deck and in the dining rooms and the increased numbers offered the anonymity I had not been able to find when surrounded by fewer faces. The swell of travelers suited me. I was not traveling to France to make friends. In fact, the fewer persons to notice my presence the better. I smiled and made cursory conversation when necessary but showed only a shallow interest in the affairs of my fellow travelers and volunteered no personal information of my own. Despite my intention of keeping to myself, I usually met Lucy March somewhere on deck at least once a day. There was nothing intrusive or compelling about her and she always looked surprised to see me, but in her own unique way she managed to make our sharing a stroll seem so natural and inevitable that it became a daily ritual almost without my realizing it. Sometimes I even caught myself looking up and down the hall for her when I stepped out of my cabin, as if she should be waiting there specifically for my appearance.

Once the seas calmed, I noticed a change in the ship's rhythm and commented on it to Miss March as she fell into step beside me one evening, bundled as usual in her woolen cloak with her pale, narrow face shadowed by the heavy hood.

"Have you noticed the change in people's conversations, too?" she asked. At my blank look, she went on, "There's too much laughter, and I hear a kind of jerkiness to everyone's words. We must have hit Channel waters." Looking over at me, she added, "That change in the feel of the ship, a kind of zigzag motion, is the prescribed course for eluding anything or anyone that might be on our tail."

"I hope it's a successful strategy for evading torpedoes."

"I don't see how it can be successful, not really. I mean, if I've heard about the tactic, the German submarine captains must also be aware of it and have worked out some kind of counter ploy." She sounded remarkably cheerful about being a bull's-eye for a German submarine, and I had to laugh.

"I suppose being stoic in the face of disaster is a prerequisite for a nurse," I observed.

"Do I sound stoic?" Her expression held sincere surprise. "Believe me, I'm not, not in the least. I may sleep in my life belt, but I'm not anxious to try it out. I dislike cold weather, in general and would especially hate being drenched in cold water."

"But didn't you say your hospital was somewhere on the northern coast of France?"

"I'm afraid so. Unfortunately, no one asked my advice before selecting the hospital's location so I'm headed for St. Valery-en-Caux." Her pronunciation of the name with an accent that held a touch of the American South made me wince, and I repeated the village's name.

"That's how it should sound, isn't it?" she asked with a smile. "It's quite lovely when you pronounce it. Like poetry almost. I took some French at school so I'm sure I can make myself understood, but my French doesn't sound anything like yours. I sound like an American attempting to speak French. You sound like a French woman born and bred."

"At one time, maybe," I admitted, "but not now. I'm too rusty, but after a few weeks in France, you'll be hard-pressed to hear any American accent in my speech at all."

We walked a brisk pace. Despite the fact that Lucy March was three inches shorter than I, she kept up with my longer stride without apparent effort.

"That will suit your purpose quite nicely, won't it? Because then you can disappear completely." She made the remarkable statement with only friendly inflection, no pause in her step and not even a glance in my direction. From the corner of my eye, I saw her grasp the edge of her cloak at her throat and pull it closer together for warmth, evidently interested only in staying warm. I was not fooled. I thought she had intended the words to startle me and could not let them pass without some kind of equal challenge.

"What on earth do you mean by that?" I heard the suspicion and an edge of hostility in my tone and tried to soften the effect by adding, "That's an odd observation to make, Miss March." We had slowed a little, and she turned her head to look at me at last.

"I know you don't want to be friends with me and I certainly respect your wishes, but you could call me Lucy without being my friend, couldn't you? My family knows me as Lucy Rose, but I won't ask that of you. Only *Miss March* this and *Miss March* that makes it sound like we're at a formal dinner or back in the school room."

"All right," I replied pleasantly, not bothering to refute her comment about our being friends or to offer her a similar familiarity. I paused briefly for effect and repeated, "That's an odd observation to make, Lucy," saying her name with a touch of temper I hoped would quell her curiosity.

Even with short acquaintance, however, I had learned that Lucy March was not easily distracted, even by a tone of voice intended to warn that she was treading on dangerous ground.

"But true, I think," she said with undaunted cheerfulness. "My guess is that, for reasons known only to her, Miss Meg Pritchard is on a mission to disappear."

I stopped completely, somewhat breathless and not from the cold wind off the water. "What an astonishing thing to say!"

"Is it? Well, perhaps I'm wrong." She stopped, too, and we stood facing each other on the breezy deck.

"Of course, you're wrong! Do I look like a magician that makes people disappear?"

"Not at all, but I still think I'm right." She peered at me from under her dark hood and said suddenly, "I'm sorry. I've startled you or frightened you, haven't I? How stupid and rude of me! I was just talking. Please forgive me."

"I am not startled or frightened," I retorted.

"Of course, you're not, and I'm just making matters worse. I don't know what I was thinking to blurt out such nonsense. I wasn't thinking at all, more like it. That's what my father sometimes said when I was a little girl and jabbering on about this or that." She resumed walking with deliberate steps and changed the topic of conversation. "We should dock in Southampton in two days. Dr. Fitch said someone will be waiting there to meet my companions and me and get us east to the Channel. I'll be relieved to land in France and be done with water crossings for a while. I may have a sound stomach, but that doesn't mean I enjoy traveling on anything other than solid ground." She wanted her general chit-chat to move the conversation onto another topic, and I participated in the attempt.

With my breathing returned to normal and the uncomfortable flutter of alarm I'd felt in the pit of my stomach gone, I took a long step, caught up with Lucy, and made a noncommittal response to her shared travel plans. As I did so, however, I thought with concealed admiration, well, aren't you the clever little thing? Hidden depths there that I had certainly failed to recognize and appreciate. For all her simple appearance and unsophisticated manners, for just a moment Lucy March had seemed as frightening in her own sharp and relentless way as any German submarine. If I were ever forced to choose between the two, I told myself ruefully, I might very well stand a better chance with the Hun.

Whether because of the ship's zigzagging progress or in spite of it, we arrived in Southampton safely and on schedule. Watching the British coast line take shape, I realized with sudden clarity that once I stepped onto foreign soil, I would leave behind everything familiar and start a brand new life. The idea, planned and intentional as it was, still caused a pang of sadness for which I could not account. I had anticipated the moment but not the accompanying emotion. Of course, I told myself, there's a natural trepidation that comes with the unknown, but the thought did not comfort. I was haunted by my mother's face, haggard from worry and grief, and by the expression in my brother's eyes at our last meeting. Only sixteen and always high-spirited, he had lost all his natural ebullience and was cool, withdrawn, and taciturn, hiding whatever he felt with a few clipped phrases. Not my dear Scotty any longer but a stranger. I tried to shake off the memory. Surely time would restore the cheerful young man who seemed to have vanished, and I believed my absence would aid in the recovery. They had each other, Scotty and Mother, and that would help the healing.

In the morning's cool sunshine, I watched the four nurses carrying their satchels disembark and stop at the bottom of the gangplank to speak with a waiting driver wearing a cap and warm coat. He swept off his cap respectfully before gesturing toward the vehicle waiting behind him. An ambulance appropriately enough, and I was not the only one that found the choice of transportation amusing. All the nurses burst out laughing at the sight. One girl said something to the driver, he nodded a response, and they all headed for the rear of the ambulance and the wooden portable steps that led into the back of the vehicle. At the last minute, Lucy Rose looked over her shoulder to where I stood on the deck waiting my own disembarkation. She waved with a childlike energy, the white nurse's cap she wore bobbing with the effort. Despite myself, I raised a hand and responded, then wished I hadn't, although I couldn't imagine why I felt the sudden regret. The driver lifted the nurses' bags after them into the vehicle, returned to the front, cranked the motor, and climbed into the driver's seat. The ambulance gave an audible backfire and lurched into the street. Headed for the Dover coast where I was also headed, but I'd given Lucy March and her fellow nurses a head start on purpose. Hers was the last familiar face I wanted to see for a very long time. She had been right, that serious young woman with the messy hair: I was on a mission to disappear and the sooner the better.

When I finally stood on solid ground, I hailed a cab, horse-drawn because it was the first one at hand, and asked to be taken to the train station. The driver gave me a look kind yet patronizing.

"Which station, Miss?" The first—but certainly not the last—time my ignorance and presumption would make me feel like an idiot. I must get used to being a pilgrim in a new land and a new life.

"I'm on my way to France," I responded, giving the man a straightforward look and not apologizing for my lack of knowledge, "and I'm booked on a channel crossing from Dover tomorrow morning. What station would that be?"

"You'll need the London, Chatham and Dover line, then. The South Eastern line's been blocked for nigh on two years." I climbed into the cab as he picked up the reins but could still hear the end of his advice. "You'll want to get off at the Harbour Town Station and don't be surprised by the crowd. There's a war on, you know, and Dover's a right popular spot for coming and going."

The cabbie was right about the crowd, but I was comforted, not intimidated, by the throngs around me. Being one among hundreds suited me just fine. I had prepared for an overnight stay by writing in advance to a small hotel called Harbour

House that I'd heard critiqued at a stateside lecture. Modest but adequate, the guest speaker, a middle-aged widow who enjoyed traveling, had said. She was regaling her audience with her European adventures when I commented in an innocent and only slightly skeptical tone that surely it would be impossible for a single female to find acceptable and secure accommodation in any coastal British town but especially Dover because of troop transports.

The story teller rose to the challenge by declaring that Harbour House had been more than acceptable. "Not grand, mind you," she added, "but secure, adequate, and reasonably priced." Adequate and reasonably priced, I mentally repeated to myself. How perfect for my purpose because even then, months ago, I'd begun to consider a plan to disappear completely, exactly as the clever Lucy Rose March had guessed.

Harbour House, I eventually discovered, sat at the top of a rise that overlooked the Channel and was approached by wide but steep wooden steps that scaled the incline to the front porch. My unwitting informant had failed to mention that particular feature in her story, and I felt a pang of something between annoyance and dismay as I stood at the foot of the steps, my portmanteau resting at my feet and the hotel looking as far away as the moon. It was not a climb I felt much like making just then but there was no use postponing the inevitable, and I reached for my case only to find that someone else's hand had gotten there ahead of mine, had grabbed hold of the handle and hefted my bag off the ground.

I turned in surprise to face a man wearing the uniform of an American soldier holding my bag in one hand and what must have been his own smaller duffel in the other. I would like to say that at that moment, at my very first meeting with McDermott Chesney—Mac to his friends—I felt a premonition of the wartime experiences and emotional attachment he and I would come to share. But if I tried to say so, it would be one of those lies created out of one simple, prosaic memory and embellished after the fact by a desire for dramatic effect. I had no such intuition. None at all. What I saw was a young man wearing the uniform of an American Marine and a soft-brimmed military hat. I thought the insignia on his tunic probably meant he held an officer's rank of some kind, but I had no idea what rank and no interest in finding out. The face beneath the hat's brim looked agreeable enough, was clean-shaven and lean with friendly hazel eyes and a pleasant expression. He was tall and broad-shouldered, possessed of an easy grace that allowed him to heft my case without losing either balance or eye contact. In his late twenties, I guessed, with a face as open and uncomplicated as a summer sunrise.

"I'm headed in the same direction," he explained, nodding his head up toward the hotel, "and if I may, I'd be happy to assist with your bag."

Never one to stand on pride when faced with an obvious need, I gave the soldier my warmest smile and said, "I appreciate the offer. Thank you." He waited for me to take the first step and then fell into step behind me. Had it not been for the sound of his boots on the wooden steps, I wouldn't have known he was there. No heavy breathing from the climb, not the slightest gasp or grunt despite his burdens while I held my bunched skirts in both hands and tried to maintain my dignity as the ascent robbed me of both breath and balance. Once I reached the porch, I turned to face him, a drop of sweat tickling its way down the side of my face. I let it go, damned if I'd acknowledge its presence or the fact that I was breathing harder than he was.

"Thank you. I'm sure a porter can take it the rest of the way," I said and reached for the purse slung over my forearm. "Please let me give—"

He handled my fumbling attempt to pay him with the same ease he'd used to heft my luggage. "Absolutely not. It was my pleasure entirely, Miss—"

I had no desire to tell this man my name or give him the slightest encouragement to advance our acquaintance, but the silence stretched out, he standing with a half smile and waiting, just waiting, so finally and with an unmistakable lack of cordiality I replied, "Pritchard." Then I turned and with a hand on the doorknob of one of the front double doors repeated, "Thank you," before I pulled open the door and stepped briskly to the front desk.

The man behind that desk recognized my name and my reservation and quickly summoned assistance for my bag that waited on the front porch. It wasn't until I was following the porter up a curving staircase to my room that I saw the American soldier step to the front desk and heard the clerk say, "Ah, yes—Captain Chesney. We were told to expect you."

Except for that first meeting with Captain Mac Chesney, I recall little of my first visit to Dover. I was exhausted from my pell-mell departure from the States, from the ocean voyage, and from the train trip to Dover, and in a way I could not have articulated even to myself, I believe I was caught up in a kind of unnatural—even for me—emotional detachment and had been so through all the days on board the *Ausonia*. I was not nor ever had been a woman at the mercy of her emotions. Not one to cry or shriek or faint or flutter about helplessly. Rather, one who kept her own counsel and was known to make gentle and not-so-gentle mockery of even the most serious occasion, a protective device learned years before and one that has continued to serve me well up to the present. That early May night in Dover, I can recall no feelings whatsoever, only a hasty meal in the hotel's modest dining room followed by a deep, dark sleep. No dreams of the past. No hopes for the future. Nothing but a black tunnel of sleep.

The transport that would carry me across the Channel to Calais was a mid-sized ferry that appeared to have seen better days. I examined its weather-worn appearance with a skepticism that must have somehow shown on my face because the cabbie that dropped my bag to the rough pavement said, "She's safe enough, miss. It's not her you need to worry about," giving me a look that told me there were other dangers more serious than an aged British ferryboat.

"I'm not worried," I replied in absent-minded response as I tossed him a coin, which he caught adeptly. "Not about the ferry or the Germans. Like the rest of my companions, I'll take my chances with them both." I reached for my bag only to discover that, exactly as the previous afternoon, someone's hand was already on the handle. I looked into the smiling face of the same young Marine officer of yesterday. Captain Chesney, the hotel clerk had called him.

"It may appear somewhat suspicious that I am once again on hand to assist you with your luggage, Miss Pritchard, but I assure you it's nothing but serendipity. I'm traveling to Calais aboard the same ferry as you, and it would be ungentlemanly of me not to offer assistance, though I can appreciate that you might harbor suspicions about a man who pops up whenever and wherever you stand next to a suitcase."

I studied the captain without bothering to hide the inspection before I rejoined, "Let me rephrase my previous statement: I'll take my chances with the ferry, the Germans, and with the Marines. I have no suspicions about you, Captain Chesney, and if you're willing to haul my luggage all over kingdom come, far be it from me to interfere with your good deed." I caught his surprise at the use of his name and added, "The hotel clerk's voice carried up the stairs." Without a backward glance at my helper, I walked forward onto the gangway and boarded the ferry, and with an almost amusing replication of yesterday, the only hint I had of the man's presence behind me was the sound of his military boots on the wooden plank.

From the deck of the ferry, I stared out at the Channel and thought that in roughly two hours I would step foot in France, would make my way to the train station and without a great deal of trouble would soon be heading into the French heartland, to Paris, and to a new existence. For the first time since I'd left America, I felt the stirring of anticipatory excitement mixed with curiosity and a vague regret. The regret surprised me. There was little of my past life I would miss, after all—only two names came to mind—and my departure from the broad tree-lined streets of Cleveland was both strategic and smart. So why that niggle of regret? I might have pondered the question longer had not Captain Chesney appeared beside me.

I had expected him to pursue a conversation and felt a smug satisfaction at my accurate prophecy. No doubt there were many things, an absolute excess of things, of which I had no knowledge but men certainly weren't among them. Even as a young woman, I understood men and prided myself on my ability to read them. As a sex, they were so very, so tiresomely predictable.

"You have the look of a sailor about you, Miss Pritchard, very steady on your feet. You must be accustomed to the water."

I gave him a quick, sideways glance and caught a slight wobble to his walk as he grasped the railing. No sailor there, I thought, and said, "I swam and sailed before I was old enough to walk, and we kept a schooner on the river. The yacht—" I stopped mid-sentence, conscious that my comments were indiscreet and too revealing, and concluded, "—the yachting crowd that lived nearby would sometimes condescend to take me out on their boat." To distract the conversation from myself, I added, "Have you a similar familiarity with the water, Captain?"

My comment made him turn to smile directly at me, warm hazel eyes meeting mine with open good humor as if he were well aware that I had seen his unsteadiness and asked the question with mockery and a desire to distract. It was the first time I felt a grudging admiration for the man's self-deprecating charm, but not the last. He could be very charming, that one.

"I have a landlocked heritage, I'm afraid," Captain Chesney answered, as rueful as if he were admitting to a foolish and serious social faux pas. "As I recall, a full bathtub on Saturday night was the largest body of water I'd ever seen before I arrived in New York City. All I can figure is that I'm able to remain upright on board ship because the vessel's motion bears a slight resemblance to standing in the back of a wagon, and that's something I learned to do before I was old enough to talk in complete sentences. I grew up accustomed to working outdoors but surrounded by flat, treeless plains, not water." The words explained his tanned face and the muscled chest and broad shoulders that allowed him to heft a heavy bag as if it were a simple hatbox.

I had mastered the art of the effective snub years ago, but I could not bring myself to snub the young captain just then. I did not want his company and was not especially interested in his conversation, but an inexplicable caution warned me that the man possessed sharp eyes and a sharper intelligence, and I had no desire to fuel speculation about me or my intentions.

After a prolonged silence and unable to help himself, Chesney prodded the conversation along by remarking, "You're traveling into a war, Miss Pritchard. Perhaps you're working with the Red Cross." An off-hand statement with the slightest lilt of a question at its tail, no overt inquiry and no curiosity about me or my intentions in his tone.

"I'm not with any organization, but I read about the American Fund for French Wounded and may visit their office while I'm in Paris. If I like what I see, I might volunteer for a while. My trip is really intended to be just a bit of fun more than anything else."

"Fun," he said in a voice without inflection. I don't know why it was that I enjoyed setting people on their ear—I recalled I'd made a similar remark to Lucy March on board the *Ausonia*—some childish need to show how little I respected pretense and propriety, I suppose, but while I've never been accused of being very sensitive to other people's feelings, I thought my lighthearted approach to war in the presence of a soldier might appear to be more insensitive than was acceptable.

"Not fun, exactly," I amended. "It could hardly be called fun. More like an adventure, I'd say."

Captain Chesney nodded but remained quiet and I clamped my lips together. Lark. Fun. Adventure. No more explanations for him. Let the man think what he wanted. What did I care? Once in Calais, our paths would part and what did it matter what he thought, as long as he did not give serious contemplation to me or to any of the nonsense I spouted?

Our conversation moved on to other topics, I can't recall exactly what, and the time passed. At first, having been solitary for the past few weeks, I felt a spurt of annoyance at finding myself with an unsolicited traveling companion, but Captain Chesney's intermittent, innocuous, sometimes amusing, and always intelligent observations made the time pass quickly and, truth be told, also kept me from dwelling on either my past or my future.

So when the outline of the French shore appeared at the horizon, I said with more sincerity than I'd imagined I would feel, "Thank you for your company, Captain." I again received his disconcertingly direct gaze, one tinged with a humor I'd already come to expect from him.

"You are a gracious woman, Miss Pritchard." He spoke simply but for an unsettling moment I thought he might be aware of both my initial annoyance at his presence and my self-serving tolerance of his company and conversation.

The discomfort I felt at his clear-sightedness made my reply sound sharper than I intended. "I am nothing that resembles gracious, Captain Chesney. Nothing at all. Please excuse me. I'm going below deck."

That verbal exchange would have been a fitting conclusion to our Channel conversation, but the fact that I still had baggage to lug to the Calais train station almost predestined me to spend additional time in the captain's company. I was not surprised, then, to see Captain Chesney standing on the dock next to my bag when I disembarked.

"No doubt," he said without preamble, "you're feeling more skeptical every time you see me, and I don't blame you, but there's a cab waiting to take me to the train station and I wondered if you'd care to share it. You said you were en route to Paris, too. I won't be a boor, I promise."

In one part of my mind, I thought it might be wise to separate from the man sooner rather than later but not taking advantage of his offer seemed unnecessary and foolish. Why spend time looking for a porter and requesting transportation to the train station when it was looking right at me?

"That's very kind of you, Captain Chesney. Thank you. I appreciate not having to make that arrangement myself, but I wouldn't want you to sacrifice your comfort for me."

"Miss Pritchard, your company could never in any way be considered a sacrifice," and how could I find fault with that pretty phrase, even if I knew he had spoken it only to get in the last word?

I followed the captain's lead as he strode toward a cab that waited for us outside on the street. The morning was lit by a pale sun, and I was able to observe the streets of Calais that bustled with pedestrians, carts, and a few motorcars. A typical port made busier by the hectic comings and goings of war time. Once at the station, however, my mood changed when I discovered with dismay that the train to Paris was not expected for three hours. Chesney, not appearing at all annoyed by the news, sat down beside me on a backless bench facing the tracks.

We remained wordless for several minutes until he said, "We passed a patisserie on our way and I think I can find it again. May I bring you something?"

Restless, I stood and replied, "No, I'll come with you. I'm not good at waiting." Then remembering that he hadn't invited me I added, "If I may."

"Of course, you may." The captain set our luggage inside the station next to the attendant's counter with a stern request directing the clerk to guard our bags—actually, in his barely passable French he told him to *save* our bags but there was no misunderstanding of intent on either side. No doubt the bags would be waiting for us secure and untouched upon our return.

I thought my companion must have quite a homing instinct because when we stepped out of the door on the street side of the train station, he hesitated only briefly, took a quick look up and down the street, and then led me straight to a small storefront that displayed a few delectable pastries in its front window. Once inside, we were overwhelmed with the redolent fragrances of freshly baked bread and cakes and a mix of aromatic spices. I could pick out cinnamon, rosemary, dill, and something sharp I thought might be mustard. A heavenly mix.

I took a deep breath and with the exhale murmured, "Divine."

"Yes, isn't it? What would you like?"

"I haven't decided. You go ahead while I look."

In amateurish French, he asked the shopkeeper for a thick slice of olive bread and when the man apologized for not having any butter, Chesney smiled and said with kindness that I thought was second nature to him, "I wouldn't think of spoiling your perfect creation with butter." Gratified, the man watched Chesney tear off a chunk of bread and nodded at the appreciative murmurs the captain somehow managed to make as he chewed.

I asked for an apple tart and with the tender pastry in hand repeated, "Merci," several times between chews and swallows. The elderly man behind the counter observed the two of us with the same indulgence he might have spent on two favorite grandchildren before shifting his attention to another customer. The day was too breezy and cool to take a seat outside and Chesney and I finished our treats at the one of the small tables the shop offered. I had eaten at some of the finest restaurants in the United States, meals of several courses prepared by masters of cuisine, but could not recall anything that matched the sheer bliss of that apple tart.

"My mother needs the recipe," Chesney said, waving the last corner of his bread in the air to indicate what recipe he meant. "She's a great cook and used to a hungry family waiting at the table. My dad would love this."

When he spoke of his family, I detected in his tone what I might under other circumstances have considered pride. That day, however, as we sat together in the shabby patisserie with the sea breeze rattling the window in a subdued but insistent reminder that it was still spring and uncharacteristically cool, I did not hear so much pride as the warmth of sincere affection.

His words put me into rare charity and I let down my guard enough to ask, "Where's home for you, then?"

"Winner, South Dakota." I must have looked at him blankly because he laughed and said, "South Dakota. Fortieth state in the union. North central United States. Shares a border with Nebraska and —"

"I know that," I replied, sounding too defensive.

He raised an eyebrow. "Miss Pritchard, I believe I'd have seen more recognition on your face if I'd said I hailed from the Struma Valley in Bulgaria."

"You may have recently called me gracious, but you must also consider me ignorant of my own country's geography. You really know how to flatter a girl, Captain Chesney!"

He wanted to make sharp retort but thought better of it, flushed a little (from the effort it took to hold his tongue, I decided) and stood, not looking at me as he brushed a few crumbs from his pants. When he finally shifted his glance to mine, he wore a slight smile.

"Ah, Miss Pritchard, I fear I have attempted a levity which was neither appropriate nor effective. Please forgive my feeble efforts at light-hearted conversation. My sisters have told me I haven't the knack for it and as much as it pains me to admit it, I believe they're right." He pulled out his watch from a pocket. "Only an hour now before our train. Are you ready to return to the station?"

I briefly regretted that I had squelched his good humor. He had meant no harm, and I'd experienced little enough of that kind of good-natured harmless banter in my lifetime, which was the only thing Chesney had been guilty of. I had appreciated the unguarded affection in his tone when he spoke of his family, an affection with an undertone of longing, because I felt the same warm ache when I recalled my mother's laughter or Scotty as a little boy slamming through the back door with his latest discovery—a shell, a bird's nest, a toad cupped in both hands—and his face lit by curiosity and delight. At our last meeting, there'd been no sign of that delight or the joy that was always so much a part of my brother, but I hoped that time would restore the cheerful young man who seemed to have vanished, and I knew my absence would aid in his recovery. I could never speak of my own family to anyone but because I recognized the warmth in Chesney's voice when he spoke of his, I should not have used that tone of cutting mockery with which I was so experienced.

Still, I was unpracticed and thus inept at apology and so I answered only, "Yes," and rose to my feet, vaguely unhappy at my own conduct but with no intention of sharing my regret. I murmured a quiet, "au revoir" to the shopkeeper as we exited and once outside turned for a final look at the shop's shabby exterior, with its sign weathered by wind and its faded and peeling door that still bore traces of the cheerful bright blue it had once been. I had enjoyed that brief stop more than the occasion warranted because it was as close to comfortable and safe as I had felt in a long time. In my present situation, however, safety was a luxury and a deceptive luxury at that. I knew I was not safe, would not be safe for a long time, if ever, which was why I sought the anonymity of a large cosmopolitan city in a war-torn country. Lucy Rose March had said it with uncanny perception: "Miss Meg Pritchard is on a mission to disappear," and Lucy Rose March had been exactly right.

Our train to Paris arrived on time and when the captain expressed his surprise that it did so, I said, "The French are very prompt and very courteous."

"Yes, ma'am. Point taken." His meek tone made me laugh in spite of myself.

"I was not chiding you, Captain Chesney, on either of those points, just offering an observation that might prove helpful as you continue your journey. You said you would be spending time in Paris, didn't you?"

He nodded and I realized that I knew nothing of the reason for his presence in France. The United States had declared a state of war with Germany last month, but the American military was still being made combat-ready and no American soldier had yet set foot anywhere outside of the borders of the United States. Why this lone Marine was on French soil was something of a mystery. In the patisserie, he had volunteered sketchy information about his background in South Dakota and his vocation of the law but had said nothing of his reason for traveling to Paris. Neither had I, of course, and I found the idea of mutual mysteries entertaining. Neither of us asked anything very probing of the other for fear we would have to share something significant about ourselves. Captain Chesney carried himself with a quiet poise that came from an innate intelligence and confidence, and it might only have been kindness that kept him from asking prying questions, but I was convinced, without any tangible proof that the reason for his lack of persistent inquiry into my personal plans was because he needed to protect his own secrets. I couldn't help but wonder if he suspected my reticence was for similar reasons. We could both have been German spies for all we really knew of the other.

"Well, then," I continued, "remember always to be on time, to greet with *bonjour*, and depart with an *au revoir*. If you do so, your travels will go much more smoothly."

"Thank you."

"Merci," I corrected.

"Oui. Merci," he agreed, and I did not think he was teasing me just then.

We found seats next to each other on the train and to my chagrin, I fell asleep an hour into the trip and awoke with my cheek against Chesney's right arm. The abrupt way I awoke and drew away from him almost caused some of the papers he was studying to flutter to the floor, but he had quick reflexes and was able to snatch them up before they hit the ground and hastily push them into his traveling case.

"What time is it?" I asked, deciding to ignore the familiarity of my head on his shoulder. What was there to say, after all? I must have been more tired than I'd thought and it wasn't like I was going to see him again once we parted in Paris. I rubbed my cheek with the back of my hand and wondered if the wool of his sleeve had left an impression there.

"Thirty minutes from Paris," he answered with a smile. I had slept, and slept soundly, for over two hours despite the rough rhythm of the train.

Outside was an early afternoon sky of gray blue with scudding clouds and pale sunlight. I turned my head to peer out the train window and watched neat compact farms give way to more traffic and the urban outskirts of Paris, to neighborhoods of narrow houses and children at play in the streets enjoying the disappearing warmth of the afternoon sun. I felt the train slow. We're almost there, I thought, and experienced a queer mix of excitement and regret, the sadness of good-bye mixed with the hope of an anticipated future. Everything would work out. I had done the right thing, taken the right action. Everything would work out.

Standing in the station, my satchel at my feet, I saw a man in a French military uniform approach Chesney and extend a hand in greeting. They spoke for a moment and the Frenchman turned, expecting the Marine captain to follow him out of the station, but instead of following, Chesney walked briskly back to me.

"Could we drop you off at your destination, Miss Pritchard?" A small crease of concern showed between his brows. "I don't like the idea of leaving you here on your own."

I swallowed an ungrateful response and said, "That's kind of you, Captain, but I am expected and will take a cab to my hostess's address. I'll be fine. My French will see me through, I'm sure."

"Better than mine will support me. Still—"

"Really," I insisted, now anxious to be rid of him and his relentlessly thoughtful attention. "I feel quite at home here. Thank you for your assistance on the trip. I hope your mission in France, whatever it is, will be successful." He did not miss the dismissal in my voice.

"I hope so, too," he replied. He hesitated, almost extended his hand, thought better of it, and finally gave a slight nod of his head in farewell. "You can reach me with a message to 73 Rue de Varenne here in Paris if there's any service I can offer you."

"I'll remember," I responded, smiling slightly. "Now, I think your companion is growing a little impatient. I advised you about the French temperament, you'll recall."

He looked over his shoulder at the man in the French military uniform who stood slapping his gloves against his leg in an agitated manner.

"Yes. Timely and courteous. I see what you mean. Well, good-bye, then."

"*Au revoir*, Capitaine Chesney."

"*Au revoir*, Mademoiselle Pritchard," his well-intentioned French holding a flat American accent he would never be able to eliminate, no matter how long he remained in Paris. He turned and strode toward the waiting man without another word or glance in my direction. With relief I watched the tall figure disappear among the people crowding the train platform and turned to locate a porter.

"I need a cab, please," I told him after I'd got his attention, "and will you arrange for my bag to accompany me?" I handed the man several coins with the same nonchalance with which he received them, and he gave a respectful nod of understanding.

"But, of course, mademoiselle, I would be happy to do so." He matched his cheerfulness with admirable efficiency and grabbed my bag, leading me outside to the street where a motorcar waited. I handed him a second supply of coins and thanked him profusely as, my bag securely loaded into the cab, he assisted me into the vehicle. I gave the driver a number on the Alcazar d'Ete.

"The office of the American Fund for French Wounded, mademoiselle?"

"Yes."

"I am in your debt, then," the driver said gallantly but when we arrived at the house, he did not refuse either my fare or my tip.

During the trip, we had passed British soldiers in heavy khaki greatcoats, Frenchmen in their uniforms of horizon blue, what I guessed to be Canadians in coarse gray-brown, even some Scot soldiers wearing kilts topped by unexpectedly formal jackets. Surely they didn't go to the front lines dressed in kilts, I told myself, but when I made such a comment to the driver, he lifted a hand from the wheel and shook his finger in the air as a schoolmaster might have done to make an important point.

"Ha!" he replied with enthusiasm. "The Scot, he is a fearsome thing to *le Boche*. A fearsome thing. The Scots kill everything, *le Boche* say." There was no denying the admiration in the man's voice.

"It's fortunate they're on our side, then," I said.

"And you Americans, too, eh? At last! I tell my friends, when the Americans come that will be the end of this madness."

I thought he was right about our entering the war but wondered if American fighting troops, needing to be trained and then delivered across the Atlantic, would end the war quite as easily or as quickly as the driver predicted. I hadn't the heart to disagree, however. With so many long years of fighting, the man voiced the hope of his entire nation.

# *"~Autumn softly fell~"*

# Chapter 2

The central depot of the American Fund for French Wounded was situated in a large elegant house set back from the street. With my bag placed discreetly to one side of the front door, I waited until a young woman answered my ring.

"I'm here to see Mrs. Lathrop," I told her quickly. "She knew I would be arriving sometime today. My name is Meg Pritchard."

The woman smiled and opened the door all the way. "Of course, Miss Pritchard," she replied in American English. "Please come in. Mrs. Lathrop mentioned to expect you. If you'll wait here, I'll tell her you've arrived."

I stepped inside the hallway and waited until Isabel Stevens Lathrop, the chairman of the organization, appeared walking briskly down the hallway toward me. I would find that my first impression of the woman was common to everyone that met her—here was a woman of purpose and boundless vigor. In another venue she might have seemed overwhelming, but her personality was perfect for a large metropolis threatened and bombarded by its enemies. Had I been a German soldier, I'd have given careful thought to approaching the lady with anything but amiable intentions.

"Hello, Miss Pritchard. I trust you aren't too exhausted from your trip. You look in good spirits and good health, I must say. Come join me for tea and what little luxury of refreshment we have available."

I tried to protest any special treatment, but she would not be diverted, turning back the way she'd come without another word and expecting me to follow. The woman's overflowing energy could not be denied or disobeyed. Once in her office, we made polite conversation until the young woman I'd met at the door brought in a tea tray, set it on the side table beside Mrs. Lathrop, and vanished as wordlessly as she arrived.

My hostess poured and handed me a cup of steaming tea, saying as she did so, "Now tell me about your trip."

I did so, conscious of the woman's intent gaze on my face as I spoke, gauging me, hearing more than the words. She made me uneasy in a trifling way, but I knew I had successfully handled listeners as perceptive as she and in much more pressured situations than this pleasant room, so I spoke of the initial ocean voyage, fellow passengers on board the *Ausonia*, the threat of maritime attack, the Channel crossing—those matters I believed she wanted to hear.

"So here you are safe and sound, Miss Pritchard," Mrs. Lathrop said when I finally concluded. "When Letty Tankard wrote that you would be arriving and asked that I take you under my wing for a while, she didn't elucidate why you were coming. She only mentioned that you had had a personal loss in your family, would be arriving in Paris, and asked if I would be willing to be of some service to you upon your arrival." She paused with proficient delicacy and eyed me, waiting for further information.

"My father passed away very unexpectedly," I said, "and he was my only immediate family. I didn't know what to do with myself."

"I'm so sorry," Mrs. Lathrop's murmur one of perfunctory sympathy. "How kind of Mrs. Tankard to take an interest in you! You must be good friends of long standing." Another question veiled as a statement.

"She's been like a mother to me for several years."

"Everyone always speaks so kindly of her," Mrs. Lathrop told me. "I've never met her personally, but my husband knew her first husband, Owen Phelps, and spoke of him with admiration. My Benjamin had enormous respect for Mr. Phelps as an industrialist and even more so as a philanthropist. In fact, years ago Owen Phelps once did a service for our family that we felt we could never repay. We lost touch with his wife after he died, I'm afraid, and it was only recently that we learned she had remarried and resumed our acquaintance with her. Mrs. Tankard's letter asking for my aid came out of the blue."

"She admires you and the work you do here," I said, "and it would be fair to say that Letty Tankard is the main reason I'm sitting with you today."

Mrs. Lathrop smiled. "Well, having never met Mrs. Tankard in person, I wouldn't recognize her if I passed her on the street, but I assure you that any friend of hers is also a friend of mine. She and her first husband had children, as I recall."

I responded with casual warmth, "Two, a boy and a girl, but I don't know either of them well. I've really only known Letty since her second marriage. When I decided to volunteer my services in France, she didn't encourage the trip considering the present state of ocean travel, but I was determined to follow my own course. When she realized I wouldn't be dissuaded, she volunteered to contact you on my behalf. Please understand that I don't want to be any kind of burden to you or an impediment to your work with the A.F.F.W."

A silence followed our conversation, and I felt a momentary panic. Had I sounded too practiced, too facile? For all my confidence, Mrs. Lathrop remained a woman of uncommon discernment, perhaps more so than I had first realized, a woman sure to recognize any word or tone that was not quite right or credible. Still, there was enough truth in my words and enough first-hand knowledge in my background to be convincing, and I did not see suspicion on the other woman's face, only a quick sympathy and an even quicker understanding.

"Loss affects all of us differently, Miss Pritchard. Now, if I may, I'll give you a quick tour of our depot and by then Agnes should be here and will take you to her apartment."

"Agnes?"

"Agnes Beechum, an extraordinary woman who has no equal in my opinion, though that is not to say she has no faults." She took my arm and gently propelled me toward the door. "I have yet to find words to adequately describe Agnes Beechum. She needs to be met in the flesh to be fully appreciated." With those enigmatic comments, Mrs. Lathrop led me out of the room.

The Paris depot of the A.F.F.W. over which Mrs. Lathrop presided was made up of fourteen departments that supplied the Allied war hospitals with valuable medical supplies purchased by the organization's New York City home office and its vast network of smaller branches throughout the United States. I hadn't known all those impressive details beforehand, but Mrs. Lathrop shared the information—and additional particulars that

I have long since forgotten—with enthusiasm. She was proud of the cavernous rooms of heavy tables where women, uniformed neatly in gray dresses and crisp white caps, counted and packed bandages, syringes, rolls of tape, and a variety of other tools, medicines, and materials.

The warehouse area with its piles of stacked, sealed, and labeled boxes was busy, as well, with a rather pitiful array of vehicles and carts aligned for loading. Mrs. Lathrop had to raise her voice over the noise made by the motor cars and trucks, the old Renault taxis that misfired with alarming frequency, and the even older horse-drawn wagons that stood at a distance from the noisy motor vehicles with the hope of keeping the animals relatively calm despite the racket. One especially loud backfire that sounded more like the thunder of a fired shotgun than an engine caused all the horses to shift nervously and made my guide turn her head toward the large loading area.

"Ah," Mrs. Lathrop remarked, "there's Agnes now." She added with a casual innocence that I did not realize until much later was neither casual nor innocent, "Do you drive, Miss Pritchard?"

"Yes," I answered, falling right into her trap without a second thought. "I enjoy it very much. In fact, I was once told by someone who purported to be a motoring expert that I drove like a man. I think he meant it as a compliment."

"Really? How—" Mrs. Lathrop paused, searched for the right word, and finally settled on opportune, which she repeated "—opportune, Miss Pritchard! How very opportune!" She spoke with a thoughtfulness that held the merest hint of awe, but before I could ask for an explanation she hurried me toward the Ford wagon that had just pulled off the street into the broad loading area. The figure behind the wagon's steering wheel wore a long coat and was so swathed in scarves that it was impossible to make out its true size and shape and except for Mrs. Lathrop's introductory comment could have been either man or woman, human or beast. It clambered down and began to unwind the layers of scarves wrapped around its neck and head until first a blue felt hat with the initials A.F.F.W. on the hatband emerged, and then a woman's face.

"Aggie," said Mrs. Lathrop, pulling me forward, her hand gripping my forearm, "here's Miss Pritchard. You remember I told you she was arriving today."

"Of course, I remember. I may not be aging as gracefully as I wish, but I've managed to retain the use of my brain, even if there are some who'd argue the fact with me."

Well, I thought, making an assumption from Agnes Beechum's tone and words that was never to change throughout our acquaintance, here's a woman who possesses even less patience than I. I found the thought cheering.

"How'd you do, Miss Pritchard?" the newcomer said and stuck out a large hand in my general direction.

"Miss Pritchard knows how to drive, Aggie."

"I know how to drive, too, so don't expect me to be bowled over by the news. More to the point, does she know how to go in reverse?" Aggie Beechum turned her broad face with its wind-reddened cheeks to me. "Well, do you?"

"Yes," I answered, trying to sound suitably meek. "I can go forward and in reverse."

"Well, thank God for that. We'll be one up on Stein, after all." Aggie gave a sudden grin. "What do you think of my truck?"

"It looks serviceable," I answered with caution, seeking a word that would be true and yet wouldn't offend. She gave a cackle that it took me a moment to identify as laughter.

"Serviceable! That's a good one! Serviceable! Ha! Well, it's like me, not pretty and no longer young, so maybe serviceable is a fitting word for both of us. I like you, Miss Pritchard. I believe we'll do all right together." To Mrs. Lathrop she added, "She has a bad backfire"—I assumed Aggie meant the truck and not me—"and I need someone to take a look at her."

"I don't know who's around, Aggie, but I'll find somebody quick. Go in with Miss Pritchard and search out some tea. You look like you could use it."

"How long have you been in the city, Miss Pritchard?" asked Agnes Beechum.

"Only hours and please call me Meg." Together we entered the warmth of the main house.

"I'm Aggie. Crazy Aggie they call me when they think I can't hear 'em." She tacked on the latter comment as an afterthought and looked sideways to see my reaction. There was something about the tall, big-boned woman that put me in good humor.

"I imagine it helps to be crazy if you want to survive during a war," I replied. "Too much sanity and good sense can't be healthy." She cackled at that.

"It's not healthy anytime but especially during a war. If you try to make sense of the poor troops and the stupid, arrogant old bastards who sit on their fat asses behind the lines and send them off to die in the mud, you'll end up murdering the first general you meet. And that might feel good but it won't help the legless boys or the ones with their faces shot to hell or their lungs burned up by gas. Being crazy helps me stay sane, Meg. If you see what I mean." Somehow I did see.

"Lulu!" Aggie called down the hallway. "Where are you, girl? I need tea and I need it now!" The perky girl who'd met me at the front door when I'd first arrived stepped quickly from one of the side doors of the hall and without a word came and threw her arms around Aggie Beechum in a hug so vigorous that the scarf Lulu wore threatened to slip off the back of her head.

"I haven't seen you forever!" Lulu disengaged herself from the hug, rearranged her scarf to its proper angle, and went past us. "Go wait in the front room while I bring your tea. I'm sorry the fire's small, but we've used up nearly all our coal supply and Mrs. Lathrop won't let me break up any more chairs for firewood."

Aggie Beechum looked after the girl with a smile. "That Lulu's a good girl," she said. "Young, of course, but she's got a good head on her shoulders, and there's no job she's above doing. Ask Lulu to do something and it gets done. Ask her to find something and she finds it. The only advice I have is don't ask her for the details because if she told you, you'd probably have to report her to the authorities," adding after a thoughtful pause, "We could use a dozen just like her."

Once seated in the small front room, Aggie Beechum and I examined each other from opposing chairs. I saw a large woman with frowsy, gray-streaked hair, light eyes, an uneven complexion, and a strong jaw. What she saw I don't really know, but after a moment she relaxed and sat back, stretching her legs out in front of her in a posture that was not very ladylike but was decidedly human.

"I said you could stay with me as long as you were willing to drive once in a while, so I hope that's all right with you."

"Drive where?"

"Wherever we're told to go. I don't ask questions. I just get out the map. I can read maps just fine, but I cannot put that damned truck in reverse." Aggie Beechum was the most profane woman I had ever met and while I didn't really care, I would still have to get used to her language. She grinned, reading my mind. "I was raised in Beaumont, Texas, Meg, smack in the middle of nowhere. My mother died before I was two. If my daddy, God rest his soul, hadn't struck oil sixteen years ago, I'd still be in Beaumont, running a boarding house or taking in laundry, I expect, but he did strike oil, a great gusher of oil that hasn't dried up yet, though by then it was too late to make a lady out of me. My daddy meant well, but I'd grown up around roustabouts and cowboys with no one bothering to tell me not to copy their ways and their talk. Daddy wanted to send me away to a school for young ladies—in Switzerland, of all places—but I said no thank you, I was perfectly happy just the way I was, and I guess at the end he saw the wisdom of what I said. Still, it wasn't too late for me to use some of the money from those oil fields to see the world and maybe make a difference somewhere. I could tell from the moment I met you that we came from backgrounds so different we might as well have lived on different planets so if how I act or how I talk bothers you, just say so. No hard feelings. I'm a woman who likes to have things out in the open." She gave a broad wink. "I don't have any intention of changing my ways, of course, but it's still good to know where we stand."

We're more different than you realize, I thought, because I don't like things out in the open at all. I have too many secrets and I like things hidden, but I could appreciate Aggie Beechum for exactly what she was—a woman with no dark corners. A woman easy for me to manage.

"You don't bother me and I hope it's the same for you. I think we'll deal together all right, Aggie, at least for a while." I leaned back, smiled, and thrust out my legs in an imitation of her casual but unorthodox posture. "Besides, I know how to shift into reverse. I must be an answer to prayer."

At Aggie's nod, half-smiling but still serious, I realized she and I had reached an understanding of sorts, an understanding that would suit me until I got my bearings and could decide on my next step. I didn't have the intention or the desire to deliver medical supplies to French hospitals for any length of time, but it would do very well for a while. I couldn't have planned anything better.

Warmed by tea, Aggie stood abruptly. "Now I feel better, though to tell the truth I'd have welcomed something a little stronger than tea, but rules are rules and even Lulu has to draw the line somewhere. Besides, if we did manage to lay our hands on a bottle of brandy, I'd pack it up and take it straight to the boys at the hospital. Or the doctors and nurses. God knows they need it more than I do. Do you have baggage with you?"

"A traveling case I left by the front door."

"Well, I'll go see if anyone's had a chance to check out the old girl's backfire. Do you know anything about a Ford engine?"

The sudden mental picture I had of me brandishing a wrench and digging around under the hood of our luxurious Pierce-Arrow made me smile. As if that had ever happened or had even crossed my mind, for that matter! Louis, my father's chauffeur for many years, would have been outraged at the idea of anyone but himself touching that elegant, powerful vehicle.

"No. I'm sorry for my lack of education." I tried to sound contrite.

"Oh, we'll remedy your ignorance soon enough," Aggie replied cheerfully. "The first time we can't get that Ford cranked, I'm putting you under the hood. You've got to start someplace. Go wait by the front door, and I'll come around and pick you up."

After standing for at least thirty minutes in solitary expectation next to my bag, I heard the quick clip of Mrs. Lathrop's heels on the hallway's wooden floor and turned to meet her.

"I'm sorry you've been here by yourself, Miss Pritchard. I got snagged by an official of the Ambulance Corps and lost track of time. Aggie said to tell you she'll be around to the front to get you in just a minute."

I smiled a polite response. "I appreciated having some time to catch my breath after my conversation with her."

"Yes, Aggie affects people like that, but there's no soldier who's ever met her that wouldn't cheerfully die for her. And the doctors—! When we get an emergency request from a hospital that's in desperate need of one supply or another, it always ends with *Send Aggie.* They trust her to get them what they need safely and on time." Mrs. Lathrop opened the front door as she concluded the sentence. "And speaking of on time, there she is now." She took hold of one side handle of my traveling case and I grabbed the other. Together we hefted it across the threshold and down the walk to the curb where the paneled truck and Aggie waited. With one final tandem swing, Mrs. Lathrop and I loaded the case into the back of the truck. For a moment the sun glinted off the initials MP engraved in gold script on the side of the handsome leather case.

With everything loaded, Mrs. Lathrop observed, "I'm afraid you might lose that little frippery thing on your head, Miss Pritchard. Aggie's driving speed has separated many a hat from its owner."

"I have a scarf packed somewhere."

Aggie unwound one of the several scarves wrapped around her head and shoulders and handed it to me. "Here." When I hesitated, she said, "No use worrying about how you look. There's no young men left in town any more to see you."

I wasn't going to give Aggie the satisfaction of seeing that she'd surmised correctly—the part about my vanity, anyway. I was in no mood to care about the opinion of men of any age, but I did take a certain pride in my appearance. Like Aggie, I had grown up in circumstances that had made me the woman I was, whether I liked that woman or not. Appearance, I had once been told, was the most important part of a woman and could either make or ruin her future, and appearance wasn't found only in face and figure. It included everything about a woman that could be observed: the way she walked and talked and sat and danced and ate and laughed and listened. Certainly, sitting unprotected from the elements on the seat of a Ford truck with an old scarf wrapped several times around my head would not have passed the test of acceptable exposure.

I shrugged off Aggie's comment and took the scarf, saying as I wrapped it over my head several times and finally tied it with a flourish under my chin, "Well, when you put it like that, I suppose I'll have to put off finding a husband until after the war."

Aggie sent me a sharp glance then relaxed into a grin. "Maybe. Maybe not. Though to tell the truth, I'd be surprised if you're after a husband." I felt a moment of uneasiness at her comment until she concluded, "No intelligent woman—and while I don't know you well, I can tell you're not lacking upstairs—would go to a country that's been sending its young men off to die as soldiers for the last three years and expect to find material for a husband there. The good old U.S.A. would have more fish in that particular pond, I'd be bound." She didn't give me time to react. "I'll be by tomorrow afternoon to load up," she called to Mrs. Lathrop and shifted the Ford into gear. The truck jerked forward abruptly with a terrible grinding noise, and I had to clutch the edge of the seat for support, managing to dislodge one hand long enough for a quick wave to Mrs. Lathrop.

"Sorry!" Aggie shouted to me cheerfully. "It always does that. You'll get used to it!"

I doubt that, I thought to myself. I felt suddenly tired and windblown and more than a little cranky but despite my pique, as we chugged through the streets, I turned from watching the passing houses and shops and people to take a good look at the profile of the woman at the wheel. I like Aggie Beechum, I thought, surprised to find that it was so, and it's going to work out. Haring around the French countryside means it might be difficult to locate me and that fits in very nicely with my plan—or to use Lucy March's word, my *mission*. How had she phrased it during that evening shipboard promenade? "Meg Pritchard is on a mission to disappear." Smart girl, that Lucy Rose March.

Aggie parked the truck at the curb of a quiet block of stores and apartments, and between the two of us we managed to carry my bag up three flights of stairs to a surprisingly spacious apartment located in the Hotel Premier. Even with its general air of abandonment, I could tell from the small hotel's lobby and the luxurious rooms into which I stepped that it had once been a destination for those with good taste and ample money. Aggie caught the expression on my face and grinned.

"I'm not one to spend money on jewels and clothes and such, but there are certain luxuries I don't skimp on. I pay a pretty penny for central heating to stay reasonably comfortable. It's true that coal's at a premium for everyone, rich and poor alike, but I've been here long enough to have a regular acquaintance with the right people." She didn't explain any further but I understood. Anything could be got for the right price. Anything. Anytime. Anywhere. Wartime or peace didn't matter as long as you knew the right people and had the cash. What a universal and international truth that was!

The front room into which we entered held good furniture, nothing fancy but everything cushioned and well-made. Aggie Beechum liked her comfort indeed. She went a few steps down a side hall and pushed open a door.

"This should suit you. There's a toilet there at the end. Take your time. Are you hungrier than you are tired?"

I didn't need to give my answer thought. "Yes," I replied, aware that I was ravenous.

"We'll eat downstairs. I have a kitchen and a woman who cooks in when I ask, but we'll use the hotel's kitchen tonight. Your first night in Paris, after all."

The room designated for me was as spacious and comfy as the rest of the apartment and included a bed covered by a deep featherbed and a layer of quilts folded back at the foot that almost made me reconsider my answer to Aggie's question. I was tired as well as hungry and the idea of snuggling into that soft bed with those warm coverings was nearly irresistible. The small bunk I'd had on board the *Ausonia* had not offered very restful slumber at its best, and I'd lost even the pretense of sleep during the last few days of the voyage when all the passengers had been advised to sleep wearing their life belts. Except for the unnaturally deep slumber I experienced at my Dover hotel, I hadn't had a night of healthy sleep in a long while. At the moment, this room was more inviting than any hotel room I'd ever visited, and I had stayed at some of the finest in America.

With a faint trace of regret I left my bag unpacked, spent time enjoying warm water and soap that bore the gentle fragrance of lavender, and met Aggie in the front room where she sat leafing through a paper. She looked up as I entered.

"You look like a hungry woman to me," she announced and promptly stood to lead me into the outer hallway and down the stairs to the hotel's small restaurant located off the lobby. A man dressed in a neat black suit met us, greeted Aggie by name, and directed us to one of the room's few tables, all of which were empty of diners.

"I can recommend anything with chicken," Aggie told me in a low voice. "I'm not really sure that any of the other meats on the menu are what they claim to be, but I trust the chicken. The war has added a certain level of creativity to French cuisine that we will all want to forget when it's peacetime again." By then, I felt—to my discredit—that I would have eaten anything without asking questions, but I took her advice and was soon presented with a bowl of something thick and creamy loaded with chunks of chicken (or so I presumed) and vegetables and covered with a thick pastry. I thought at the time that it was the most delicious meal I had ever tasted and its memory still has the power to make my stomach growl.

Neither of us talked much, at first intent solely on eating and both of us fatigued from our days' activities, but once we were upstairs again, Aggie said, "You're welcome to come along tomorrow or not. That's up to you, and I can understand if you want to sleep a little later after your long trip. I need to take the truck to the depot to load up so we can get an early start the next morning."

"An early start?" I repeated. "Where are we going?"

"I was told you wanted to help the A.F.F.W. so you might as well get a taste of what we do. We're scheduled to make a swing to some of the hospitals that lie up along the northwest coast to deliver supplies to the doctors and donated items to the patients. It's been wet and the roads are a mess, but I'm not going to put off the trip. Not now that I have someone to travel with."

"I suppose having a person along who knows how to get the Ford into reverse will be helpful."

"Damned right. Whenever I cross paths with that fat Gertrude Stein, she reminds me that she's made twice the trips I have, and I know for a fact she can't drive in reverse, either. Of course, she's got Alice. Well, now I've got you."

"That would be Gertrude Stein, the writer?"

"If you want to call her that." Aggie's disdain was obvious. "I'll take a good Zane Grey story anytime. Now that's writing! Have you read Stein's *Tender Buttons*? I tried, but it was nonsense pure and simple. And she calls herself a writer! The words ought to make sense, at least. Edith Wharton's another thing altogether. I've met her, too, and at least she can write, though I can't say I have much sympathy for her characters. Take that Lily Bart in *The House of Mirth*. If ever there was a woman who deserved what happened to her it was Lily Bart. As useless a female as I ever read about. But it was a good story, and I suppose there really are society women like Lily Bart that Wharton felt she needed to write about. Tells us all how not to act and that's worth something, I suppose."

Not willing to admit that I knew a lot of women with exactly the same priorities and motivation as the protagonist of *The House of Mirth,* I tried to steer the conversation back to its original direction.

"I think I'll relax a little tomorrow," I said, "if you don't need me."

Aggie shook her head. "Not tomorrow. You can sleep as late as you'd like in the morning, and I'll have them send something up from the kitchen for your breakfast. Take a walk, if you want. The city's different than it used to be, I'm told, but I was never here in the days before the war so I can't say. Be sure the curtains are drawn tight in your room tonight because your room's got a window on the street and there's a blackout every night. No lights are allowed to show, not even the tip of a lit cigarette, so if you need a smoke, you need to step into the hallway." At my questioning look, she added, "It's to protect against the Zeppelins and the German *Taubes*. Nothing dove-like about those flying machines, I can tell you. When we go closer to the front, you'll see the kind of damage they can do if you give them a target, and I've grown kind of fond of having a roof over my head. You're not home any more, Meg. You're in a country at war, so you'll have to learn the rules if you want to stay in one piece."

"I understand," I replied humbly. "I will. Good night, Aggie. Thank you for your hospitality." Back in my room, I unpacked my bag and then sat on the edge of the bed for a while deep in thought. I'd had a plan of sorts when I arrived but after talking to Mrs. Lathrop and Aggie, I realized I would have to be more flexible and open to the situation than I'd originally thought. It wouldn't be as simple as I first imagined to get lost among the population of a chaotic, war-ravaged country, not when people knew me and expected me to be part of an effort for which I had volunteered, never mind that I'd volunteered out of purely selfish motives. I had needed a legitimate purpose to visit France and the American Fund for French Wounded had seemed an ideal cover for my trip. Even better if I could get hold of one of their vehicles and wander around the French countryside for a while before settling in some small town that would provide anonymity and allow me to relax long enough to catch my breath and decide on my next step. But I had been adopted in a way by Aggie Beechum, who was no desperate Lily Bart but a woman that knew her own mind, brooked no nonsense, and seemed heedless of other people's opinions, a woman with a purpose of her own into which I had been recruited with ruthless assumption. I did not suppose Aggie Beechum's passions would ever be mine, but it was true that I knew how to shift into reverse and it seemed a shame to waste the talent.

I was awakened in the morning by the bell at the door and groggy for a moment, felt completely mystified by the sound. Then I recalled where I was and rose, belted on a dressing gown, and opened the door to a young woman waiting with a tray. She was a chubby, dark-haired girl whose figure was an endorsement of the hotel's cuisine.

"Good morning, miss," she greeted in cheerful and heavily accented English, adding in her native language, "Mademoiselle Beechum asked me to bring up your breakfast. Where shall I set it?" I motioned toward the closest table. After she deposited her burden, she turned back to me and introduced herself. "I am Giselle."

"Hello, Giselle," I responded, also in French. "My name's Meg Pritchard. Will you wait here a moment?" I went back to my room and returned with a coin that I tried to give her.

"Oh, no, no, no!" She backed away from me hands out, palms forward, the picture of someone warding off a threat. "Mademoiselle Beechum has already been generous. I cannot accept anything from you. You are her guest. It would offend her."

"She needn't ever know," I replied.

"But I would know, mademoiselle. I, Giselle, would know." Her response held a dignified simplicity.

I thrust the coin into my dressing gown pocket. "Of course. I understand. I didn't mean to offend you." I felt unaccountably ashamed of myself, but I spoke the truth: I hadn't meant any insult or dishonesty with either my coin or my words.

Giselle was sunny again. "Mademoiselle Beechum has been very good to me and my brother, and we can never repay her." Changing the subject, she said, "She told me she would be gone most of the day but that you might wish to spend some time touring the city in her absence. The wind has died down and the sun is bright. It will be a good day for such a venture."

After she departed I poured out a cup of hot and fragrant dark coffee, gulped it down so quickly I almost seared my throat, and proceeded to eat every bite on the tray Giselle had left on the table. Then I wandered to the toilet, murmured a word of wonder at the warm water available from the taps, and ran myself a bath. I knew I had once taken all such luxuries for granted and supposed I would be blasé about hot coffee and warm running water again someday, but for the time being I viewed both as miraculous.

When I stepped outside, I realized just how accurate Giselle had been about the day's weather. Yesterday's biting wind had vanished and the sun felt warm on the back of my neck. Lovely. I set out on a walk with no destination in mind and my only purpose to stretch my legs. Before my departure, I'd read several accounts in American papers and journals of the toll the war had taken on France, but at first glance Paris did not seem much affected by the hostilities. Shop doors stood open in invitation, busy people engaged in lively conversation as they waited on corners or walked together toward a common destination, cabs rumbled down the streets. The more I walked, however, the more I realized that most of the civilians on the street were women and children, and the shopkeepers standing in doorways were old men. The younger men I saw were in the blue military uniform of the French army, soldiers all, and many of them with terrible injuries. I began unconsciously to count the number of men I saw with sleeves pinned back or trouser legs pinned up, men that wore eye patches or walked on crutches or lumbered along with a splinted limb. After a while, I had to stop the count. The number was overwhelming.

Many of the vehicles I had first identified as cabs busy with passengers turned out to have bright red crosses painted on their sides. Still carrying passengers, I realized, just not the kind I first imagined.

A column of people trudged down the opposite side of the street where I walked, and I tried to observe them without seeming to stare. They walked with a profound weariness, feet dragging and faces all similarly expressionless. They looked so lost and exhausted that for a moment I was shaken out of my absorption in my own situation. Something about the drawn, bleak faces, the unresisting children pulled along by women who never bothered to glance down at them, the slow-paced feet, and the complete silence of the group affected, even frightened me. I didn't know what it was I saw, who they were, where they had come from, or where they were going, but they were people who seemed to lack any spark of humanity. I turned to watch them as they walked away from me, the curve of their backs reflecting the same hopeless fatigue I had seen on their faces. Even with the bright sun, I shivered and could not stop staring after them.

When I finally turned to resume my walk, I found a fair woman not much older than I watching me, though not unkindly, and I flushed at the thought that she seemed to be eyeing me with the same focused attention I had just given the group of people on the opposite side of the street. I found the idea of being scrutinized distasteful and wondered if the people who'd just passed by had been aware of my intense inspection. I wished suddenly that I had not stared at them.

"Bonjour," the woman said with a slight smile and would have turned away without another word except I asked impulsively, "Who were those people? They looked so—" I paused to find the right word.

"Desperate? Lost? Hopeless?" she supplied with gentle bitterness. "Yes, I suppose they are all those things. They are refugees from the Somme. Everything they had has been taken from them. Not just houses and farms and fields and shops but even those things one cannot touch. Joy and hope and pleasure have all been stolen, too. They are people who belong nowhere and have nothing left. Nothing at all."

"What will happen to them?"

She answered with a Gallic shrug, both shoulders lifting slightly. "Who knows? There are so many here now, you see, and we are all lost one way or another. It is hard to think what to do, hard to give direction." The woman turned away, her face sad and I noticed what I should have seen immediately: that she was dressed all in widow's black, her small hat black, too, with a dark veil that covered the back of her head.

The day that had first seemed so bright and sunny now carried the kind of chill that came when a cloud covered the sun, and I turned quickly to retrace my steps to the hotel. *People who belong nowhere.* At that moment I saw myself part of that gray-faced group, one more person who belonged nowhere. I recalled my feelings of pleasure over hot coffee and warm water with the same odd shame I'd felt when Giselle had rebuffed my monetary offer. I had done nothing wrong so why did it feel as if I had?

Aggie was already at the apartment when I got there, studying a map spread across her lap. "We're scheduled to stop at Rouen first," she said, looking up, "then travel northwest to St. Val, follow the coastline east to Dieppe, and return to Paris from there. It's pretty enough country, but the weather's changeable that far north, and it could be cold. Wear something warm. How was your city excursion?"

I felt an odd reluctance to mention the refugees I had seen or my conversation with the young woman in black, so I replied, "Pleasant, but I saw a lot of soldiers, most of them injured or impaired in some way."

"Naturally. Healthy soldiers are busy elsewhere, Meg, not out enjoying a Parisian stroll. Sometimes you'll see able-bodied men but they're on leave—the French call it *permission.* You can recognize them easily enough from the expression on their faces, grim and gray and haunted somehow. It takes more than a week away from the fighting to get them to relax. You can tell that the idea of returning to the front is all they're thinking about, no matter how much time and money they spend on women and drink. Did you notice that the city cabs have been appropriated by the government for ambulance duty? They carry injured and sick soldiers from the rail station to a number of hospitals in the city."

"Yes. I spotted that." The conversation lagged and Aggie gave me a quick, sharp glance.

"Is everything all right?"

"Everything's fine," I replied and went on to cover what seemed to be an awkward silence. "I met Giselle this morning, and I'm afraid I insulted her by offering her a tip for delivering my breakfast tray. She acted like I tried to bribe her to divulge military secrets to the enemy."

"Giselle's a good girl," Aggie said complacently. "She's had a rough time of it and she wants to be sure I know how grateful she is."

"Grateful? For what?"

Aggie shook her head with a look on her face that said she regretted the words she'd just spoken. "That's not important. Don't let Giselle's reaction bother you. I'll tell her next time to take whatever you offer. She can use it." Aggie folded the map into rectangles. "I think we should plan on an early night. It's eighty-five kilometers to Rouen, and I want to get there in the morning and leave for St. Val by lunch. We'll go downstairs again for supper tonight." She rose and stretched. "I suppose I should put on something that doesn't smell like *eau de petrol*." Her wry tone made me smile, which made her smile in return. "I don't have your flair for fashion, Meg. Used to wish I did and I spent more money than I should have before I realized that was never going to happen. For all the money my daddy made, there wasn't enough to turn me into a beauty."

She nodded her approval when I remained silent and didn't try to rebut her comment with inanities. Aggie Beechum wasn't a beauty and never would be, but I surprised myself by thinking it didn't matter. She possessed character and courage, and that suited her more than a pretty face or the latest fashion.

"Good girl. No use arguing when a thing is obvious, and I've seen enough since I've been in France to be content with who I am and what I have." She gave me an appraising look. "A woman like you, Meg, may not believe I really mean what I say. You're no doubt used to the attention that beauty and style generate because there's nothing plain about you. You're the kind of woman that men notice. I always wondered what that would be like, but you must be used to it."

"I've had my share of notice," I admitted, allowing too much emotion into my tone, "and not always the good kind, either. I had to learn the hard way that sometimes there's a price to pay for the kind of attention you're talking about. I haven't known you very long, Aggie, but it's long enough for me to realize you're a woman with no patience for pretense. It seems to me you've figured out something that many women struggle with." I turned away. "I think I'll freshen up, too." I went down the hallway and into my room, closing the door softly behind me. I feared my response had revealed too much about myself, and I needed to escape Aggie Beechum's intelligent, curious gaze. For some reason—the sights and sounds of the day or the memories that the conversation with Aggie stirred or perhaps a combination of the two—I felt close to tears and that would never do. I had not wept in many, many months and now was not the time to start.

We shared another enjoyable evening meal, retired early, rose before sunrise, and left for Rouen just as morning light began to creep along the city streets. Unfortunately, we had our first flat tire before we even made it outside the city limits.

"Oh, hell," said Aggie and turned sideways to look at me. It took me a moment to realize that she wanted me to take care of the problem.

"I've watched someone change a tire," I protested to her unspoken expectation, "but I've never done it myself."

"Well, I have, but it's as good a time as any for you to learn to be useful. I guarantee this won't be the last flat, and we can take turns if you want, but right now you go ahead and change this one," her tone implacable and not open to discussion.

Wordlessly, I clambered out of the truck, Aggie behind me. I suspected this was some kind of test, the details of which only Aggie understood, and felt trepidation mixed with resentment. I fumbled and guessed my way through the task and thought I had acquitted myself as well as could be expected, sending silent thanks to Louis for the years he spent letting me watch him work in the garage without letting on to anyone where I was. Girls weren't supposed to understand engines or even like them, but he always had a soft spot for me and seemed to understand my need to learn new things and prove people wrong in the process. He liked to talk, too, especially about automobiles, and I had listened and learned. Louis was a childhood memory that always made me smile.

It had taken time to figure out what I needed to do, but remarkably, once I started, I didn't need further help until the last struggle to get the tire back on the rim. I had figured out how to jack up the truck, had pried the tire off and extricated the punctured inner tube, inserted a fresh tube into the tire, and used the pump that was kept in the mechanical parts box to inflate the new tube. Feeling pretty proud of myself—a woman who had little first-hand experience with the mechanical and manual trades—I mistakenly thought the worst was behind me.

As I occupied myself with the tire, Aggie had busied herself rearranging the boxes that had slid off their stacks in the rear of the truck. She finished, came around to my side, and watched me wrestle with the tire, the last step.

"That's the worst part for me, too," she told me. "I think it's easiest with two pairs of hands." She was right. Between the two of us, we were able to get the tire back on the rim and the rim back on the vehicle. We had a moment of heart-sinking fear when the truck sputtered and died with the first crank, but at the second try the engine came to life and we were on our way again.

I studied my dirty hands with amusement: two broken nails and a deposit of grease along the knuckles of both hands.

Aggie looked over at me. She didn't commend or compliment, only grinned and said, "The carburetor will need work next."

A nonchalant shrug was my only response. I'll pass that test, too, I thought to myself, see if I don't, and for a moment I experienced a ripple of undiluted power and confidence. I liked feeling that I had the wit and will to do any task set before me and found the sense of authority the feeling generated to be as intoxicating as champagne.

# *"~Winter of the world~"*

# Chapter 3

We arrived at our first destination—a hospital set in an old chalet in the countryside southeast of Rouen—before noon, rolled through two large iron gates that hung open, and pulled into a courtyard.

"It's beautiful here in the summer," Aggie said. "Climbing roses cover the walls and the air's filled with their perfume. Not so nice now but it won't be long before it warms up. We've had an unusually long and cold spring this year." We squished our way through a few muddy puddles to the heavy wooden front door, but before we could raise its knocker, the door opened before us to reveal the figure of a woman.

"Mademoiselle Beechum!" the woman cried with delight and sidestepped Aggie's outstretched hand to embrace her and then step back to kiss her gently on both cheeks. "How very good of you to make the trip!" Despite her gaunt face and faded blond hair, the woman carried herself with an elegance that would have fit the most sophisticated drawing room. Her English was impeccable, her welcome gracious, her emotions sincere.

"Countess, this is Meg Pritchard, newly arrived from the United States. Meg, meet Countess Desmarais."

"I am Cecile," the woman replied. "I am not Countess anything." To an elderly man hovering behind her she said, "Paul, unload the truck and bring the boxes into the front room."

"Only those boxes marked with Rouen," Aggie interjected. "We have other stops," and Paul nodded his understanding.

As he slid behind us and exited the front door, Cecile took Aggie's elbow and propelled her into the house and then into the first room off the hallway, a room of graceful proportions that must once have been beautiful but had been transformed into a nearly empty utilitarian office. A large, rather ugly desk stood in one corner and only the window curtains, striped in elegant green and blue satin, hinted at what the room must once have been. I could envision it with a large rug of rich colors covering the scarred wooden floor and filled with furniture delicately designed with curved backs and slender legs, furniture that in its own way resembled Cecile herself.

"I hope your trip was not too fatiguing or the roads too crowded," the Countess said to me as Aggie counted the boxes that Paul carried into the room in which we stood.

"No," I replied, not even remembering my frustration with the flat tire. "It was pleasant enough, and we met very few others on the road, just farm wagons."

"I told the men of your arrival only today because I was afraid something would happen to delay you. They anticipate visitors with such pleasure, and I can't bear to give them disappointing news of any kind. I prefer to leave that to the doctors."

"It's very generous of you to open your home to them," I said, making conversation, and was unprepared for the passion of her response.

"Generous?! Generous to these brave men who have suffered so much? No, no, not at all, Miss Pritchard. It is they who are the generous ones." The tears that suddenly filled her mild eyes made me uncomfortable and embarrassed. I had forgotten how open the French were with their emotions.

"I'm sorry," I said hastily. "I didn't mean to—"

She placed a hand on my arm. "You did nothing for which to apologize. This is your first visit and I spoke too quickly, but it was from my heart, you see. Sometimes it's more than I— but you and Miss Beechum should come with me. Then you will understand."

Aggie came over to us, her arms filled with a pile of small cloth bags. "Here, Meg, take some of these." Obediently, I stretched out my hands for the felt sacks and realized each one was filled with several small items. "We're ready now," Aggie told Cecile and the three of us filed out of the room, down the hall, and up a handsome double staircase.

Once upstairs, we stepped into what I guessed had once been a ballroom, with a row of small windows high along the east wall, windows that had probably never provided quite enough ventilation when the room was crowded with dancers. No one was dancing now, however. Ten beds lined each side of the long room, and in each bed lay a wounded man. A nursing sister stood by the far door.

My first thought was how very clean the room appeared, how pristine the walls and how white the linen that covered each cot. The light coming in the windows intensified the impression. They were a variety of men, from a young man I didn't think could have been older than fourteen to men of middle-age and beyond, at least two old enough to be grandfathers, but all of them pleasant and smiling. Like children doing their best to practice good manners, each man thanked us for the small gift first and then as we moved on to the next patient dug into his cloth bag and pulled out a razor, playing cards, chewing gum, and a pencil—each gift a grab bag of thoughtful trinkets.

When we finished distributing the small pouches and stood at the other end of the long room next to the quiet nurse, I looked back at the men who no longer lay in inanimate stillness but called to each other. Many held up an item for a neighbor's attention.

Aggie must have seen the surprise on my face. They were such commonplace items, as ordinary as penny toys to children, that the men's reactions seemed out of proportion to the triteness of the offerings.

"They're men grateful for small favors," she said gruffly. "It's been a hell of a war for them."

We left without much additional discussion, Aggie Beechum not being a woman to spend her time on the inconsequential. After repeating the same procedure at a hospital set up inside the local church in a small town called Yerville, we accepted the offer of lunch from the nursing sisters there before we left again and motored even farther north. I could feel the tang of the sea in the air long before we reached St. Valery. The hospital there was grand by any standard, located as it was inside a large resort hotel, but it seemed especially so compared to the two we had visited earlier in the day.

"Over a hundred and fifty beds here," Aggie told me. "This place used to be where the weary rich came from all over Europe to recuperate from their strenuous lives of spending money. Now it's where some of the most seriously injured are brought. We'll sleep here tonight and head back to Paris tomorrow." I had the nagging idea that I'd heard of St. Valery before but despite the presence of a grand hotel, it was really only a picturesque fishing village with a fine view of the sea, not a town I would have had any cause to recognize. We turned the boxes of gift pouches over to the head matron for her to distribute, and Aggie and I unloaded the last of the medical supply boxes from the back of the truck.

"Just leave them outside," Matron instructed. "I'll have someone take care of them later. Could I interest you in some tea? I have coffee, too, if you prefer the French custom."

"Coffee would be perfect," I said, and we trooped through the front doors of the hotel *cum* hospital. It had been a day of jolting over rutted roads on the hard seat of an old Ford interspersed with dragging boxes of hospital supplies down hallways and over thresholds. I was ready for coffee and would have taken something stronger but didn't suppose the hospital matron was going to crack open anything with alcoholic content. What predominated through my jumble of thoughts from the day's activities was the sobering realization that if this was what my days would be like assisting the A.F.F.W., I would hardly have the opportunity to vanish into the French countryside and strike out on my own. Clearly, I needed another plan but I needed the coffee first. The charitable life of volunteer work was more physically taxing than I expected.

We passed through a ward on our way to the matron's office when I heard my name spoken in a low voice at my elbow. Surprised, I turned and looked directly into the face of Lucy Rose March. I admit, tired as I was, that it took me a moment to place the face. She wore the white wimple-like head scarf that all the nurses wore and which from a distance and in multiples turned them into a group of alarmingly similar figures, but once I met her serious gaze, I recalled both her and the reason the name *St. Valery* had held a vague familiarity. St. Valery-en-Caux. Lucy March and I had at one time discussed the village situated on the cold northern coast. I had not paid much attention at the time and once the conversation ended, I had had no reason to commit the name to memory, not expecting or desiring to meet the young nurse again in a country the size of France. My intention was then, and still was, to disappear, not pop up at unexpected times like a child's jack-in-the-box.

"It is Meg Pritchard, isn't it? I almost didn't recognize you without a life belt strapped around your waist." Perhaps my brief inability to place her had shown on my face.

"Hello, Miss March," I replied, even as I mentally cursed the idea of meeting someone who would recognize and thus also remember me. What were the chances of finding a familiar face along the wild north coast of France? Yet here she was: Lucy Rose March. I gave a quick, obligatory smile at her comment and corrected myself. "Hello, Lucy, I mean. I recall now that you told me you'd be working at St. Valery-en-Caux. It's a very impressive facility. And call me Meg."

She gave me one of the quick smiles I recalled from our time on board the *Ausonia*, a smile that turned her fleetingly into a beauty.

"It truly is impressive," she agreed, "and Dr. Fitch is wonderful. I'm learning so much." She looked toward the doorway where Aggie and the matron waited for me. "I see someone's waiting for you and I'm on shift for a while yet, but if you have some free time later, maybe you'd like to take a quick stroll along the coast. The wind will be colder than you'd expect for May, but the view is glorious and I recall that you seemed to find the ocean appealing."

I should have pleaded weariness and begged off but caught unawares found myself accepting her offer.

"Good," she said. "How about six o'clock in the front lobby? Remember to dress warmly." She smiled at me again and turned back to the row of beds along the wall, all filled with the still figures of bandaged soldiers. These were the most seriously injured, Matron had told us earlier, and from bed to bed I could see motionless figures with heavily bandaged limbs and faces so swathed in bandages that only their eyes and a gaping hole for a mouth showed. They did not look quite human and the thought caused an involuntary shudder. What kind of life did the future hold for them, even if they survived the sudden and immediate trauma of their dreadful wounds?

I saw Aggie shift from one foot to another where she waited at the door and recognized that sign of her impatience.

She was as tired as I and just as eager for a warm beverage so I picked up my pace to join her, wishing I could go back and tell Lucy I'd changed my mind about that walk. I had no wish to be included in her circle of friends so maybe I'd do just that when I met her in the lobby: plead fatigue and beg off the outing. The young woman's quiet nature was the kind that seduced confidences, and I had no intention of sharing anything of importance with her. It must have been the compassionate nature of her profession that made a person want to talk to Lucy March, and I would have to be on my guard with her, a prospect that was, in its own way, as fatiguing to contemplate as the thought of dragging more boxes up more steps.

After coffee with Matron, Aggie, and I made our way to a small room, long but so narrow that the two cot-like beds located there fit only because they were arranged foot to foot. I was reminded of the cramped quarters on board the *Ausonia*. We dropped our travel duffels, mine on loan from Aggie, beside the beds and together went in search of the dining room where the staff had their meals and where Matron had assured us we would not be too early—or too late, for that matter—to find warm food. Aggie and I ate without much conversation between us and when I told her I was going to renew my acquaintance with a nurse I'd met on my trans-Atlantic crossing and take a walk through town toward the coastline, I asked if she wanted to join us. At the last minute I'd thought that it might be a good idea to have my fellow volunteer along when I met Lucy. Aggie's blunt-spoken company might be just the thing to keep any inadvertent confidences from slipping into the conversation, but at the suggestion Aggie heaved herself to her feet, shaking her head as she did so.

"No, thank you. You're a better woman than I am, Meg, and that's a fact. The wind off the water will be too cold for me and I've been spoiled by central heating and a featherbed. I'm tired, besides. You go ahead." Aggie looked tired and all her age as she stood in front of me. I watched her walk away, her pace slower than it had been that morning, before I rose, too, and went out to the lobby. The lobby clock said ten minutes to the hour, then ten minutes after before Lucy came hurrying into the lobby.

"I'm sorry," she told me, trying to catch her breath. "We had an emergency just as I was leaving." I didn't ask my question, just raised my brows in query, and for a moment Lucy's thin face looked stricken and desperately young.

"The young Scot in the bed by the door—you must have seen him; you walked right by his bed when you left—hemorrhaged. He'd lost an arm and a leg, but we all thought he was healing. It was on my last round that I saw the blood. Some of the sutures had split. Another thirty minutes and he might have bled to death!"

Without giving my words much thought, I commented, "Maybe he would have preferred that."

I heard Lucy's quick, sharp intake of breath and expected a retort of some kind, a scold, perhaps, or a lecture on the sanctity of life, and when nothing was forthcoming, took a quick look at her face. She was partially hidden by the hood of the heavy cape she wore, but I could see she was looking straight ahead and not at me. She's counting to ten, I thought with a little humor. I didn't recall any kind of temper on her part from our earlier shipboard conversations, but admittedly I'd been preoccupied and hadn't paid a lot of attention to much of what she said at the time.

After a long silence, she finally responded, "Maybe he would have, but he's not in a mental condition to make that kind of decision right now. A year from now, or two years, or ten, he may appreciate being alive." I wondered if she really believed that or was just repeating some kind of nurse's credo she'd learned in school, but I hadn't the heart for an argument just then and changed the subject.

"You seem to have learned your way around town in only a few days," I commented. Lucy had set a brisk pace, leading me through narrow streets and alleys until we came out in the center of town next to a long canal.

"I generally walk before bed. The exercise helps me sleep." We came up to a short rock wall that separated the street from the descent toward the shore of the Channel. Just a few days before I had been looking at the same body of water from the British side. Regardless of manmade borders, the Channel possessed no real politics or patriotism. It was water, plain and simple. I stepped up onto the wall and took a long, leisurely moment to absorb the view. It was very late afternoon and the setting sun illuminated streaks of orange and red in the rocks of the cliffs, a striking scene.

Lucy stepped up onto the wall beside me. "It's glorious, isn't it?"

"Yes." I took a deep breath of the sea air. Around me gulls dove and called to one another with raucous insistence. I felt a brief but piercing homesickness and stepped back down onto the ground. "Thank you for bringing me here."

She stepped down, too, and without a word we both turned and started back the way we'd come.

"Is it what you expected?" I asked. Somehow she knew I wasn't asking about France or the sea or the village or even the hospital itself.

"I don't know what I expected, exactly, but it's almost too safe and too—" she searched for a word "—clean, somehow."

"Hospitals are supposed to be clean, aren't they?"

She made a clicking noise with her tongue in response to my purposeful dimwittedness. "You know what I mean."

"You expected bombs and trenches of mud, I suppose."

"It's silly, I know, because I signed up to work with Dr. Fitch and I knew he wasn't working at the Front but was at one of the largest hospitals in northern France, but still…" Her voice trailed off. "I feel I should be doing more."

"Why?" We both walked steadily without looking at each other as we talked.

"Because I—well, I've lived in peace and plenty all my life, and I should pay something back."

"Why?" I asked again.

She answered my question with a question of her own. "Haven't you ever felt the slightest curiosity about why some people have so much and others so little?"

"No, I can't say that I have." I could almost hear her mulling over my frank admission.

"Well, since childhood I have wondered about it and felt I needed to try to balance things out."

"It seems like a presumptuous undertaking for a single human to put herself in charge of making the universe fair and equitable. Presumptuous and impractical."

She surprised me by laughing. "When you say it out loud like that, it does sound presumptuous, doesn't it?" The hospital was now visible ahead of us in the distance.

"Anyway, you've just begun. It hasn't even been a week. Hopefully, once you get more settled you'll discover a variety of ways to assuage your conscience."

Lucy laughed again. "You're probably right." We trudged on in silence until we reached the hotel, climbed the steps to its porch, and entered the lobby area where most of the chairs were filled with recuperating patients. "I'm going to find some supper. Have you already eaten?" she asked, and at my nod thrust out her hand. "Thanks for the company, Meg. I was glad to see you again. The A.F.F.W. makes regular deliveries so I hope I see you at your next visit. Promise you'll look me up if you get back this way." I hesitated but she waited patiently for my response.

"I will." My words sounded grudging, like a child promising to eat her vegetables or do her chores.

"Good. I'll look forward to it. Take care, Meg." She gave me one of her sweet smiles, although describing it as sweet offers a wrong impression. There was nothing weak or false or even sweet about Lucy March's smile. *Pure* might offer a better description, or *transparent*.

"You, too," I said, and we both headed off in opposite directions, she to the dining room and I to the narrow, closet-like space where I found Aggie already asleep.

We made a direct return trip to Paris from St. Valery-en-Caux and after only one more flat tire, which I was able to handle more quickly than the first time, we pulled up outside the A.F.F.W. depot in the very late afternoon. The condition of the roads being what they were—rutted, rough, and pocked with holes—it was a wonder we didn't have a regular procession of flat tires for the full 120 kilometers of the trip. As it was, a trip that would have taken four hours under non-wartime conditions took twice that. By the time we signed ourselves in at the depot, climbed back in the Ford, rattled our way to the Hotel Premier, found a spot on a side street to leave the truck, and plodded into the hotel lobby, neither Aggie nor I was in much of a mood for conversation. I couldn't recall the last time I'd felt so tired to the bone.

Aggie disappeared briefly into the rear kitchen and said as she reappeared, "Someone will bring supper upstairs in an hour, which will give us enough time for a couple of hot baths first." The thought of both the bath and the supper brought a faint smile to my face, all I could muster at the moment, but by Aggie's nod I could tell she read my approval.

We found our voices again later, once we tasted the chicken stewed in white wine and served with apples and managed a few inarticulate murmurs of endorsement as we ate. Finally, warm and full and content, we looked at each other across the small table.

"Perfect," I said.

"Damn straight," Aggie replied. I wanted a cigarette but Aggie had made it clear she didn't approve of it in the apartment and by then I was too sluggish to walk down to the hotel kitchen or even step out into the hallway. In lieu of the tobacco, I refilled my wine glass and held it up between us.

"Here's to the Ford," I announced. "Long may she prosper." In perfect concord with the sentiment, Aggie finished her wine with a final swig.

"You did all right for your first time," Aggie told me, "but it was an easy enough trip. Weather was good and the roads fairly dry. Everything changes right after a rain." I could well imagine how the dirt roads would turn muddy and the deep ruts fill with water. "We'll hope the weather holds through Saturday."

"Saturday?"

"We're off on Friday again, only farther east this time."

"How far east?" I asked.

Aggie smiled. "Not as far as the Front, if that worries you, but you might be able to hear the guns if the wind's right. Up to Amiens and then down to St. Quentin. Just one overnight." She rose, stacked all our dishes except my wineglass on a tray, and carried everything to the hallway outside the door where she left it on the floor. Returning, she stood in the entry way of the small kitchen. "I'm for bed. Not as young as I used to be."

"I'll have another glass," I said, adding "if you don't mind" as an afterthought. She was still the hostess, I supposed, but our trip together had changed my original feeling of being a stranger and a guest.

"Finish off the bottle if you want, Meg. When I was your age, I wouldn't have stopped with one glass either."

Sitting there by myself, nursing a glass of ruby red wine, I thought through the preceding days. My lack of altruism allowed me to disregard the recurring image of rows of pristine hospital beds with their exhausted and immobile inhabitants. War, after all, so, of course, there would be injured men, but I hadn't expected so many catastrophic injuries, multiple missing limbs and heads swathed in bandages that indicated a man whose face would no longer be recognizable to his family. I didn't let myself dwell on the columns of the trudging dispossessed, either, even while I admitted to myself that the memory of those curiously passive, blank-faced women, children, and old men who had had the misfortune to live within the range of the big guns and had seen their villages blown into oblivion was harder to ignore. What I needed to spend serious contemplative time on was how to ditch Aggie Beechum long enough to disappear into the French countryside. Added to that was the question of where I was going to go once I did so. I had once considered taking the truck along with me, but it had taken only one laughable second to give up that thought. Remaining unnoticed in a backfiring Ford truck with the emblem of the A.F.F.W. painted proudly on its doors was a disappearing act beyond the talents of even the famed Harry Houdini. I sat there long enough to refill my glass yet again, but despite—or perhaps because of—the wine, I did not have a single flash of inspiration. I seemed unable to plan for the future when I was tired and various parts of my anatomy ached from being bounced around on the seat of the Ford. Never a woman to belabor the obvious, I emptied my glass with one final gulp and went to bed.

We made the scheduled trip to Amiens with only one mishap: the fan belt stopped working. After taking a studied look at our predicament, however, I used a hairpin to fix the problem and we made it the rest of the way home without further incident. I felt inordinately proud of the hairpin solution, and my sense of accomplishment made the entire trip enjoyable. St. Quentin was the farthest east Aggie had ever traveled, and we listened for the echoes of artillery but to no avail. All we heard besides the chugging of the truck was birdsong heralding the pleasures of spring. The roads farther east were worse than the ones we'd experienced the week before, probably because they were used more frequently by heavy military equipment moving toward the Front, but we didn't meet any such vehicles on our trip. Only the heavy ruts gave evidence of their presence.

The day after we returned from that second trip, Aggie tossed a copy of the Paris *Herald* onto the table where I sat with my afternoon tea.

"Look at that," she ordered. "My French is pretty bad, but I managed to get the gist of it."

I set down my cup and spread the front page out on the table. The "it" was a front page article with a bold headline announcing that President Woodrow Wilson of the United States of America had appointed Major General John J. Pershing to head the American Expeditionary Forces. Thousands of American forces would land in France by the end of June, the article stated firmly, and the war was as good as over. I studied Pershing's distinguished face in the grainy photo beside the article. A handsome man of stellar reputation and exceptional military pedigree, but I still thought the tone of the newspaper's announcement was too exultant and too optimistic. America's standing army, while made up of competent and brave men, was untrained and untried. Surely Pershing would not send over soldiers that were not fully prepared for combat, and becoming combat ready would take time, regardless of France's enthusiasm for the decision. For the first time since we had parted ways, I remembered Captain Chesney and wondered if he were somehow part of the Pershing entourage, an advance emissary, as it were, to pave the way for American solders. He had been met at the train station by a French officer of high rank, after all. I don't know why or how I came to such a conclusion but would find out later that it was surprisingly accurate.

Aggie poured herself a cup of tea and came to sit across from me holding the steaming cup in both hands.

"What do you think about this?" I asked.

"I suppose it's for the best," she answered with grudging concession. "Europe is running out of young men and I can't blame England and France for crowing about having the Americans on their side. Germany has to be running low on soldiers, too. The mud and the shells don't discriminate nationality. But I hate the idea that we'll be seeing American boys laid out in those hospital beds. Hate it like hell. It's not those damned kings and czars and kaisers getting their legs blown off. Not presidents either."

"But how could Wilson ignore the fact that Germany tried to form an alliance with Mexico and promised to hand over some of the United States if Mexico agreed to the arrangement? I mean, what other interpretation can anyone put on it except that Germany planned to invade and conquer the U.S. and then apportion it out as they chose?"

"Politics, Meg. It's nothing but damned politics or I'm not an old maid from Texas with more money than sense."

"But if the Americans can shorten, even end the war—" I let my voice trickle off, seeing the trade-off as Aggie saw it, fresh dead in exchange for fewer dead. Seeing it that way robbed the news of any triumph.

"A fresh supply of energetic Yanks will make short work of the war," Aggie agreed in a sober tone, "but it won't be without cost. It's a devil's bargain. Bring men in to get killed in order to save men from being killed. Doesn't sound right somehow, but there's nothing you or I can do to change things."

"It's not just soldiers getting killed in war," I said. "Maybe it means that fewer villages will be leveled and fewer people left homeless."

Aggie gave me a searching look. "Those people on the road bother you more than the wounded soldiers, don't they?"

"I wouldn't say *bother*," I retorted, but I had never forgotten how unsettled I felt after seeing that procession of refugees my first day in Paris. For a reason I did not understand, the plodding, lost refugees with their soulless stares affected me in a more profound and lasting way than any of the injured soldiers I'd seen lying in hospital beds. Perhaps I identified with the displaced more than I cared to admit.

Aggie rose. "Well, we'll deliver what we're told to deliver and it won't make no nevermind what country those poor boys in their beds and bandages came from. We're scheduled to leave again the day after tomorrow, a long trip due east to the depot at Quimper where we load up with as many supplies as we can carry. One overnight stop at Chartres on the way home and that's all."

"That's five hundred kilometers one way! So what is that, three hundred miles, maybe? That's at least a nine hour trip if we're lucky enough not to have any mechanical problems, which we both know isn't going to happen. And where do we find enough petrol for that kind of trip?"

Aggie grinned at me. "I never pegged you for a whiner."

"I'm just pointing out the practicalities." I felt unaccountably offended by the accusation and my reply was short and cool.

"If you say so. Anytime you want to stay behind, Meg, you only have to say the word. I wouldn't want to offend your delicate sensibilities."

I glared at her a moment, then said, "Oh, shut up," taking a page from Aggie's book of blunt speaking. "Don't even think about going alone but be sure to bring along a good supply of hairpins because something tells me we're going to need them." I stood up. "Now I'm going to go for a walk."

The only reason I minded a lengthier trip, I told myself, was because it tied me to Paris and Aggie and the A.F.F.W. when I knew I should be headed into the anonymous countryside. One more trip couldn't be helped, however. After that, unless I was visited by some kind of inspiration, I might have to pack my bags and slip out to the train station in the dead of night. A fine thank you to Aggie for her hospitality but I couldn't help that. Self-preservation always trumped good manners.

The ride to Quimper was bone-rattling. The plains and hills of northeastern France were bare and the wind off the water cut through layers of clothing. Later, the A.F.F.W. depot personnel would confirm what Aggie and I had already heard: that it was unusually cold weather for the season, that by late May the sun was typically warm and the jonquils, primrose, gorse, and violets already in full bloom. The information, meant to assuage the cold misery of the drive, was small comfort, however. In addition, we had two flat tires on the way and by the time we reached Quimper the gasoline pipe had become unsoldered and bounced along with us over the ruts in a way that made me expect to blow up like an incendiary bomb at any moment.

Combined with the petrol we carried, the explosion would have blown Aggie, me, and the Ford into thin air. That was one way of vanishing into the French countryside, but I had hoped for a less fatal way of disappearing without a trace.

Once we pulled into the Quimper supplies depot, we turned the Ford over for repair to a boy named Gerard, who couldn't have been older than fourteen. He was small for his age and managed to slither under the truck without needing to lift the vehicle off the ground. When he explained about the gasoline pipe in halting English and told us what he needed to do to fix it, both Aggie and I nodded like we understood a word he said and told him to go ahead with whatever he thought needed to be done.

"You might want to take a look," he suggested, having given Aggie's bulk a dismissive glance and turning his attention to me, "so if it happens again, you'll know what to do."

"What? Crawl under there with you, you mean?" I asked in skeptical French. At his nod, I didn't bother to protest, just divested myself of my top layer of clothing and joined him under the Ford. He pointed out the wire he'd used on the pipe. "It needs to be resoldered, but there's no one here who can do that for you. I did the best I could, but I can't guarantee it will hold all the way back to Paris. I'll throw extra wire in the back so you can restring it if you have to." I nodded and the two of us wiggled our way out from under the truck.

"Thank you," I said to the boy. To Aggie, I added, "Don't worry. Gerard and I have it under control." As I spoke, it occurred to me that the words were true in their own odd way, and it was the first time I'd felt in control of anything for several months. I had to believe that was a good sign, even if the only thing I felt in control of was a gasoline pipe.

We slept overnight in a spare room volunteered by a woman whose entire house was smaller than the front foyer of the house in which I'd lived for the last ten years. The room itself was the size of one of my childhood closets. But the two tiny beds both had featherbeds and warm woolen covers and even Aggie, who was longer and broader than her bed, fell asleep quickly without a word of complaint. We left early the next morning, the truck loaded with supplies for Chartres and Paris and had to stop along the way more than once because as

Gerard had prophesied, the wire he used to hold the pipe together jostled loose because of the bumping and thumping caused by roads that were so rough they were nearly inaccessible. The first time I wiggled under the chassis I was somewhat uncertain if I'd remember what to do, but by the third repair my manner was so offhand that a person might have thought I'd spent years working under a truck instead of having seen the undercarriage of a Ford for the first time only one day earlier. When we finally reached Chartres, I was muddy and messy and I didn't care about my appearance one bit. We had made the trip in good time, and I had enough wire left to fix the blasted gasoline pipe two more times, which I thought would be just enough to get us the last eighty kilometers to Paris.

After our overnight stay at the local hospital in a room saved for visitors, Aggie insisted we stop in town long enough to view the cathedral before making the final leg of our journey home to Paris.

"I've seen my share of churches," I replied to her suggestion, "and I'm sure I can survive quite nicely without seeing this one."

"Calling the Cathedral of Our Lady a church is like saying the Rocky Mountains are mole hills. It won't take long, and I promise you won't regret the stop."

She was right. The Cathédrale Notre-Dame de Chartres rose over the city like some great medieval guardian, mammoth, stern, and gray with years. Only the windows warmed the structure, their brilliant, gem-like hues splashing onto the stone floor and giving the interior beauty and warmth. If a worshipper could make it past the imposing exterior without being terror-stricken by the divine foreboding and implacable judgment its design implied, he might be able to find a touch of grace in the colors within. Not being a religious woman, I was hardly the person to form a conclusion about the attraction of the cathedral to its congregation, but I could see that its size would make all the individuals gathered inside seem small and insignificant— and unrecognizable, which held more personal appeal than the idea of religious fervor.

Holding a conversation in the truck as we traveled was always a challenge due to engine noise and because we were wrapped in scarves and hats. Even so, our recent viewing of the cathedral caused Aggie to shout just as the Ford rumbled into life, "Pretty spectacular, wasn't it?"

I hopped in beside her, nodded, and shouted in return, "Yes, but right now your apartment is a lot more enticing, that and a bowl of soup."

She grinned and nodded in agreement. "Just a couple more hours to go."

"If the gasoline pipe behaves itself," I grumbled under my breath, and while Aggie couldn't have heard me, she sent me a look that indicated she read my thoughts. Don't count on that happening, her expression said, and she gave a shrug as Gallic as one native-born to the countryside through which we rattled.

"Nous vivons dans des temps troublés," she said over the noise, and even in French heavily tinged with a Texas drawl Aggie was right. These were indeed troubled times, more so on my part than she realized.

After being forced to stop to repair another flat tire along the way, which gave me the opportunity to tighten the wiring under the truck and preempt a breakdown, we arrived at the Paris A.F.F.W. depot in late afternoon. We left the truck behind for repairs, took a taxi home, and traipsed up the stairs to the welcoming apartment.

"You've got a knack for the mechanical, Meg," Aggie observed later over supper.

"And," I said, "I can shift into reverse."

"That, too." She lifted her glass. "Here's to a successful partnership." I touched my glass to hers and we both drank.

Aggie was right; we were a partnership of sorts. The two of us dealt well together despite our differences in characters and ages and backgrounds. I liked Aggie and surprised myself by also liking driving and—to an extent— the challenge of making that old Ford get us where we needed to go. Aggie never pried into my life or asked questions about my past. It was as if we had both been freshly hatched in France for one singular and solitary purpose. If I hadn't had other, more pressing personal matters on my mind, I could have settled in for the duration of the war right where I was and been content, but as tempting as that idea was, I couldn't allow the thought. Having a home address wouldn't do for me. Not then and maybe not ever.

Paris in late May was a city of surprises, still cool enough some days that I needed a sweater for my walk, brilliantly sunny and warm other times, with no rhyme or reason to the changes in temperature. Aggie helped out at the A.F.F.W. depot on the days we weren't driving and delivering, but I preferred to spend my time exploring the city, discovering great splashes of flowers in nearby parks and spending too much time on the Rue de Rivoli looking in the display windows at that street's many ladies' stores. I'd always had a weakness for fashion and stylish garments—still have to this day, for that matter—and despite the deprivations of war, Paris remained Paris, the world leader of fashionable dress. Colors were universally somber but hemlines were gradually creeping up to reveal a shocking amount of leg. There was a languid and subdued elegance in the revealing lines of Grecian tea gowns, leaving little of the female form to the imagination. Had I worn such a gown I would not have been accepted into the polite American society I'd left behind, but it seemed the only way to be considered scandalous in Paris was to be commonplace. Women's full and sweeping skirts of the past had become straight and were topped by utilitarian jackets that still managed to offer an indefinable style totally and recognizably French. I had a quick mental picture of myself in my old skirt, shirtwaist, man's jacket three sizes too large, and a cloche hat pulled down on my head as far as it would go to protect my hair as I crawled under the Ford on the verge of a muddy road. As far as couture was concerned, I had become a lost cause. No one who had known me in my earlier life, that leisurely life of privilege and wealth, could have imagined—or better yet—recognized me. Which, while an unplanned and unforeseen result of my present circumstance, was exactly the way I wanted it.

Aggie and I made a quick one-day trip that same week, and then were without assignment for several days while a mechanic tried to identify a noticeable hissing sound that occurred every time we accelerated. It was during those quiet days—days when I knew I should be planning my disappearance but instead strolled the city, visited the shops, explored the parks, and found inordinate pleasure basking in the morning sun at a nearby café while I clutched a small cup of bitter coffee in one hand and the local newspaper in the other—that Giselle came scurrying up the stairs to knock at our apartment door one late afternoon. Aggie was out, but I was the person Giselle wanted.

"You have a visitor, mademoiselle."

"I do?" I thought she must be mistaken because no one knew where I was. "Are you sure?"

"Yes. She asked for you most specifically."

*She.* Not *he*, at least, but Giselle's words still inspired in me a sense of foreboding. I couldn't think of a person who would know to come looking for me at the Hotel Premier. Not one person. How had someone managed to track me to this nondescript hotel when I hadn't told a single soul I was here? I followed Giselle down the stairs to the front desk, and when I reached the bottom Lucy March rose from the worn lobby chair where she sat. She wore civilian clothes, her nursing headdress, gray dress, and white apron exchanged for a plain white shirtwaist blouse and straight skirt in a lightweight rose-colored fabric, both garments emphasizing her slim, boyish figure. Her light brown hair, unruly with curls, was tied back with a wide ribbon the same color as her skirt. Despite being well past her schoolgirl years, at that moment Lucy Rose March did not look a day over fifteen, and I remember wondering at the time if nursing the horribly damaged and the dying would eventually rob her of her bright, youthful simplicity. I know for a fact that it never did—at least, not in the way a person would have expected.

"Meg," she said and came toward me. Something tense and watchful inside me dissolved at the sight of her.

"Hello," I greeted her. "This is a surprise. How did you find me?"

Lucy gave me a quick searching glance, somehow sensing my ambivalence at her presence, before replying with a slight smile, "I went to the A.F.F.W. depot and Mrs. Lathrop gave me the address." She looked around her. "It's an elegant place."

"Old but elegant, yes. We should all age as gracefully as the Premier." After a brief silence, I asked, "Is everything all right?"

"Yes, everything's fine. I accompanied some injured Brits from the hospital to the train station in Paris and had some free time after we got them boarded, so I decided to tour the great city before I went back."

"Have you just arrived?"

"No, I got here yesterday. I'm staying with an acquaintance who works at one of the city's hospitals and she's on call today. Then I thought of you. I knew you might have been on the road but decided to take my chances."

"I'm glad you did." I surprised myself by nearly telling the truth. There was something so engaging about the woman that I almost *was* glad to see her. Almost.

"I thought—well, of course, this is last minute and you probably have plans already but if you don't, I thought you might want to join me at one of the little sidewalk cafes I saw on my way here. My treat. It's nice to see a familiar face. I have to head back to St. Val tomorrow morning and I thought it would be—you know—a pleasant end to my little adventure." Her voice faded and I thought she was suddenly embarrassed and wishing she had never looked me up. I rather wished the same, but she was here now and for all her slight stature it was difficult to ignore Lucy Rose March. Besides, I still felt some residual relief that it had been only Lucy waiting for me in the lobby, and that relief put me in a good mood. I made up my mind as her words trickled away.

"Good idea. As it happens I don't have plans and I'm hungry. Let me go grab a sweater. I'll just be a minute."

Her thin face brightened. "Really? I thought you were trying to figure out a way to get rid of me and I was mentally going through sensible sounding reasons for taking back my offer." Her grin forced a smile from me.

"Let's not examine motives too closely. I know just the place for the best fresh vegetable stew, with brioche and a wonderful local wine to wash it all down. You'd never know there was a war on."

Several minutes later Lucy and I sat at an outdoor café, our table strategically located to enjoy the late afternoon sun. We had ordered our stew and were making cursory conversation as we sipped a lovely pale wine from earthenware glasses. I was thinking that if Lucy and I had both remained stateside our paths would never have crossed in a hundred years and yet here we were chatting like old friends—well, old acquaintances, at least—when a shadow blocked out the streak of sun in which we sat. Both Lucy and I turned, our hands shading our eyes to get a clearer view of the figure beside our table.

A tall young man dressed in khaki uniform—the uniform of lighter weight and different color than the last time I'd seen him but a man with the same hazel eyes I remembered—stood smiling down at me. With his hat secure under his arm, the setting sun gave his dark brown hair a gleam of gold I didn't recall from our earlier meetings.

"Miss Pritchard." Captain Chesney said my name with the formality of a debutante ball. "I thought it was you."

I looked up at him, narrowed my eyes a moment against the sun behind him, and saw his smile. That was different than I remembered, too. Much more attractive.

"None other than, Captain Chesney. You have the eyes of a hawk, I must say. Lucy, this is an acquaintance I met when I crossed the Channel: Captain Chesney. Captain, please meet my friend, Lucy March."

"How do you do, Miss March?" Chesney said and turned toward her with that same engaging smile. He held out his hand and when Lucy didn't immediately reach for it with her own, I gave a quick glance at her face. She was absorbed in the man, looking up at him with such intensity that she might have been memorizing his face for an examination she must later take. I can't think of a better word for it than *absorbed*, either. It was as if she had never seen a man before in her life and couldn't quite get enough of the novel creature that stood before her.

Finally recollecting herself, Lucy flushed slightly, stretched her hand to his, murmured a greeting, and replaced her hand in her lap, eyes downcast by then.

"Are you taking in the sights, Captain," I asked, "or simply stretching your legs between important meetings?"

"Oh, the sights. I haven't had a lot of time to see the city since I arrived and I had the afternoon to myself today. It seemed the perfect opportunity." After a momentary pause, he concluded, "Well, it was nice to see you again, Miss Pritchard, and nice to meet you, Miss March."

I heard the words, a prelude to departure, with relief but Lucy did not share my feelings because without so much as a look at me she said, "Please join us, Captain. We've just ordered bowls of the house specialty, a vegetable stew Meg assures me is delicious, and I'm sure they can rustle up another bowl for you."

"Rustle up," Chesney repeated, as if the words pleased him. He gave her a quick grin. "The words bring out the cowboy in me." With a look at me he added, "Thank you. I'd like to try the stew—if you're agreeable to my company as well, Miss Pritchard."

There was only one response I could make—did he really think I'd be able to say, "No, I'm not agreeable; go away"?— and in a few minutes the three of us were happily occupied with savory stew and brioche and a wine so light in taste it was almost lemony. The conversation seemed to flow as smoothly as the wine, too, but that was primarily due to Lucy's questions. She had a knack for making a person feel the center of attention, her questions appropriate, her head tilted slightly to the side bird-like as she listened with rapt attention to the answers. She was not pretending interest that evening, either. Even if such pretense had been part of her character, a ridiculous notion from what I knew of her, something about Captain Chesney of the United States Marine Corps had grabbed her interest from her first sight of him. Even then, at first acquaintance and with nothing very tangible to go on, I realized that Lucy Rose March had fallen head over heels for the captain. Fallen just like that. With just one look. It must have been the uniform, I thought with disappointed skepticism. I had pegged Lucy as someone with enough inherent good sense not to be bowled over by a handsome young man in a handsome uniform, but obviously I was wrong. I had always reacted to tales of love at first sight with the derision they deserved, but that afternoon for the first and frankly the only time in my life, thank God, I observed the unnatural phenomenon firsthand. Poor Lucy, I remember thinking with unbecoming arrogance and the slightest hint of wicked humor, though later when I saw the effect such an unplanned, unexpected, and even unwelcome emotion could have, I would find my arrogance replaced by pity and surprising admiration. That early evening, however, the three of us sitting in rickety chairs outside a modest French bistro at the tail end of a warm May afternoon, I felt no shred of either pity or admiration. I was very nearly bored by then, wondering if Lucy would thank me or curse me if I made my excuses and left her to continue her admiring interrogation of the captain when she stood abruptly.

"Oh, dear," she said, grabbing for her gloves and purse. "I don't know what I was thinking. I've lost track of time, I'm afraid, and my friend will be home and worrying that I'm not there." Captain Chesney, ever the gentleman, stood as soon as Lucy rose, and I could see a dilemma of good manners in his expression. Should he offer to accompany Lucy home and leave me sitting alone or let her depart by herself in order to keep me company? I was just about to propose the former when Lucy said to me, "Meg, thank you for suggesting this place. I loved it. It was perfect," before asking Chesney, "Captain, would you be kind enough to find a cab for me? I think I see one coming in our direction so maybe I'll be able to get home on time after all."

His etiquette decision made for him, Chesney sprinted down the sidewalk, one arm raised in solicitation for the cab, as Lucy turned once more to me.

"Thank you, Meg, for letting me interrupt your day. I really enjoyed spending the afternoon with you, and I hope I see you again." I merely smiled at that until her words, "It's not as easy as you think to disappear, you know. Life can get in the way of the best laid plans," sobered me, forced me to remember the observant shrewdness that lay at the core of Lucy Rose March. Before I could respond to her words, if I'd even known how to respond in any credible way, Captain Chesney returned at a lope.

"He's waiting for you, Miss March."

She put a hand on his forearm, a very light, brief touch, and said, "Thank you, Captain. Good luck to you," and with the quick vitality that was so much a part of her stepped to the waiting cab in the street. She did not look back at us as the cab carried her away down the street, around the corner, and out of sight. A small whirlwind of energy swirled in her wake and then stilled. Captain Chesney and I remained standing across from each other at our little table, both of us looking in the direction the cab had taken as if we expected it to reappear at any moment. I had just made up my mind to say my own good-bye when he asked, "Could you stand another coffee and a little more time in my company?" My companion signaled to the waiter, came around to pull out my chair, and ordered coffees in his barely passable French, all without waiting for an answer from me.

Despite my earlier intention to depart and against my better judgment, I sat down to wait for the coffee, sipped at it when it arrived, and wordlessly studied the man.

He met my gaze and gave the attractive smile I hadn't remembered. "Are you having as much fun as you anticipated, Miss Pritchard?"

Remembering the columns of refugees, the hospitals I'd visited, the wards of wounded soldiers, and the haggard nurses and doctors scurrying along corridors, I almost flushed. I suppose he had a right to throw my words back at me, but I still didn't like it.

I wrestled with the urge to make a snappy comeback and finally admitted with as much humility as I was capable of, "Fun in a different way than I expected. I've discovered that I have an affinity for crawling under Ford trucks and that's been fun. Sort of. In its own way." Even I didn't find my tone convincing.

"Was that part of your efforts for the A.F.F.W.?"

"Yes. My partner Aggie Beechum and I deliver goods to the hospitals along the coast and the roads are rough on the old thing. Rough on the Ford, I mean. I can change a tire without turning a hair and I've learned to work automotive miracles with a three inch piece of wire and a little chewing gum."

"I'm dutifully impressed." He asked another question and for a reason I cannot explain to this day, I began to tell him about our trips: the chateaus turned into hospitals, the soldiers in their pristine beds waiting for their bundles of small surprises, the delight a few boxes of gauze generated, how the rutted roads could jar your teeth enough to make them ache and how there weren't enough layers of clothing to keep the wind off the sea from cutting to the bone. I talked and he listened through several more cups of coffee until it was nearly dark and the waiter was sweeping around us with a broom.

"Well, Captain—" I began, suddenly aware that the earlier roles had in their own way repeated themselves, only he'd become the interested questioner a'la Lucy Rose and I was the one satisfying his curiosity just as he'd done for Lucy.

He sat back in his chair. "It's Mac. My mother did not name me Captain. I was christened McDermott Alan Chesney so couldn't you force yourself to call me Mac?" He was only half joking.

"It's the uniform. It doesn't seem right."

"Even soldiers have first names, Miss Pritchard, even captains."

I found a certain amusement in his calling me Miss Pritchard as he beseeched me to use his first name.

"I suppose I can force it out if I must." I stood. "But I think I should call it a day."

"I'll walk you back to wherever it is you're staying."

"No, that's not necessary. I live close and I often take an evening walk before we shut down for the blackout."

"Really, Miss Pritchard—"

I stopped in the middle of reaching for my handbag and said with a dangerous coolness he did not miss, "I suppose it will have to be Meg since you're so insistent on our being on a first name basis." He didn't look at all abashed.

"I'd like that, thank you."

I knew he'd backed me into the familiarity and he knew I knew. For all his farm-fresh appearance he shared some of Lucy's craftier qualities.

"Really, Meg," he started again, "I can't let you leave unescorted."

"You aren't in a position to *let* me do anything." My tone held no compromise. "I am quite capable of walking home by myself and, in fact, I prefer it. If you follow me, I will report you to the first gendarme I find and your superiors will have to come fetch you from a French jail. How would you explain that, I wonder?"

"Since you put it like that, I guess I don't have a choice. I admit my defeat. You win. No doubt you are always right." He grinned a bit when he said the words. I found Captain Mac Chesney difficult to put in his place. Either he had an unusually high level of self-confidence or I was losing my touch.

In the dim light of a day almost gone we peered at each other, and I was the one who finally laughed out loud.

"No doubt. And don't forget it." I paused long enough to make my point before I added, "Mac." I thought I should say something else: that I had enjoyed spending time with him or that he was a good audience, but I didn't. Instead, I spoke a simple good-night and turned away.

"Perhaps we could do this again," he said hastily to my back. "Meet for coffee, I mean, or lunch. I'll be in Paris a few days yet."

I shook my head without turning around. In the dusk it was unlikely he saw the movement. "Sorry," I tossed over my shoulder, "but Aggie and I are off tomorrow morning. We'll be gone for a week, and after that it's hard to tell what the future holds. Good night."

I didn't wait to hear his reply but walked quickly away toward the corner, suddenly eager to escape—an odd word to use, but it was how I felt at the time—yet in a contrary way, conscious of a vague but very real regret at the necessity of so final a good-bye.

## *"~rich with wild increase~"*

# Chapter 4

Aggie and I made two grueling delivery trips in early June, the weeks slipping by without fanfare. I was well aware that I was no closer to escaping Paris for parts unknown than when I'd first arrived, but I couldn't find a way to elude Aggie's presence. We lived together and traveled together. Whenever I thought I should simply gather my belongings and head for the train station some dark early morning, I would be pulled up short by a vision of me eventually disembarking the train. I'd be noticed, for sure, an American woman with no vehicle dragging behind her a large portmanteau with her initials engraved in gold. And where would I go? On at least two occasions while on the road I considered sneaking out into the night and taking the Ford truck with me, but on both occasions I stopped yet again, unsure about Aggie's response to my disappearance. Would she report the truck stolen and put all the efforts of the A.F.F.W into finding it? I rather thought she would. Aggie might part from me easily enough, but I didn't believe she'd act the same with that old truck. I'd allowed myself to be trapped by circumstances and had to fight a feeling of complacent safety. I was not safe, and in my heart of hearts I knew it.

Sometime mid-June I became conscious of a change in the atmosphere of the city, a palpable excitement that seemed to affect not only the people of Paris but coursed down the streets and alleys, as well, swept through the parks and gardens clearing away fear and despondency much like a wind might blow away dead leaves and litter. I couldn't put my finger on what it was I felt or why, but the surge of animation I saw in everything around me was surely caused by some new emotion not previously found in Paris, not since my arrival, anyway. Something livelier than the unfurling of late spring flowers. Something warmer and brighter than the June sun. What I sensed winding its way through the city might almost have been hope.

Then, the morning after Aggie and I returned from our second trip north, I grabbed a newspaper during my morning walk and saw the reason for the energy. On the front page was a photo of General John Pershing, the commander of the American Expeditionary Force, as he arrived in Paris. General Pershing was a handsome man, dignified and stalwart, a man of physical stature who appeared to tower over the French commanders. U.S. ARMY NOT FAR BEHIND ITS LEADER the headline stated with assurance. I thought that was probably true. The United States had entered the war in April and the French had been awaiting the appearance of American troops ever since. At last, fresh blood: the source of the hope that had changed the very air of Paris and cleansed it of the accumulated despair and fear of the past three years. The thought did not cheer me quite as much as it cheered the French. I had seen too many bandaged faces and damaged bodies to cheer the arrival of American boys. What if it were Scotty headed for the Front? The idea made me wince. I tossed coins to the newspaper seller and looked at Pershing's front page picture again, then looked more carefully a third time. The great man was surrounded by his officers, a crowd of them, but I recognized the man at the general's right hand immediately. He was not Army, that tall, muscled figure with the open face standing with serious expression almost but not quite at Pershing's side, but Marine. That much I knew because despite the crowd of uniformed officers in the front page picture, there was no mistaking Captain Mac Chesney.

Should I have known that Chesney was one of Pershing's men? Admittedly, I had not paid as close attention as I might have to the indefatigable stream of questions Lucy had earlier posed to the captain as the three of us sat over stew and wine. Had he said something about the reason for his presence in France then? Surely, even if I'd periodically drifted off, any mention of American troops in Europe led by "Black Jack" Pershing would have jerked me back to the conversation. I had the vague recollection that Chesney had mentioned being an attorney by trade because I remembered wondering how much use a lawyer would be in combat. I realized now that although he might be all thumbs behind a gun, an attorney could prove very useful for diplomacy or negotiation. I guessed that was exactly what Chesney had been up to for the months he'd been in France. An intelligent man, I'd realized from our first meeting, and someone just pleasant, just ordinary enough not to attract too much attention. Perfect for diplomacy, now that I thought about it, and perhaps even more perfect for spying. He had a non-threatening, almost common, look about him that would allow him, in everyday clothes, to be seen and then without much effort and with even less fanfare forgotten. Once home, I tore out the photo and tucked it into my cloth purse. I couldn't have said why.

Later, trusting a rumor, Aggie and I made the two hundred kilometer train trip southeast to the coast and watched 14,000 American troops step onto French soil. I was there against my better judgment and kept to the rear of the crowd, careful to cover my fair hair with a soft-brimmed hat. The cool Channel breeze gave me a reason to wear a drab jacket large enough and long enough to camouflage my form and the hat's brim shaded my face as we viewed the disembarkation.

I couldn't have dressed with more anonymity but felt edgy and restless, nevertheless, and finally said to Aggie, "I'm going to take a stroll along the dock. I'll be back in a few minutes." She shot a quick, keen look at my face, nodded, and returned to watching what appeared to be an endless stream of young men, most of them not much more than boys, march into a crowd of excited French citizens waving American flags. Obviously, Aggie and I weren't the only people who had heard the rumor about arriving American soldiers.

Mac Chesney and I spied each other at almost exactly the same time. Once the train station came into view, I could see that trains commandeered to carry the troops were in place and waiting for soldiers. I slowed my pace and decided to head back to Aggie. With only cursory attention, I noted groups of officers huddled in several separate discussions between me and the station when as if on cue, the two officers closest to me concluded their talk. The man facing in my direction lifted his head just as my glance settled casually and briefly on him and his companion. Mac Chesney stared at me and I at him, both of us surprised and one of us happy at the accidental meeting. He said something in a low voice to the other officer, saluted smartly, and came quickly in my direction.

"Meg!"

Only someone both blind and stupid could have missed the delight in Mac's voice and on his face at my appearance and I had neither of those handicaps. The man had given something away just then that I had already guessed. Surprisingly, at the moment I thought briefly of Lucy Rose March and felt an unexpected regret on her behalf.

The indistinct and out of character sympathy vanished as Chesney grinned and said, "I told the general it was impossible to keep a secret in Paris. I suppose we'll have more parades along the line."

I nodded. "The word's been out for days. Aggie heard it at the depot and Giselle, who works at our hotel, told me about the arrival last week already. At least with the speed and reliability of French gossip, you won't have to worry about missing important messages if the lines go down." After a pause, I added, "What exactly is it that you do, Captain?"

He shrugged. "Anything I'm told to do."

"But you had a role in arranging all this, didn't you?" I waved my hand toward the lines of soldiers headed for the train depot.

"A little role, yes, but all I really did was act as a courier. I'm a very small cog in a very large machine."

I examined his face, not believing a word of it. How deceptively mild the man was! Somehow I knew he'd had a much more important role in arranging the arrival of these troops than he would ever admit. But I wasn't interested enough to press the issue further.

"Are you still driving for the A.F.F.W.?"

"Yes."

"Having American soldiers on the continent might change that role, you know."

"Why should it?" I couldn't figure out what he meant and his only explanation was another oblique comment.

"We have a call out for ambulance drivers. I'm only being realistic when I say we'll need more than we have right now, which is none."

In little more than six weeks I would remember his remark and wonder at its prescience but then I laughed. "I'm barely competent to carry cardboard boxes so don't expect to see me transporting wounded soldiers any time soon."

"You never know."

"*I* know," I replied with emphasis. "Look, Aggie's waiting for me and I've got to go. If we don't catch a train back to Paris while we have the chance, we may be stuck here for days behind all those railcars of doughboys."

"Doughboys?" He must not have realized the term had made its way across the ocean ahead of the troops.

"The French are way ahead of you, Captain."

"I see." He smiled. "Take care of yourself, Meg."

"I'm not the one marching into battle," I retorted. "My only enemy is an old Ford truck and I've just about got the thing conquered. You're the one that needs to take care, Captain." After a moment I volunteered, "I'll tell Lucy I saw you." I didn't know where the words came from or why I felt compelled to say them but my reward was a brief, blank look.

"My friend, the nurse. Lucy Rose March. The three of us spent an afternoon together?" I ended my explanation with the lilt of a question and he had the grace to color slightly.

"Yes, of course. Miss March. I remember." But he hadn't, and I felt again the unexpected and vague pity for Lucy that I'd experienced earlier.

I gave him a look that expressed my opinion of his lame words but said only, "Good-bye, Captain. Good luck."

"Good-by, *Mac,*" he amended but I shook my head at that, gave a quick wave of one hand, and turned back the way I'd come. Odd to think of the times I'd run into Mac Chesney or he into me. If I believed in that kind of thing, I might have credited Fate and thought some kind of destiny was at work. But I didn't believe in that kind of thing, not in fate or destiny or even in God, believed instead that life was made up of chance encounters and luck, both good and bad, and accidents and coincidences. No chess board with a chess master moving the pieces. If there was a master at all, and I very much doubted there was, its name was Chaos.

Aggie and I returned to Paris that evening, made four supply runs in six weeks and on Tuesday, July 31, left for our fifth trip of the month. Our very last trip together, in fact, but I had no way of knowing that at the time. I remember the date even now, decades later. We planned to make the familiar trip to St.Valery-en-Caux, to what I thought would be another meeting with Lucy March and perhaps another walk along the water as we had done previously. This visit I would remember to give her the newspaper photograph I'd torn out, the one of Mac Chesney striding at the side of General Pershing, to see if I could detect the same unmistakable enchantment for the captain I had detected in her that warm late spring night weeks ago. I didn't know why it mattered or whether I cared about her feelings or was just nosey, but I admitted to myself that for some inexplicable reason I was interested in that relationship, however one-sided it might be. Lucy was a pragmatic young woman. Whatever was there about Mac Chesney to make her fall head-over-heels for him and so quickly, practically at first glance? I recalled the look on her face when she'd first seen him. Obviously, I hadn't seen what she saw that afternoon, still didn't, and couldn't understand her reaction. Human behavior is so curious sometimes.

We pulled up at the delivery entrance to the resort-turned-hospital at St. Valery, had our cargo unloaded, and parked the Ford in its usual spot. Usually there were several ambulances parked there, as well, ready to carry recovering patients to the St. Val train station or even, as Lucy had once mentioned, to carry those who were seriously injured all the way to Paris for specialized treatment available there. That day, however, the only ambulance in sight was an old model that looked the worse for wear with tires and running board caked thick with mud, one headlight broken, and a deep gouge on the same side as the damaged light. The gash ran the entire length of the vehicle, denting the side badly, marking through the words of identification printed there, and defacing the bright red cross that displayed its ambulance status.

"Somebody cut their turn too short," Aggie observed as we trudged past the ambulance into the hospital.

Once inside, Aggie went in search of someone to sign off on the delivery and I went to find Lucy. The hospital buzzed with unusual energy. Several orderlies pushed empty beds down corridors, and when I poked my head into a ward in search of

Lucy, I saw the nurses there rearranging the patients' beds, pushing them closer together to make room for more beds as if they anticipated an influx of additional patients. An ominous sign, I thought. What had happened to cause the stir?

Lucy, when I finally located her, filled me in, her eyes sober, her face pale, her hair stuffed so unsuccessfully under her white nurse's cap that the cap tilted crookedly on her head.

"Haig opened up an attack on the Germans this morning near Ypres. Three thousand guns. Nine divisions. Heavy casualties. The hospitals closest to the Front are already full and we just sent all our ambulances to the clearing station there to pick up wounded."

"Ypres," I repeated, trying to place the name. "That's in Belgium, isn't it?"

"Yes, just over the border." Lucy replied. "The Brits call it Wipers but that's not how the French pronounce it. Anyway, it's a hundred and thirty kilometers due east from here to Arras and then another seventy-five kilometers north from there."

"A hell of a drive," I told her. "We've been on some of those roads and calling them roads is a kindness. That's at least a five hour trip from St. Valery." At my words Lucy grew still.

"You say you've driven on those roads, Meg?"

"Well, as far as Abbeville," I amended. "Not as close to the Front as Arras but close enough to hear the guns. That was earlier this month." Her continued stare made me uneasy.

"You're looking at me like a cat considering an especially fat mouse."

"Am I?" Her slow smile was not reassuring. "Did you see the ambulance out in the yard?"

"I saw just the one, and it was so banged up I could hardly tell it was an ambulance. I didn't think it looked drivable."

"All cosmetic damage," Lucy said with a dismissive wave of one hand. "Except for a hairline crack in an axle, our mechanic said, and how bad can a hairline crack be, after all? I've seen hairline fractures, you know, and they practically heal themselves."

"Spoken like a true angel of mercy. Lucy, I am not an ambulance driver."

"Not yet."

"I drive supplies, not wounded soldiers. I don't want the responsibility."

"No doubt that's true." A rather grim censure crept into Lucy's voice; I thought the tone of a New England Puritan condemning dancing would have carried similar disapproval. "But what you want is not the issue here. I need a driver to get me to the Front and to collect injured soldiers from Ypres."

"Where's the driver that came with the ambulance?" I could feel my control of both the conversation and the situation slipping away.

"Broke his arm in two places. The roads were so muddy that they slid into the ditch and he got tossed into the mud. If they'd been going any faster the ambulance would have fallen on top of him but it came to rest upright—well, halfway upright—only the front wheel rolled right over his arm before it came to a stop. Miraculously, all the injured soldiers stayed strapped in and weren't injured. Charlotte, the nurse that was with him, ended up driving the rest of the way and she'd never driven before. They struck a bargain of sorts. Charlotte splinted Tommy's arm and he gave her driving instructions for the rest of the trip. Now we've got an ambulance and no driver. Except you, Meg. I'm approved to get to the Front and you're taking me."

I could have said no. Should have. But that day Lucy Rose March would not have been swayed no matter what I said or did, and it seemed silly to waste time in argument.

"Aggie will have something to say about it," I warned and she did, but it wasn't what I expected.

"I can get the Ford back to the depot without you, Meg. If they need you, they need you. It's that simple."

"But how will I get back to Paris?"

"Ah, Meg, use your head. You're not coming back. Not for a while, at least. If I know how these generals think, they'll keep shooting at each other for the next eight weeks with no success on either side, just a lot of mangled up boys, which will keep your ambulance full and you on the road. You've got a change of clothes in your duffel and I'll send your satchel up here on the next run from the depot and have them forward it on to wherever you finally end up. With the increase in patients, there'll be a need for more supplies and someone will be willing to throw your bag into the back of whatever they're driving. I'll see to it. You'll be fine. Might even find you like it."

"Like it?" I echoed. "Are you crazy, Aggie? People are shooting at each other out there."

She gave her loud laugh. "Can't argue with the obvious. Now go tell your friend it's a deal and you'll head out for Ypres at daybreak. That will give you a chance to have some supper and get a little sleep first."

The same look was on Aggie's face that had been on Lucy's. The look of a done deal, of something preordained and inevitable and right. I suddenly remembered my conversation with Mac Chesney, my confident rebuttal of his vague suggestion that I might one day be useful as an ambulance driver and his smiling response of, "You never know." It seemed that I was the only person unsure of my ability to handle the role, and if I were honest with myself, the notion did hold a certain tug of appeal for its adventure. What really clinched the idea in my mind, however, was the practical realization that there were few places less likely than a battered ambulance on the front line of war for someone to expect to find me. Smiling to myself at the irony of it, I thought that the safest place for me might well be right in the middle of a war zone.

Lucy Rose and I left at sunup the next morning. The two of us nodded wordlessly at each other when we met next to the solitary ambulance that waited in the yard. At least it was a recognizable Ford Model T, but it looked worse than yesterday, battered and dented with much of the bright red cross on its side scraped away. We'd still be recognizable as medical transport but just barely. A young man pushed himself from under the ambulance, wiped his hands on his trousers, and gave us a good-natured grin.

"She'll run better than she looks," he told us cheerfully and when Lucy and I had climbed into our seats, he started us with two easy cranks and we were off. I looked over at the hospital and saw Aggie on the front porch, not waving, just watching and I lifted one hand from the wheel long enough to give her a broad and unmistakable salute. She returned a wave before we pulled out of the yard and onto the road. I wouldn't see Aggie again for a long time, for months.

There's no way to make intelligible conversation while bouncing along a rough road in the front seat of a Ford ambulance, and Lucy and I didn't try. I was busy driving and my companion was busy not falling out of the vehicle. She held on firmly to the bar in front of her and stared straight ahead, clearly pretending there was a side door available to keep her from falling out when there was no such thing. When we stopped I kept the ambulance idling while we stretched and took care of any personal needs, and by mid-morning we arrived at a hospital just south of Arras. The hospital had formerly been a country chateau as had the hospital run by the countess near Rouen, but the Arras facility was larger, busier, and more crowded. I went in search of sustenance while Lucy sought out the hospital matron, and we met back by the ambulance within the hour. An orderly was loading supplies into the back of the ambulance under Lucy's supervision. She thanked the man and turned to me.

"We're less than two hours from the clearing station. This will be where you bring the injured, Meg, and where you'll most often find food and a place to sleep. I left your bag with the matron, whose name is Agate Diamond. I've told her about you."

"Oh?"

Lucy grinned at my tone, her small face lit by mischief. "All good, Meg. Don't look so skeptical. She thinks you're part angel and part mechanic, that you wear coveralls and a halo. Didn't I get it right?"

I couldn't help but grin in return. Lucy Rose March can have that effect sometimes. "Close enough," I said. "Are we ready?"

We drove around the city of Arras, which I would discover later was a pleasant town with a wide central square and a curious underground, interlocking cave system that had been around for centuries. Once north of Arras, we heard the booms of the guns, and the whole experience suddenly seemed extraordinary: I was driving a Ford ambulance straight into a battle zone. How it had come to this I didn't really know and how I would ever extricate myself from the situation was equally as baffling. For a moment everything seemed muddled in my head, but then I looked over at Lucy's profile and thought to myself that if she could make the trip into war without flinching, I could, too. That was the last time I had any self doubts for many months.

We were not alone on the roads. Passing us on the other side were ambulances already filled with patients. Meeting any kind of vehicle, machine or horse-drawn, on the narrow, rutted thoroughfares was always a maneuver fraught with peril. There was no guarantee that one or both would not slide into a side ditch, and I quickly learned that it was the empty vehicle that was expected to give way to the ambulance carrying the injured. Besides transports of injured soldiers, there were guns being hauled to the front by weary, straining horses, wagons of supplies, and always, always groups of men trudging away from the Front, the walking wounded with arms slung over a neighbor's shoulder for support, some with swaths of bandages traversing their heads or with arms in slings, some holding themselves upright with only a makeshift crutch in place of an injured leg or foot that could not bear their weight. I remember my first sight of such a group of men, the same as I remember my first glimpse of refugees on a Paris street, but it didn't take long for the sight—of both injured soldiers and displaced civilians—to become so commonplace that their presence often ceased to register in my mind.

The casualty clearing station was set up in front of a burned out farmhouse off the main road, easily identified by its line of stretchers that held injured men. We had recently passed two loaded ambulances headed back toward Arras and when we pulled into the muddy drive, I saw that men were busy loading some of the stretchers into another ambulance. My ambulance had room for six stretchers and an additional two, maybe three, less seriously injured soldiers if they could sit in the aisle. At the rate of eight or nine men per vehicle, it seemed to me it would take many days to transport all the wounded, and that only if no more wounded arrived on the scene. Later, I grew accustomed to the contrast between the frantic pace immediately following a battle—an endless line of stretchers waiting to be loaded, bodies set to the side awaiting burial, and medical personnel moving from stretcher to stretcher—and the quiet of the clearing station between battles, where only the surgical tent showed activity and a few wordless nurses and ambulatory patients stood outside smoking, trying to catch a moment of peace.

I'd hardly come to a complete stop when Lucy hopped out, tossing, "Wait here," over her shoulder as she headed for a man in a bloody smock crouched over one of the stretchers. I watched her wait for the man to finish his examination of the wounded soldier and rise before she put out a hand to his forearm and begin speaking. For all her slight stature and that unbecoming frizz of hair she could never quite tame, there was nothing retiring about Lucy Rose March. She spoke to the doctor without a hint of bashfulness, waited for his answer, and with a quick nod pivoted and came back to where I sat.

"Pull over there, Meg." She motioned toward a broad area of ruts and mud that would bring me as close as possible to the line of recumbent injured soldiers. "They have men ready and waiting to get to the Arras hospital."

I did as directed—I would quickly come to recognize the times when one's only action was to do exactly what Lucy said—and after orderlies had loaded the wounded men, Lucy stood in front of me. As usual, I had to tilt my head slightly downwards to meet her gaze.

"I'll be in the back with the patients," she told me, "and try not to hit every rut and bump you see coming, okay? We've got seriously wounded men here."

"You want to drive?" I eyed her without smiling before I tossed my cigarette past her shoulder. "No? Then let's agree that I won't tell you how to take care of patients and you won't tell me how to drive."

A smile tugged at a corner of her mouth but all she said was, "Deal." She handed her satchel to one of the orderlies. "Leave this for me in the nurses' tent, please," Lucy told him and didn't wait for his nod before she climbed into the back of the ambulance.

I met the young man's gaze and shrugged. "Don't argue with that woman," I said, "or there'll be hell to pay."

He was a wearied man that I guessed looked older than his age and he had a smudge of blood down one cheek, but he had a cheeky grin.

"Appreciate the warning. We already got hell," he said, "and I sure as shit don't need any more."

I wondered how Lucy would take to the language of the trenches, so often coarse and profane, but I had a quick memory of her climbing monkeylike down the escape rope on board the *Ausonia* with her skirts bunched around her legs and thought she would not allow herself to be distracted by anything that got in the way of her vocation. In our own unique ways, we were two of a kind. Both of us women on a mission, both of us finding what we desired at the Front, but Lucy Rose March's desire had a nobility to it that I could not match.

The guns were never quiet that day, but as we put distance between us and the clearing station, their sound became muted, like distant thunder on a stormy summer day. In the hubbub of arrival and departure I had somehow stopped hearing their constant pounding, and I would find that a not unusual phenomenon. It was only those times when the guns ceased altogether that I was shocked out of complacency by the quiet. Like everything to do with the war, life and its commonplace occurrences were backwards. Anything normal became peculiar and only the abnormal comforted because it was repetitious, and because of repetition also expected and commonplace.

With our patients delivered to the Arras hospital, Lucy and I stood for a moment in the front hallway.

"I'll park the ambulance at the mechanical garage," I told Lucy. "Someone needs to take a look at the fuel line."

"Well, don't take too long about it," she said. "All we have time for is a quick bite to eat before we head back."

I stared at her. "What?"

"There are wounded men waiting for us, Meg." At my continued silence, Lucy sighed. "This is the plan," she said. "You need to grab an orderly from here and make him your traveling companion. Then you need to get me back to Ypres, which is where I'll be located permanently. The station is down a nurse and I'm needed there. You and your orderly and your ambulance are a taxi service, Meg. There's little enough time for sleeping and eating and you'll eventually make the trip we just made so often that you'll be able to do it in your sleep. Not that I recommend you doing it in your sleep but—" she held out a hand as if stopping traffic "—I know I'm not allowed to tell you how to drive so as long as you get the wounded safely to hospital you can drive standing on your head for all I care."

Somehow at some time Lucy March had taken charge of both me and my vehicle, and I saw that it was useless to attempt any kind of rebuttal. Without a word, I turned on my heel and headed outside to the mechanical yard.

Once there, I walked around the ambulance and nearly tripped over a pair of legs protruding from beneath the vehicle. The skinny young man that eventually emerged, wrench in hand, gave me a quick look and a grin.

"I've met you before, haven't I?" I asked, taking in the pointed jaw and bright eyes.

"Yes. Quimper. Gerard."

"Right." I had a vague recollection of crawling under the Ford truck with the boy. "What are you doing in Arras?"

"Brought an ambulance for their use and just stayed. Got a little boring there in Quimper and I don't like boring."

"Don't you now? Have you been to the Front yet?" A little spark of interest showed in his eyes.

"I tried to get there by enlisting but they wouldn't take me. Said I was too young." His tone told me what he thought of that rejection.

"Not too young for ambulance work, though," I said, "and I need someone to make the trip between Arras and the Front with me, someone that knows motors and doesn't faint at the sight of blood. Interested?"

"Sure. When do we leave?"

"An hour," I said, "and don't make Lucy Rose March wait or we'll all be sorry."

"Lucy Rose March?"

"Our commander," I said. "You'll find out soon enough. Just don't be late."

He wasn't and later, the next supply of wounded loaded from the Ypres clearing station, Lucy already vanished into the surgical tent, and the ambulance turned for departure, Gerard stopped beside me long enough to say, "More than commander." He shook his head. "Commander-in-chief, more like it."

"I warned you."

He nodded. "You did. I'll pay more attention to what you say next time."

"It would be worth your while," I agreed. "Ready to go?"

Gerard climbed into the back with the patients by way of answer and we were off, the first of countless trips the three of us—Gerard, the old Ford ambulance, and I—would make throughout the summer and fall of 1917, loaded with men and their terrible wounds, the floor of the vehicle always slick with the endless mud that was often mixed with the blood of the wounded soldiers. Some died en route, and I would come to know by my first look at Gerard's face upon arrival at the Arras hospital when that happened, but more lived. I slid off the road half a dozen times and needed help from passing troops to get pushed back in place. Gerard was undoubtedly shaken up on each occasion. I would remember the gleam in his eyes when I first offered him the chance to get to the Front. That gleam disappeared soon enough, but he wasn't a boy to complain or panic and I don't think it ever crossed his mind that he was there purely as a volunteer and could leave the messy, dangerous business anytime he felt like it. Who would stop him? The same could have been said of me, too, I suppose, and for all my desire to remain unnoticed and invisible, I never once considered walking away. How strange that seems now! I think unless you were there in the middle of it, you could not understand the imperative under which we worked. Without overstatement, it was life and death. Always life and death. I did not realize it at the time but the road—a kind word *road*, giving the benefit of the doubt—between Ypres and Arras changed me. For better or worse I didn't know at the time, only that in some respects one woman began the work and another woman ended it.

# *"~a slow grand age~"*

# Chapter 5

"**M**eg, watch it!"

I stopped immediately, replaced my foot with gentle care onto the plank where I stood, and looked over at the surgical tent. After eight weeks I was well acquainted with Lucy March's voice, able to recognize it even if it came out of the darkness as at that particular moment.

"Why?" I called back.

"They just replaced the board and I don't think it's steady. We just cleaned up some poor sap who tipped it over. Sank up to his knees. Come around the other way."

I took Lucy's suggestion and backed up one careful step at a time until I stood once more on what passed for solid ground at the Ypres Clearing Station. The fall of 1917 had seen a constant deluge for weather, a deluge that turned everything into mud including the roads and worse, the battlefields. The past days Gerard and I had slid along the last few miles as if the road was covered with ice instead of mud. I had personally given up on ever feeling dry and clean again, and the thought of tumbling from one of the rough boardwalks into the sea of mud over which it was placed caused me a literal shudder.

By the time I took a different route to the surgery, the slight drizzle in the air had ceased and the clouds had parted to allow a watery moonlight through. Just enough that I could make out Lucy Rose March's pale face and the dark smudges on her apron that I knew were not mud but something else entirely.

"Here," she said by way of greeting and handed me a cigarette, its lit end a small radiant circle in the darkness.

"Thanks." I inhaled deeply, exhaled, repeated. God bless Lucy Rose. I had offered my last cigarette to a soldier on a stretcher, had lit it and held it to his lips. He had lost one arm at the shoulder and might keep the other above the elbow if he was lucky. Lucky. I shook my head at the word, at the thought.

Everything had taken on a different meaning after weeks of transporting mangled, ruined young men. Lucky meant alive. That was all. Alive.

"Are you all right?" I asked. It was not like Lucy to be so still, and I could hear that her breathing was ragged.

"Yes." She stood leaning against one of the side poles that supported the tent, her arms crossed over her chest, staring out into the darkness. I could just make out her profile.

"Sure?"

"Yes." Then immediately, "No. No, I'm not sure. What is this all about?"

"The war, you mean? Or life in general? Not that I have an answer for either. It's all lunacy." At my words, she looked over at me, and I thought I could see a glisten of tears in her eyes. Tears! That shook me. Lucy March was Gibraltar.

Once I saw her respond to a dying man's request to sing a chorus of *If You Were the Only Girl in the World*—"If you were the only girl in the world / And I were the only boy / Nothing else would matter in the world today / We would go on lovin' in the same old way / A garden of Eden just made for two"— holding his intestines as they spilled from his gut into her hands, keeping her eyes on the poor bastard's face, smiling, her voice slightly off tune and sweet as honey. As far from a garden as it was possible to be, but no tears then, or at any of the other times little Lucy Rose turned into an Amazon warrior before my eyes. But tears tonight, I thought. I am a woman of negligible sentiment, a woman that craves her own comfort but has little inclination to offer comfort to other human beings, and so I was silent and kept puffing on my cigarette. With selfish relief I heard Lucy take a deep breath and then another one, less shaky; I did not relish the idea of patting the nurse on the shoulder and saying "there, there."

"You're right. It is lunacy. All of it." A long pause, followed by, "Did you manage to stay on the road on the way to Arras?"

"Barely. That damned mud is slicker than ice."

"I never knew it could rain so steadily and so constantly. Wouldn't you think the sky would run out of water eventually?"

"The romance of France must be in its mud."

She gave a small chuckle before she said, "Well, I'm glad you and Gerard are back safe and sound. I don't think we have any cargo for you right now."

"I noticed. Are you expecting some in the near future?" I felt more than saw Lucy shake her head.

"I doubt it. Listen."

We both tilted our heads, two quizzical puppies listening for the voice of the master, the booming sound of the guns being our master in this circumstance. I heard—or rather, didn't hear—what Lucy meant. That close to the Front, we could always hear the guns, but that night the booms were sporadic, almost obligatory, certainly not the constant, deep-throated threat I knew meant men fighting, men dying. Even more noticeable, there were no shell whistles, either, no high-pitched whine that acted as a delayed warning to the listener to dive for cover. That September night in Ypres in the fall of 1917 held the relative quiet of a nursery.

"What's up?" I wondered, more a question for myself than my companion.

Lucy shrugged. "We don't know, but maybe they're getting ready for another assault."

"The Brits or the Huns?"

"Brits, we think. Haig can't admit that he might have made an error in the initial assault so he'll just keep throwing his soldiers at the line. If it didn't work the first time, maybe it will the second."

"Or third or fourth." Lucy made no response, and I threw my tiny cigarette butt into the night. "I'm going to bed. Are you on tonight?"

"Yes. Linda and Jo are there and no doubt asleep so go in quiet. It was a long day for them."

"A long night ahead for you and Mary, too, I imagine."

"Yes."

She turned to step around the corner of the tent but halted when I spoke her name and said, "Thanks for the cigarette."

"My pleasure," she replied before she disappeared.

I made my way along the planks to the nurses' tent where I always borrowed a bed on my overnight stays. There were four nurses at that clearing station and two of them were always on duty, which meant there were two beds always available. It never mattered whose. By the time I slipped inside the tent, the night drizzle had returned. I left my mud-encrusted boots just inside the flap and led by the muted snores made my way to Lucy's small bed where I flopped onto my back, reached for the folded blanket at the foot, and fell immediately asleep.

The morning saw a break in the dismal weather, patches of light breaking through behind clouds and even the glimpse of a watery sun. No warmth to speak of, too late in the year for that, but the sight was still welcome enough that when I stepped outside, I stopped for a moment and closed my eyes, allowing the tepid sunlight to rest against my face. More the absence of rain than the weak sun made me almost giddy with pleasure.

Since I'd awakened to an empty nurses' tent, I realized the two who'd been asleep when I arrived had left for their shift, and that meant Lucy was probably eating something before she headed for her own bed. When I pushed back the flap of the cook's tent, I found Lucy immediately. She sat on a bench at a long table, her elbows resting on the tabletop and her eyes fixed on the person across from her. I could see only the back of the man's head and his cropped dark-brown hair, but the olive drab uniform gave notice that it was an American soldier. That was unusual to start with. We were nowhere near the Americans' military quadrant and did not see many doughboys along the Ypres Front. Then I studied Lucy again, noticed how intently she listened to her companion, saw the expression on her pixie face and the way she tilted her head like a little bird trying not to miss anything, and I knew who it must be that sat across from her. I had seen that exact same expression and posture weeks ago at a sidewalk Paris café.

I would have turned around and exited, leaving Lucy and Mac Chesney to their own company, but at that moment Lucy looked up, perhaps feeling the chill of the morning enter along with me, spied me, and gave a welcoming wave. For neither the first nor the last time I considered how remarkable Lucy Rose March was. Any other woman, finding herself the sole recipient of the attention of a man she favored, would have wished an arriving second woman to the devil. Not Lucy. There must be a limit to her unselfishness, I thought to myself, not with admiration, and I hope I'm around to see it. She would have labeled her actions friendly. I found them foolish and just short of incomprehensible.

Chesney looked over his shoulder to find the recipient of Lucy's wave, saw me, and, doing his best to control the kind of double-take one might see in a stage comedy, rose and turned toward me.

"Captain Chesney," I said when I approached. "You manage to turn up in the most unexpected places and at the most unexpected times."

"I'm grateful you chose the word *unexpected*, Miss Pritchard."

"Opposed to?"

He grinned. "Oh, *unwelcome* springs to mind, or *annoying*, perhaps." He looked thinner, I thought, more tired than I remembered, perhaps even older. But war could do that to a person, that and much worse.

I smiled and looked past him to where Lucy sat watching us with an attentive, serious expression.

"How was your shift?" I asked her. I remembered the rare glisten of tears the night before.

She shrugged. "Not bad, and I'm grateful for the quiet. Mac says Ypres might be out of the action for a while." *Mac*, I thought. She's made progress, then. "Sit down for a while, Meg."

Chesney had gone in search of a cup of coffee for me so I was able to say, "I don't want to interrupt."

Lucy met my look, understanding my meaning exactly but she still shook her head and gestured to the bench across from her where Chesney had been sitting.

"You're not interrupting. Mac shows up from time to time without notice and we take the time to reminisce about home. That's all it is."

I was as surprised by the information of Mac Chesney's intermittent presence at the clearing station as I was skeptical of Lucy's dismissive tone. She couldn't know how transparent her face was and how it gave away whatever emotions she tried to hide, or she wouldn't have tried to make light of the man's presence. Just then the captain appeared with a tin cup of coffee and set it down on the table. I slid onto the bench from one end and he from the other and we came to sit shoulder to shoulder across from Lucy.

"Thanks," I told him, lifting the cup toward him before I took a sip.

"My pleasure." He smiled at me. "Lucy tells me you drive an ambulance." *Lucy.* That was telling, too.

"A diversion I chanced upon entirely by accident," I smiled so he'd understand my choice of words was intentional, "but it passes the time. And driving came highly recommended by an acquaintance of mine." I knew he would remember our conversation the day the A.E.F. landed in France.

"Sounds like a person of rare perception." He was pleased with himself.

"Perhaps."

After a pause, Lucy pivoted on the bench where she'd sat wordlessly observing Chesney and me, swung her legs over, and stood up.

"Time for this girl to get some sleep," she said. She looked tired, dark circles under her eyes and something like grief in their depths. Had something distressing occurred in the medical tent during the night or was it simply that she heard a tone in Mac Chesney's voice as he spoke to me that quenched her usual sparkle? I knew from my many exchanges with Lucy March that she could be frighteningly intuitive at times.

Chesney, ever courteous, made the same upright movement as Lucy and stood facing her. "Was it a rough night, my girl?" The pet name came easily to him; he had surely used it with her before. His tone was affectionate and concerned but it was not the tone of a lover, just that of an admiring friend or even a brother. I felt a quick pity for Lucy. Would it always be that she would love him and he would never be more than a slightly dispassionate friend? I would not wish that kind of pain on anyone and I had come to admire, sometimes even like, Lucy Rose March. She deserved more.

Lucy seemed to appreciate the inquiry, however, and answered with direct simplicity, "Yes. A young man we'd sent to the hospital at Arras a month ago with an injury that was not life-threatening—you and Gerard probably transported him, Meg—was released back to battle. They do that, you know, the powers that be, put them back on the line as quickly as they can.

Not that most of the soldiers don't want to get back. There's a strange pull to be back at the Front with their regiment, as if being wounded is a sign of disloyalty. Anyway, he was carried in yesterday and died last night. That same young man. He'd been found partially buried in the mud with a bullet in his chest."

What is this all about, Lucy had asked. Now I understood the question. What was the point of prolonging the inevitable? Why mend the young man only to send him out to his death a month later? What did it serve? Who did it serve?

"I'm sorry." Chesney's words were inadequate and he knew it the moment he spoke. He looked almost shame-faced at not having a better response.

"Stop thinking about it." My tone was as cool as his had been sympathetic. "It's done now, and you can't change it. That's not your job, anyway. Maybe the next one will stay in hospital longer. Maybe the next one will get shipped home. Maybe the next one will outlive the war."

Lucy stared at me and suddenly smiled. It was like the sun coming out after a thunderstorm. "Yes, you're right. Maybe we'll save the next one." A pause, then, "There are two fellows that need to get to Arras, Meg. I'll see you next visit." She turned to Chesney, who still stood across the table from her. "I never know when I'll see you, Mac."

He shrugged. "That's true. Take care of yourself, Lucy."

"You do the same." I must have been the only one to hear the underlying quaver of emotion in her words. Then she was gone, a slight figure with a mass of unruly hair, slipping out of the cook tent without a backward glance.

Mac Chesney stepped to the other side of the table and sat in the spot facing me that Lucy had vacated.

"Who's Gerard?" he asked, holding his coffee cup with both hands and eyeing me over its rim.

"My orderly. My ambulance companion. My traffic director. My rescuer from ditches. My one all-around necessity."

"And still just one man?"

"Just one," I agreed. "One very young man that knows his way under a truck and over French roads and who's worth his weight in gold."

"I'll have to meet him," Chesney said. "He must be a paragon to have passed your guarded and rigorous inspection."

"You find me rigorous and guarded, Captain? My goodness, I don't know how to respond to such an obliging compliment."

He said nothing, just continued to watch me with the barest hint of a smile upending the corners of his mouth. For an instant, I found the man incredibly attractive, something alluring about the lean face and warm eyes and steady gaze. It was the first time I understood how Lucy Rose could have fallen so hard so quickly. Mac was right. I was guarded around men, for a number of valid reasons, but I also missed their admiration and the pleasure a man experienced with women could offer. It had been a long time since I had thought about that, about murmurs in the dark and skin on skin, and my resentment at the warmth that came unbidden into my belly at the idea of Chesney's long-fingered, large hands on me made me stand up and say, too abruptly, "I need to find Gerard and load up our two patients while the rain holds off."

He stood up, too, but more leisurely and observed, "You never asked what I was doing here."

"Would you tell me if I asked?"

He shook his head, a tinge of regret in his expression. "No."

"Well, there you have it. I'm not a woman to waste words."

"That is true." Neither of us moved. "When you're not here, you're in Arras, I understand."

"Or on the roads between."

"You and Gerard."

"Yes. Gerard and I have been making the trip more often that we'd like, but that was when the guns were going full on. Field gossip agrees with you that Ypres is done for the time being and the action is going to shift."

"Shift where?"

My turn to shrug this time. "Oh, there's a lot of speculation, Captain," I studied his face, "but my guess is that you already know where."

"Me?"

"Yes, you. Why else would an American that has Pershing's ear show up at a small clearing station bogged down in the autumn mud of Ypres?" He made no reply. "But your secret's safe with me. I have plenty of things to worry about other than American reconnaissance."

"Such as?" Neither his voice nor his expression gave anything away.

"Staying out of ditches. Missing the shell holes in the road. Getting my cargo safely to Arras."

"Are you still having fun, Meg?" I heard only gentleness in his voice, nothing censorious or disparaging.

"Not exactly, but they still let me crawl under trucks so that's something." I would not admit to him my horror at the effects of mustard gas on a man's lungs or the wave of grief and fury I felt every time I reached Arras and found that one of the patients I carried had died en route to hospital. I would not give the man that kind of satisfaction.

"I understand the *not exactly* part," he said.

I didn't respond but turned around to leave without a good-bye. I thought he had seen too much already, too much that I wanted to keep private and secure and away from another's eyes.

"Meg." I stopped but did not look back at him as he said, "Don't be surprised if you see me in Arras."

I won't be surprised at all, I thought to myself and wondered where that would lead, but I still said nothing, just gave a slight nod that he would not have been able to see and left to find Gerard.

Sometime in the next four weeks Lucy's clearing station shifted south of Arras to the area of Amiens, a French city so old it was mentioned in documents of the ancient Romans. The city's dignified brick buildings had sustained serious damage from German shells and because Lucy's clearing station of hospital tents and crude resident quarters for the medical staff was set up within ten miles of Amiens, it seemed likely that the city could expect to experience even more destruction. What residents of the city remained had already set about fortifying homes and shops with whatever materials they could lay their hands on.

Gerard and I had to reconnoiter and learn the roads south of Arras—*roads* again too charitable a word for what we were forced to drive on—but he was a quick lad with an impressive memory and I had honed both my mechanical knowledge and my driving skills so between the two of us we were not easily fazed. We slid along on roads made treacherous by mud, watched horses trudge and strain through the mire with efforts so excruciatingly cumbersome that I often had to turn away from the painful sight. The poor beasts. The rain which Lucy had commented about weeks earlier continued in drabs and drizzles so the thoroughfares, not to mention the people, never had time to dry out. Mold and mildew appeared in the most unlikely and sometimes most extraordinary places.

I saw very little of Lucy. She was busy setting up the new station at Amiens while I still had a regular hospital run between Ypres and Arras. Despite the diminished shelling in that region, there were still wounded to transport. Well, there were always wounded, even in the quiet times. Where did they come from, all these gouged, shattered, burned, ruined young men?

One evening, just back from Ypres, patients unloaded into the capable hands of the sisters, the old Ford taken off to be scrubbed down and rewired—I had spent the better part of the trip alternately cajoling and cursing an engine that wanted to die every time I had to slow for a curve—and Gerard off to find a warm meal and a warmer bed, I came through the front door of the makeshift hospital to be met by Mac Chesney waiting for me in the entry foyer. He'd told me not to be surprised if he showed up, and I had in some recessed part of me been expecting him for a while. Not anticipating, exactly, but certainly expecting.

"Meg." He looked good, not tired or bedraggled as I certainly must have looked, just good. A tall, broad-shouldered man with warm eyes and an attractive smile. Very American. Very appealing. It was impossible to meet his gaze and not smile in return.

"You got it in one," I said.

He laughed. "You're not a woman to overlook or forget."

I removed my hat and shook out my hair before asking, "How long have you been in Arras?"

"I got in this morning. Had some business to take care of and have been hanging around the hospital since lunch." He gave me an objective look. "If you know some place that will feed us, I'll stand you for supper."

I didn't hesitate. "I do know a place. Give me fifteen minutes and I'll show you."

I thought from the fleeting look of surprise on his face that he had expected some resistance from me. He knew I wasn't always the most gregarious or forthcoming of people, but the man had caught me hungry and that made all the difference in the world.

Much later, with solitude and time for memories, I recognized that moment—Mac Chesney turning to face me with an eager expression he did not have enough time or subtlety to hide and something inside me pleased enough with the look on his face to decide that Chesney would be good filler for the dark December days and nights—as the moment that changed my intentions and in a way my future. I was right about Mac and then some because he ended up being much more than filler, ended up being the man to show me what I wanted, or more accurately didn't want, from life. But that was months in the future. For everything that passed and didn't pass between us, Mac Chesney was always useful.

The evening was innocent enough. Simple stew, tough crusty bread, and the local wine. Conversation, nothing that couldn't have been overheard by the local priest, and a little laughter. Mac was careful in his speech and I was more so, treading with light steps around the war and our roles in it.

"I'm just Pershing's lackey," Mac said with his typical self-deprecating charm. "Doing what I'm told and going where I'm sent."

"But sent to Arras of all places? The Americans are nowhere near here," my not very subtle probing.

"One American is." He grinned.

"Two," I reminded him.

"So you say." I raised my brows at the comment but said nothing. "Because, Meg, you never talk about your life back home. From your speech you're probably from the North, though not New England. Michigan, Ohio, Illinois? Somewhere thereabouts, I'd say, but then maybe not. You could as easily be from Canada so maybe not American at all."

"North American, then," I replied. "You'll give me that."

"I'll give you anything you want," his tone serious and then a quick grin, "even the last glass of the red." He held up the wine bottle we'd commandeered from the waiter. I shook my head at the offer.

"It's all yours. I'm done in."

He made careful work of finishing off the wine before he asked, "Are you off on errands of mercy in the morning?"

"No. The old clearing station is almost shut down and we haven't received a summons to the new location yet. I don't know why they picked Amiens because it's relatively quiet there but for now there's not enough death and destruction to warrant our getting on those damnable roads." I waited to see if he'd respond with a comment, however cryptic, about why the clearing station had shifted south, but when he remained quiet, I added, "Are you off in the morning?"

"No." He swigged down the last of the wine from his glass. "So there's nothing to keep us from doing this again tomorrow night." He did not look at me as he spoke but I knew he waited for my reply, something significant in my response that we both recognized regardless of the fact that neither of us would have, could have articulated what that something was.

"No," I said, and at the ambiguity of the syllable his eyes lifted quickly from his wine glass to my face. "There's nothing to keep us from doing this again. Nothing at all."

He didn't bother trying to keep the relief from his voice. "Well, good. I could get fond of the wine here, and the company, too. Especially the company."

Looking at Mac Chesney across the small table, I saw how the future might play out. We would be lovers, he and I, and in the end—and there's always an end—I would not be the one left with the heartache. Chesney was a likeable enough man and would be a pleasurable diversion whenever we were in the same general vicinity, but I did not love him in any way. We were made of different stuff. He was the kind of man to read marriage as a natural follow through and I knew I would never marry. When the time was right, I'd warn him about unrealistic hopes as I'd had to do a time or two in the past with others, but I already knew my words would not register with him. Too honorable, perhaps, or simply too constrained by the world in which he'd been raised. But with death all around us, perhaps my speculation was, if not inaccurate, at least premature. This world of war was new to me. For all I knew, and as contrary as it sounded, we might both end up dead before I had the chance to hurt him.

We repeated dinner the next night and walked back to the hospital where I had my quarters. We stopped at a dark street corner midway on the walk home and Mac turned me into his arms to kiss me, a practiced and satisfying kiss on both our parts, and then we began walking again. I appreciated that he did not feel the need to talk.

"I don't know when I'll see you again," he said as I turned to push open the front door. I turned back.

"Life's like that in war time," I said.

"Life's like that in peace time, too, Meg."

"I suppose."

"Thanks for the evening and the pleasure of your company."

A long quiet moment passed, my hand still resting on the door handle and he standing with his hands in his pockets, the moonlight behind him showing only a dark outline of his figure.

"You're welcome."

"I hope we can do this again sometime."

"No doubt you'll have to get General Pershing's permission first."

He gave a low laugh. "No doubt."

What else do you want to say, I wondered. What do you want me to offer? I lost patience with the moment and with waiting for him to say more.

"Good night, Mac," I said. "Take care of yourself."

I heard his soft reply, a mirror of my own words, as I went inside and pushed the door shut against him.

# "~for us, wild Winter~"

# Chapter 6

The guns did not begin in earnest until the new year, and in the quiet interlude before fighting resumed I managed to hitch a ride with a transport carrying injured soldiers to Paris. I felt restless with inactivity and had a sudden desire to see the city and spend time with someone not of a medical persuasion. Aggie, I decided, would be a welcome break from nursing sisters in their prim white caps and young men whose most defining color was not the uniforms they wore but the crimson that spattered the uniforms.

Aggie did not greet me with open arms exactly but with a grin and the offer of a warm meal, a bottle of wine, and a featherbed in her spare bedroom. Heaven, really, and much preferred over open arms any day of the week. I was more gratified by the pleased expression on her face when she saw me than I cared to admit and accepted everything she offered without apology.

"Are you still driving for the A.F.F.W.?" I asked.

Aggie nodded. "Yes, with Lulu keeping me company more often than not." At my blank look, Aggie added, "Lulu. You met her at the office your first day here. She's a good gal to have along and not afraid of anything, but I have to admit she doesn't have your hand with a wrench."

"Oh," I said with a grin, "I'm even better with a wrench now."

"I'm not surprised." Aggie refilled both our glasses. "There was someone looking for you several weeks ago."

"Oh?" I kept my hand steady, my expression only curious, and my tone nothing but inquisitive. "Who?"

"A good-looking American soldier. Chesney he said his name was. He was looking for you at the A.F.F.W. and I didn't tell him much. Just that you were driving ambulance along the Front somewhere. I hope that was all right."

I had relaxed almost instantly at the mention of Mac's name and said, "He found me."

"A good looking man there, Meg."

"Yes, I suppose he is." Aggie said nothing and I laughed. "Not *suppose*. He definitely is a good-looking man."

"Sure seemed disappointed you weren't in Paris."

"Life," I said, "is full of disappointment."

Aggie lifted her glass. "My friend," she said, "I'll drink to that." She paused. "Well, come to think about it, I'll drink to damn near anything," and I had to laugh again. I'd missed the woman more than I realized.

We talked about the war, especially about the difference the Americans' arrival was making. The American Expeditionary Force hadn't been involved in much fighting that I'd heard about, but just knowing that thousands upon thousands of doughboys were tramping east toward the Front seemed to invigorate the poor, decimated, exhausted Allied troops and must certainly be equally as intimidating to the Germans.

"Maybe just having their feet on the ground is enough," I suggested. "Maybe the Americans won't have to fight."

"Oh, the Huns won't give up that easily. Their generals are just as pig-headed and stiff-rumped as everybody else's. I never saw such a useless bunch of old men on both sides as the ones in charge of this war. If I could blow 'em all up at once, I could end the fighting tomorrow. Though God knows nothing will bring back the young men lost on both sides. Lost in the mud. Lost on the wire. Lost to the gas. God, it makes me sick to think about it." She paused and shook her head, her expression ferocious. "The Germans," Aggie finally continued, "will throw everything they've got at the line in the hope of making it to Paris before Black Jack Pershing gets his military house in order. You'll see your share of American blood, more's the pity, but the end of this damnable war is getting closer all the time. The Americans are the only ones that aren't sick to death of it."

Without expecting it, Mac Chesney's clear-eyed face and engaging grin came to mind, and I felt a quick, sharp pang of something almost like worry, almost like fear. I had to shake my head to clear it and blamed the wine for the intrusive mental image.

I was glad for the break and glad to spend Christmas with Aggie, who never pried or questioned or said anything but what was truly on her mind, but I surprised myself by missing the Front, at least my mechanical view of it. I knew my ambulance like it was a member of the family and missed the challenge of keeping it running and out of the ditches. I never wished for wounded, but when I had them safely stowed in the back, I took to heart the challenge of getting them all to the hospital alive. Men that died in my ambulance on my run were personal failures. Not that that happened all that often. The hopeless, those of gaping wounds and seared lungs and burnt, blackened bodies, those that could not be saved regardless of ambulances and hospitals stayed behind and died under the compassionate gaze and in the tender hands of Lucy March and nurses like her. That was their job, theirs and the doctors. To sort through the wounded and pass along to the ambulances those injured that had a chance of survival, to make godlike decisions about men's lives. I wouldn't have had that job for the world.

The first time I saw Lucy at the new clearing station she was crouched next to a man that lay on a stretcher. Her right hand rested on his shoulder to calm him while her left lifted the blanket that covered him to examine his injuries. His groans were audible even at the distance I stood. Neither she nor I had seen each other in weeks and she had not looked away from the soldier since I stepped into her view, yet somehow she was as aware of my presence as I was of hers. I halted and waited until she lifted her head, met my gaze, and gave an abrupt shake of her head. I did not react, only turned away and moved down the line of injured to find those that would be my passengers, those that had some chance of living.

Later, driving toward Amiens with Gerard situated in the back with the wounded and the cold late-January wind buffeting the vehicle enough to cause it to shudder under the weather's attack, I recalled Lucy's expression. Despite an outward appearance of objective and professional nonchalance, I was sure something wounded and sad had showed in the depths of her eyes. Perhaps I only recognized it because it was what I sometimes saw in my own mirror.

By early February of 1918, the Germans were pressing west toward Arras with every intention and, it looked, with every likelihood of reaching the town that had once been my home base. Gerard and I made runs to and from the Amiens hospital with regularity while simultaneously awaiting a summons from the hospital in Arras to evacuate the remaining injured soldiers before they fell into enemy hands.

I recall January and February as a blur of misery, wet and cold months that went on forever, filled only with the sound of the guns and driving and driving and driving some more. The mud deepened, the roads got even more rutted and slick, the trips to the Amiens hospital more challenging. Our first objective became not to make it to the hospital with the injured still alive but simply to stay on the road and out of the ditches. Sometimes my hands ached from clasping the steering wheel to keep the ambulance moving forward in some semblance of a straight line.

That February Mac Chesney appeared out of the blue at the clearing station. I saw his presence reflected on Lucy's face before I saw the man in person. I suppose Lucy March couldn't help the subdued happiness that made her eyes glow whenever she spent time with Chesney, whenever she was assured he was alive and well. I wondered at it a little, at her capacity for what must surely be love when he did not reciprocate the same feeling. She must be miserable with the knowledge, I reasoned, any woman would be, but little Lucy Rose never appeared miserable in the presence of Captain Mac Chesney. Always just the opposite, in fact. I could not imagine that kind of love.

I greeted Mac at the meal tent where he sat with Lucy, grabbed a cup of coffee, and turned to leave. The ambulance would by now be packed and waiting. When Chesney called my name, I looked back to see him say a quick word to Lucy as he stood and quickly pushed away from the table. Lucy nodded and lifted her head to look in my direction. If I were closer, I wondered what I would see in her expression. She was not a petty woman but did she wish me to the devil at that particular moment? I wouldn't have blamed her.

Mac and I stepped outside and moved to the edge of the wooden platform that had been built to keep the tent's entrance out of the mud.

"You're the first American soldier I've seen in this neck of the woods," I said. "Aren't you a little far north? I heard Pershing is training his doughboys around Verdun."

"Got a little lost, I guess." He grinned but added no additional information. I wondered what kind of work Mac Chesney really did that had him roaming all over northern France.

"Looks like," I agreed. "Maybe Lucy makes you lose your sense of direction."

"Lucy?" His initial tone was blank and it took a moment for him to find my meaning. "Oh, Lucy Rose, you mean. She's a good kid. I like her." He has no idea that she's head over heels for him, I thought with something almost like astonishment. If that wasn't like a man!

Lucy disposed of, Mac lowered his voice. "But Lucy's not the woman that got into my head."

"No?"

"No." I shifted my weight and he said, "I know you've got to go, Meg, but I might be in Amiens sometime in the next few days. Just a short stop, but if you're there—"

I pulled my hat down further over my ears. "Look me up, Mac. If I'm there." I turned and stepped carefully onto the boardwalk that led to dryer ground where the ambulance waited.

"Take care of yourself," his voice behind me casual, and without turning I lifted a hand back over one shoulder in wordless farewell.

Mac appeared at Amiens's hospital on the first of March. For some reason I remember the date, perhaps because I was so relieved I had survived January and February, or perhaps because I realized that somehow in the past few months I had forgotten my need to disappear. It was why I had left the States for Europe, after all, and yet my life was so wrapped up in transporting the wounded that I had allowed my original plan to slip into the background. Except for Mac Chesney, there were no Americans in the vicinity but it had occurred to me, despite blurry fatigue and constant driving, that that would not be the case forever. Rumors had the Americans pushing east. I might find myself surrounded by young American men at any time, and it was not out of the question that one of them might recognize me from my life stateside, something I wanted to avoid at all costs. The idea of slipping away once more infiltrated my thoughts. I'd managed to forget for a while, but in the end, Lucy March had been on target: my intention had always been, still was, to "disappear completely."

Deep in those thoughts, I did not at first notice the tall figure that rose from a chair in the hospital's entryway. Mac Chesney, a man whose patience I was coming to know well, waited for me to notice him. When I finally raised my head and saw him, he smiled and said, "A penny for those thoughts."

Despite myself, the sight of him increased my heartbeat. He was not the darkly handsome hero of popular novels, but he was good looking in an American way with eyes that held a touch of amber, well-proportioned broad shoulders and narrow hips, and a smile that lightened his face and gave him a look of mischievous boyhood. I was glad to see him and hoped it did not show on my face. Never let a man get too sure of you. There was not a one of them that could be trusted past throwing distance. Not that I wanted to throw Mac Chesney anywhere at that moment. Far from it. I was tired and in need of both comfort and attention. Chesney would do fine on both counts.

He took in the red smears on my trousers. "Did you just get in?"

"Yes, and unloaded. What are you doing here?"

"Passing through. Have you eaten?"

I looked down at my blood-stained pants and back at him without bothering to disguise my opinion of the question. He caught both the look and the opinion.

"Sorry. Of course, you haven't. I'll wait if you want to change. Unless you're not hungry."

"I'm always hungry," I said. "Yes, wait. I'll be back in a little while."

We found a small café that, like all the café's in the area, had no meat on the menu—not with troops to feed—except a rich, spicy dish made with fish carted down from the northern coast. More vegetables than fish and more spice than vegetables but still hot and satisfying.

At the end of the meal we sat without talking, the last of the wine to finish and then the walk back to the hotel. I felt warm and relaxed enough to say, "Can you stay the night?" Purposefully ambiguous and interested in his response.

For a moment he didn't look up and when he finally met my gaze across the table, he smiled.

"I would if I could. There's nothing I'd like better. You must know that by now."

"But—"

"I can't stay the night. Not in any respect, whatever you were asking."

"Black Jack beckons."

"Something like that."

I had purposefully kept the night ahead intangible, had not heightened my anticipation with defined thoughts, let alone words, and had not given in to imagination or expectation. Yet I must have counted on Mac's presence in my bed without realizing it. How else to explain the unvoiced but sharp and very real disappointment I felt at his words? And was it Mac's absence that cut or simply the idea of another night alone when I would have appreciated any distraction from the grueling work of transporting the injured day in, day out?

I shrugged and finished my wine. "Well, too bad, but Gerard and I are off to Arras first thing in the morning so it's probably just as well." I don't believe my regret showed on my face or in my tone.

"Arras? Why Arras? The clearing station is due east." His sharp tone made me stare at him across the table.

"We've been asked to finish evacuating the hospital there. The less seriously injured were moved out already, most sent on to Paris for care, but there were some patients too seriously injured to move. Matron told us that couldn't matter now, that we had to get the remaining injured out of Arras tomorrow. No delay."

Mac frowned and reached across the table for my hand. "Listen," he said, "the Germans are within ten miles of Arras. Odds are they'll take the city very soon. You shouldn't go. It's too late for the hospital now." His hand tightened on mine as I tried to pull loose.

"Don't be an idiot. Of course, I'll go. I'm the best damned driver around. That's why I was picked. I'll be fine." I knew his presumption was based on whatever it was he felt—or thought he felt—for me, but I didn't like the tone of his voice, something akin to ownership. Did he think that an invitation to spend the night gave him the right to tell me what to do? That was something I wouldn't tolerate. With a twist I freed my hand, stood up, and said, "Since we both have other plans, I think it's time to go home."

He stood, too, smart enough, perhaps attuned to me enough, to realize he had made a mistake. Later, as we walked the narrow, dark streets back to the hospital Mac stopped and reached for me, and I came into his arms willingly enough. By then I was open to whatever attention I could get from him and knew from our earlier times together that he was a man who knew his way around a woman. Practiced hands and a competent mouth that caused me to reevaluate my ideas of what went on in South Dakota. Something more enjoyable than corn fields and prairie sod certainly.

"I'm sorry, Meg."

I didn't ask him what for, just stood wrapped in his arms in the late winter darkness and wished the war and the ambulance and Pershing to the devil. I would have enjoyed spending the whole night finding out just how adept Mac Chesney was at making a woman happy. I suspected that between the two of us, we would each have figured out how to make the night memorable.

"I had no right to tell you what to do. No right even to suggest anything to you. You don't work for me. You don't report to me. You don't belong to me."

"Nobody belongs to anybody, Mac. Not any more. We fought a war about that, remember?"

"I know. I know." He paused, kissed me again, held me tightly against his rough woolen coat. "It's just that I—" I didn't want any great profession of emotion from him and put up a hand to his lips.

"Never mind, Mac. All is forgiven. Let's forget about it."

"Ah." The single syllable told me he realized he had almost said too much. How and when had he come to know me so well? The realization that I was not the mystery I thought I was made me shiver.

Mac shifted me out of his arms and took my hand in his. We began to walk again. "It's just that I try to keep the people I like out of trouble," he said, his voice light and empty of any heartfelt emotion.

"It's the hero in you, I suppose, but Gerard and I will be fine, though I admit I'm not always averse to trouble, just selective about the kind I get into."

"That's a comfort." He squeezed my hand, something almost brotherly in the gesture, and walked me to the front door of the hospital. "Watch your step tomorrow, Meg," the last words I heard before I went inside to bed. Alone.

Gerard greeted me with the same news that Mac had shared: "The Germans are within ten miles of Arras," but Gerard's voice held a nonchalance that had been absent from Mac's words. Through the last months I'd discovered what a remarkable young man Gerard Giroux was, fifteen going on fifty, bright and fearless and more reliable than sunrise.

"So I heard," I said, the sum total of our discussion about any danger that might be on the day's agenda. We were bound for the hospital at Arras and there was nothing else to be said.

We heard the guns' booms and the shells' whistles before we reached the city, and as for the city itself—how to describe the devastation that had ruined historic Arras! There simply were no words. I had to dodge the timbers of shelled buildings on the outskirts just to get to where the hospital was located, and once there was horrified to see that the northeast corner of the building had sustained a direct hit. Only a blackened shell remained where, if I remembered correctly, had once been located a long ward lit by clerestory windows and the matron's small office.

When Gerard and I pushed open the front door, the hospital seemed like something out of a ghost story: chilled, dark, vacant, and abandoned. But then a figure appeared at the end of the hall, the matron with the unforgettable name of Agate Diamond, whom I remembered from my earlier time there. She looked as starched and pristine as if she had just begun her shift in an affluent, modern metropolitan hospital. Something about the nurse's fixed and intent expression made me suddenly conjure up Lucy Rose, who would have communicated the same scorn for danger and privations when it came to her patients' well-being.

"You've come from Amiens." No introduction from this purposeful woman and the reproachful hint of an unvoiced *finally* in her tone.

"Yes, Matron."

"I have three patients prepared for travel."

"We were told five."

"Only three patients," she repeated, "now." I felt unaccountably guilty, as if somehow I had been the cause of the two deaths. "We'll have to bring them out this way, through the front. The back of the hospital has been rendered useless from the shelling."

"Looks like it took a direct hit." I said, stating the obvious. "Was anyone—?"

"Two patients. Two nurses." Her tone did not invite further conversation and I had no wish to know more. I was acquainted from earlier times with some of the nurses there and preferred to think of them as I'd last seen them: young, helpful, pleasant women. And alive.

Matron, Gerard and I brought the three French soldiers down the hallway on stretchers, the men swathed in bandages and immobile.

"I gave them something for the pain," Matron said. "No doubt the roads between here and Amiens are even worse than usual, although God knows how that could be possible."

I eyed the still figures lying on their stretchers in the back of the vehicle. "If you need us to stop, you'll have to scream at us through the flap," I told her, "but I don't recommend we pull up for any reason until we get to Amiens. She's been a hard crank of late and I can't guarantee we'd get started again if we have to stop."

Matron stepped back from me, a twist to her mouth and her eyes narrowed. "Surely you don't think that I would accompany you."

We all inadvertently ducked from the sibilant shriek of an overhead shell that landed somewhere on the same side of Arras as we stood.

"You can't stay here. Everyone's gone, and the Germans are close enough you could see the shine of their belt buckles." The specter of nurse Edith Cavell, executed by the Germans in 1916, hovered briefly between us.

But she was French, this gray-haired woman with her ramrod spine and nerves as unbending as her surname, and had seen death in all its iterations.

"This is my hospital," she said, "and this is my home. *Le Boche* may find their way in but they will not stay long, and I will be here when they leave." Her voice softened. "Be careful with my boys."

Gerard was waiting, poised to give the ambulance a crank before he crawled into the back with the soldiers, his signal that we needed to be on our way.

"Of course." When I turned away toward the cab, she placed her hand on my arm.

"For all your excellent French, I recall that you are American, n'est-ce pas?"

"Yes."

"God bless the Americans," she said with quiet dignity. "God bless you all. No doubt some of you will die, but we have no more men to offer on this pagan altar of war and we are sick to death of the carnage. God bless all of you."

I was humbled by her words—a personal state of mind with which I was not very familiar—because I knew I had not cared about the war raging in Europe as anything other than a place in which to follow my own disappearing act. A conflagration to manipulate to my own personal advantage. Men like Mac Chesney deserved her fervent good wishes. I certainly did not.

Our three patient passengers survived the trip to Amiens, but for much of the journey I wasn't sure any of us would live to tell of it. A nightmarish drive I have not forgotten to this day, nightmarish not only because the roads were slick and treacherous, but because they were crowded, as well. Civilian refugees, their cloth bags bulging with whatever goods they could carry slung across their backs, trudged roadside, away from the feared German invasion. British soldiers and military vehicles, most of them horse-drawn, made their way toward us and the front line fighting near Arras. I could usually avoid the soldiers, who seldom lifted their eyes to the ambulance but simply shifted their procession to the side of the road to let us pass, but meeting a wagon loaded down with guns or supplies was another situation entirely. How close could I get to the road's edge without sliding into the ditch? How many inches did I need between my bumper and the supply wagon's wheel hub in order to pass without collision? Neither the wagon's driver nor I ever bothered to look at each other as we passed, keeping to the precarious edge of our respective sides of the road. What would we have seen in the other's face if we had? No doubt a profound weariness in his and a semi-hysterical desperation in mine. We all just moved forward the best we could, methodically and slowly and for me at least, eventually successfully.

Once I pulled up to the front entrance of the hospital in Amiens, Gerard untied the back flap, exited the ambulance, and came around to where I sat in the driver's seat, fingers still clenched around the steering wheel.

"Alive?" I asked but wouldn't have had to. When patients died en route, Gerard had a look in his eyes hard to define, some combination of anger and grief that I had learned to recognize without needing any words.

"Yes. I'll go find an orderly to help unload." He gave me a keen look. "It was very bad, eh?"

"Yes," I said in return, as offhand as he. "Very bad."

"Well, no doubt there is worse to come." He shrugged and turned away, probably missing the smile his words brought to my face. A lovely boy, I thought, as cynical as I, both of us always expecting the worst. No wonder he and I dealt so well together.

Later, history would show that day as the start of the final great German offensive of the war called the Spring Offensive. In two weeks the Germans would be as close to Amiens as they had been to Arras. There was so little safety anywhere during the last months of the war; I was foolish to think any city could provide a refuge from the guns and the shells and from the destruction and blood and spilled guts and death that of necessity followed. Both sides suffered great loss of life, but the Americans were en route to replace the lost Allied troops and the Germans had no replacements in line for their dead. Their front line would not hold. How could it with a quarter of a million German boys gone that month, their bodies lying in battlefield piles and buried in mud? It was the beginning of the end of the war, but we had no way of knowing it at the time.

The German offensive turned the clearing stations along the Front into madhouses of activity, a constant incoming stream of damaged soldiers and of ambulances transporting those given a chance for survival to the hospital in Amiens. Gerard and I picked up and delivered, picked up and delivered until exhaustion forced us to sleep a few hours. Then we returned to the road and the same drone of bloody activity, and we were just one of many ambulances. Truthfully, during the last ten days of that March I never gave even a passing thought to trying to disappear, though I knew the Americans were reported to be en route to the very location where I worked. But where would I have gone and how would I have gotten there? I was as trapped by the war as any civilian refugee. So I mended spark plugs, wired engine repairs, changed tires at the edge of sodden ditches, cursed the rain, smoked constantly, and transported the wounded, all activities at which I had become expert.

Lucy Rose March had her hands full, literally, the next time I saw her. I did not have a chance to talk to her if she was sleeping between shifts or busy in the casualty tent, but I usually caught a daily glimpse of her. She was always noticeable to me amid the flurry of activities: the doctor pointing at the wounded lined up on stretchers—"This one. Take this one," and then nothing but a quick shake of the head at the next soldier and a step toward the next waiting injured man; a decision of life and death made as quickly as a heartbeat—the moans and groans of the wounded, the clanking of ambulance engines waiting to be loaded, and always, always the endless thudding reverberations of the guns. But Lucy, despite the disarray of her frizzy hair poking out around a nurse's cap ever askew and her slight form and the constant motion that was a part of both her profession and her character, seemed to me to be a place of tranquility. It didn't matter what was happening around her, something peaceful centered itself at the exact spot where she bent or crouched or knelt, as if someone shone a light and she was where the beams converged.

The first time I saw her following my run from the hospital at Arras, Lucy knelt beside a man over whom the doctor had just shaken his head. She knelt and smiled and reached for the boy's bloody hand and said something to him. I thought I saw him nod his head but perhaps not. He was a dying man; it could as well have been death tremors. I stopped, arrested for some reason by the sight of Lucy March holding the man against her chest and speaking—murmuring, really—with her lips against his ear. Was it a lullaby she spoke, or a prayer? Only two people would ever know. After a few moments she placed him gently back onto the ground, stood and straightened her skirt oblivious to the bloodstains, and finally raised her head from the still figure to see me staring at her across the way. As if she had been engaged in something commonplace, sweeping the steps or putting away dishes, she sent me a small smile and a smaller wave of her hand to acknowledge my presence before she moved on to the next man.

I have never forgotten that fleeting moment, only one death among thousands that month and among millions across the war years, but for the first time I understood that Lucy Rose March believed in more than the importance of one life. She believed that every death mattered, too. There was never a man rejected by the doctor's clinical headshake that she would discard. Feeling so must surely take a toll on one's heart and soul, I thought, and yet, while I knew Lucy wept the same as the rest of us caught up in the carnage, I never saw her despair or rage at the wasted lives. The intangible well of compassion that sustained her was an object of my secret envy, and I wondered how she kept that well replenished. In the hard times of my life I drank too much and took lovers where I could to endure emotions I found unbearable, but as far as I know Lucy never considered either of those escapes. She remained a mystery to me as long as I knew her.

# *"~blood for seed~"*

# Chapter 7

For all my ignorance of the fact at the time, we were only a few months away from the end of the war. It didn't seem likely despite the phantom shapes of the Americans gathering along the western horizon. Everyone knew the American Expeditionary Force was in France, over half a million strong, young men fresh off the boats, healthy and eager for combat. The knowledge brought a kind of last wind to the exhausted Brits and all their allies and a desperate ferociousness to the Germans, who had no one to fill in the places where their young men dropped. They knew they must take victory before the A.E.F. joined the battle or they would be overwhelmed by the sheer numbers and vitality of the Americans, and so the Germans renewed their offensive with fierce, dedicated determination. Germany, like the countries against which it had been at war for four years, acted as if it had an endless supply of young men to throw against the enemy's guns, and it threw them with abandon. In the end, virtually an entire generation of young men would disappear across Europe and young women of a certain age would go without husbands and children because of it. There has never been a way to measure with accuracy the loss of people and property, the loss of a meaningful future, due to what became known as The Great War. *Great?!* Well, men write the history books so we are forced to tolerate the arrogant rewriting of our past. From my perspective, there was nothing great about the war, only some small moments within it—like Lucy Rose March smoothing down her bloodied apron after whispering a man into eternity— that made one hope the world might be able to survive the brutal animosity it was so willing to turn on itself.

By the end of April the location of the main medical clearing station that sorted the wounded for transport had shifted three times to follow the fluid line of fighting, managing to stay just barely out of reach of enemy forces. The first move was to the outskirts of St. Quentin, making it a longer and more precarious trip to the hospital at Amiens, then again fifteen miles west to Peronne, and finally another fifteen miles northwest to Albert. Gerard and I would find out about the move at the last minute, confer with other drivers, sketch out a makeshift map, grab our compass, and depart. We were not lost very often; the scarcity of roads did not allow it. And there was always the sound of the guns drawing us on like a malevolent Pied Piper. Their sound beckoned, threatening death and destruction with every boom. Beside the broken wagons alongside the road lay the carcasses of horses, the stinking remains a reminder that shells could land in roads as well as battlefields and not only human combatants were shattered by this god-awful war.

Gerard and I knew we were not immune to danger. Recently, a shell had hit so close to an ambulance that it threw the vehicle into a ditch and set the thing ablaze. The driver died on impact; his aide managed to scramble out and drag the injured from the back, though the poor soldiers did not all survive. Yet we seldom gave our own precarious position a thought. As queer as it may seem, driving the ambulance between Albert and Amiens became in some way like any job one does day after day. We developed a routine and stuck with it, held our own on the road, swerved when we needed to, avoided the ruts and holes when we could, shouted over the sound of the guns, loaded soldiers, drove, unloaded, drove and loaded again. We grew a trifle careless, but we were lucky enough on the roads. Not quite as lucky at the clearing station, I suppose, but both of us survived the war and I make no complaint.

The only time I felt the breath of disaster against the back of my neck was the last day of that April. We had pulled into the cleared area by the surgical tent, waiting our turn for the next load of wounded. I pushed up my goggles, stretched my shoulders, and turned my head to see if I could spy Lucy Rose anywhere in the scene. I finally found her small figure by the opening of the tent. She stood next to a tall man in a United States Marine uniform, and my stomach gave a turn at the sight of Mac Chesney. From the little jolt my system felt at his unexpected presence, I realized the man had somehow wormed his way under my skin like an infectious parasite and while I would never have admitted it to him, I was pleased to see he was alive and well and still popping in and out of northeastern France like a mad phantom.

He lifted a hand in my direction, perhaps picking out my ambulance by the jaunty figure of young Gerard, who had hopped out and disappeared quickly in the direction of the latrine. I pushed open the driver's side door, placed one foot on the running board, lifted a hand in a return wave, and started to slide both feet to the ground when the sound of the incoming shell made me freeze.

They have a distinctive sound, incoming shells, like a woman with a lisp shrieking at the top of her lungs, and it is by the sound's volume that we learned which shells we could shrug off because they would miss us by a mile and which shells might end up in our laps. This one was close. My lap, for sure, I thought, and not a thing to be done about it. Whichever way I would throw myself might be exactly where the shell would explode. Much better odds if I simply waited where I was instead of running to meet disaster.

The mortar missed the surgical tent, thank God, sang overhead like an enormous bird of prey, and landed in the copse of trees behind me. There was an infinitesimal pause before my senses caught up with its reverberating sound and powerful push of hot air and then the explosion reached where I stood, lifted both the ambulance and me and tossed us several feet toward the tent where I'd last seen Lucy and Mac. The ambulance, old trooper that it was, landed upright on all four tires, as if it were a cat tossed from a window. I, on the other hand, was not so graceful or so considerate. The force of the shell twirled me around and threw me forward onto my back, almost but not quite under the wheels of the ambulance as it settled back to earth. From a distance I imagine it looked worse than it was, looked as if I lay crushed under the vehicle.

I couldn't hear anything for the ringing in my ears and seemed incapable of movement, stunned but not injured to any serious extent, although there was no way anyone could tell that from afar. Mac reached me first. I was conscious of the movement of his big hands on me, nothing skilled or nurse-like in his movements as he tried to detect injury. I opened my eyes enough to see the expression on his face. No emotion was hidden there. He wore the look of a desperate man, one frantic with worry and fear. I could see his lips moving and knew he was speaking but couldn't hear what he said. Something serious, though. Something heartfelt, that I knew. Because of Lucy's expression. She knelt beside Mac and had reached out to me, her expert hands much better than Mac's at feeling for broken bones, but he said something—damn this infernal ringing in my ears!— that caused her to go still. For only a brief moment, a moment hardly long enough to be noticeable to anyone except me lying helpless and immobile as I tried to regain my wind and my hearing, Lucy turned her head and gave Mac a grave, studying look. He might have been a specimen on a slide under a microscope. Mac himself seemed oblivious to anyone and anything but my recumbent form, but for the length of a breath Lucy gazed at him, an emotion registering on her face that might almost have been surprise before she turned her attention back to me. For a very brief moment, so brief I could well have imagined it—but I know in my heart I did not—we stared at each other before something clicked in her eyes and she was once more a nurse. Even as she continued to run her hands along my arms and legs, she must have said something to Mac. "Get a doctor," most likely because he was gone in an instant. We had to wait for a doctor because the three on duty already had their hands full, but eventually one came to examine me even more thoroughly than Lucy had. By then I had regained the power of speech and knew that despite a throbbing head, aching back, and intermittent hearing I would survive.

I let the doctor come to the same conclusion and did not argue when he told me to wait a few hours before making any fast movements.

"No driving until the morning."

I pushed myself upright at the command, ready to argue, but at the movement felt a serious thump of pain behind my eyes.

"Oh, all right," nothing gracious in my words or tone. The doctor shrugged and went back to the surgical tent and more important work than an ambulance driver, who might have had some sense knocked out of, or into, her.

Mac, standing behind the doctor, gave a sudden grin at my words, relief on his face and something warmer in his eyes. He crouched down to gather me into his arms and carry me to the nurses' tent, but I brushed him away.

"I'll be fine," I said. "I don't need to be carried like a baby. You'd be doing me a greater favor by finding Gerard. I need to talk to him about the condition of the truck. It took quite a jolt."

"The same could be said about you."

Lucy still stood there. She could not have missed the tenderness in Mac Chesney's voice, but nothing changed in her expression.

"You can have my bed, Meg. I'm just starting my shift."

"Thanks." I reached past Mac to Lucy. "Give me a hand up, will you?" Mac backed away as Lucy took my hand. Hers was small and warm and strong. Once up, I leaned against the ambulance for support.

"I know you're needed elsewhere," I said to Lucy, and to Mac, "Why are you still here? I need Gerard." Mac gave a mockery of a salute and disappeared from my line of vision.

"I am needed elsewhere," Lucy said, "but I don't like leaving you." She meant it, I could tell, but I could also tell she had no intention of playing nursemaid to me. Not with wounded and dying men needing her more than I ever would. Their care was her calling, mine a kind of obligation of acquaintance.

"I had a shake up but I'll survive. Go on."

She smiled slightly. "You're a tough bird, aren't you, Meg?"

"Not as tough as you, and we both know that's the truth."

As she walked away, I had the urge to call her back and ask her what Mac had said to put that brief, grave, searching look on her face. It doesn't matter, I wanted to tell her, whatever it was. Things get said in the heat of a moment that would never get said otherwise. People come together for an instant and then go their separate ways. I have no designs on your captain, no permanent, long-term designs, anyway. He's all yours. But Lucy had heard something from Mac Chesney in words or tone that made her think just the opposite.

Later, one of the station nurses popped into the tent long enough to say, "That long drink of water American captain wants to come in. Okay with you?"

125

"Yes," but I wasn't sure it was okay, not really.

Mac sat on the bunk opposite the one where I lay, both hands on his knees. After a moment he said, "You sure know how to make an entrance."

"A woman of drama, that's me."

"How do you feel?"

"I'd feel better if it were quiet."

"I don't think the guns'll be quiet for a while yet."

"I'm not talking about the guns."

He gave a quick grin and stood. "Understood. I just thought I'd check on you before I left."

I had closed my eyes as he spoke but opened them again to squint at him. "Back to Black Jack."

"Sooner or later."

"How is it that you manage to show up all over northeastern France? Don't you have a regular job to do?"

"I'm doing my regular job."

"Must be G-2, then," I said.

"What do you know about G-2?" His tone lost its easy banter, grew sharp.

"As much as anyone who has a brain and keeps her eyes and ears open. I hear things, you know. Nothing definite but I'm not stupid. Don't worry, Mac. I don't care enough about your business to give away any of your secrets."

"I know that. You don't care enough about me to give a rip about me or my business." He paused and waited for me to argue the point. When I didn't, he added, "More's the pity. You know it's not like that with me, don't you? You must've figured that out."

This was a conversation I didn't want to have and I closed my eyes again. "I was nearly blown into a hundred pieces and I have a headache as a result. You're not helping."

"Right. Well, take care of yourself, Meg. I'll see you again."

"No doubt," I retorted, keeping my eyes closed. I knew he didn't move and stood there for a long minute probably looking at me, but I was determined to keep my eyes closed. Finally, I heard the rustle of the tent flap and knew he had gone. My head really did hurt and my thinking was somewhat muddled, but not so muddled that I didn't realize Mac Chesney considered himself in love with me. I found him physically attractive and good company, thought he might be a more than adequate lover, but did not reciprocate his feelings, not in the way he would expect and perhaps deserved. On the other hand, I knew from watching Lucy Rose March whenever she was in the captain's presence that she was ready, willing, and more than able to return his feelings in spades. What a mess, I thought as I tried to will my head to stop thumping. In the middle of a war and a foreign country and yet caught up in the kind of intense emotions I wanted to leave behind. There might be some irony in the situation, but I felt too shaken up either to appreciate or react to it.

I slept for a while until I was awakened by Lucy checking to be sure I was alive. She brewed tea, handed me a cup, sat down on the same cot where Mac had planted himself earlier, and asked me how I felt.

"Like I was thrown from a very big horse. Or dropped from a dirigible. Something like that." I was always cranky when awakened suddenly.

"To be expected, but your eyes look normal, and since your temperament doesn't appear to have been affected by the blast, we can assume you'll soon be back to your usual self."

"I can drive tomorrow?"

"You can drive today," she corrected. "It's nearly daybreak. Does your head ache?"

I gave an experimental shake and answered, "Not any more than usual."

"Then wait a couple more hours before you leave. Gerard was a big help during the night and he's just taken his first break in hours. Give him some time to catch his breath." Lucy set down her cup, stood, and came to stand next to where I lay. "I'm going to sleep a while, but I'll be over in the corner if you have a sudden relapse." She paused and added, "You're very lucky, Meg."

"I know." I turned my head to watch Lucy as she stretched out on another nurse's cot—I lay in Lucy's bed—and seemed to fall asleep immediately. Nurses, like soldiers, learned to do so as a way not to waste valuable time.

I *was* lucky, I told myself, and then had the sudden realization that Lucy March had probably not been talking about bombs and explosions and narrow escapes from death at all.

Gerard had had time to work on our ambulance while I was out of action and both he and the recuperating vehicle were waiting for me when I finally made an appearance. The young man had learned, as all of us involved in ambulance driving learned, how to get the most out of an abundance of wire, how to hold mechanical parts together and keep other parts from falling off. When I think of it now, I can only shake my head with wonder at how offhand we were about wiring things together and then hoping for the best. It was not just youth that made us fearless but the times themselves and the chaos around us. That we could ever draw from rational thought, even once during those chaotic times, was inexplicable, with shells exploding overhead and guns booming from the front lines and all semblance of civilization and familiar human interactions replaced by what seemed to be nothing but madness and riot.

We had lost some hours but Gerard and I were alive, the ambulance still ran despite a new rattle that sounded like we had attached a pair of Spanish castanets to the engine, and men with dreadful wounds still needed to be carted to the hospital for a chance, however miniscule, of surviving. So we resumed where we'd left off without giving much thought to the reason for the interruption.

We saw our first Americans not long after, five young men close to death and not a Hun or gun to blame. What was called Spanish Influenza had entered the conflict, a new enemy that everyone grew to fear because it did not take sides but killed quickly and indiscriminately both east and west of the front lines.

The American Expeditionary Force was in our general vicinity because a division called The Big Red One had been attached to the French First Army and sent to repulse the Germans at a little village called Cantigny, about fifteen miles or so south of our hospital in Amiens. They would eventually lose some three thousand soldiers around that little hamlet, which in its turn would disappear under rubble and its hundred or so citizens join the ranks of countless refugees that wandered without homes and livelihoods. That small, bleak, trudging procession I'd first seen on my arrival in Paris was repeated again and again wherever I drove, walking toward us on the narrow road or crossing a muddy field, their worldly goods slung over their shoulders and their steps beast-like, disoriented, stricken dumb with suffering and loss.

Gerard and I were diverted in the direction of Cantigny to pick up the soldiers suffering from influenza. The sight of American uniforms and the sound of American voices affected me more than I expected and for a moment I rebelled at the notion that this conflagration, this damnable and heartless war, should be allowed to ruin a generation of young Americans as it had ruined Europe. We shouldn't be here at all, I thought, suddenly furious. We live an ocean away and this is not our war. The anger vanished as quickly as it appeared, however. Who was asking my opinion and what difference did it make to real life, anyway? Americans were here and that was that.

The last of the five sick doughboys grabbed my arm as he passed on his stretcher. "You're awful pretty," he said, a touch of the South in his voice. Georgia, maybe, or Virginia.

I patted his hand. "Thanks."

"Well, my lord, you sound like an American girl."

"Right now I'm the driver that's going to get you safely to the hospital." As I spoke I gently removed his hand from its grip around my arm and gave Gerard a nod, who read my message and quickly got the young man loaded.

Despite myself, I gave a quick look around before we departed but there was no Mac Chesney in sight. Of course not. He only materialized where he wasn't expected and shouldn't be. Why did I think he'd be with a division of American soldiers? Too obvious.

I sought out Lucy on my next trip to the clearing station at Albert. An unexpected and nagging worry had lodged in a small corner of my brain that whatever she saw on Mac Chesney's face or heard in his voice when he looked at me might change how she acted toward me, might dim the connection we'd forged through the past months. Was it friendship?

I'd had few women friends of any degree in my life and only one I'd call close because many of the women with whom I interacted in my former life were focused on things that I, in my usual superior way, considered shallow, boring, and unimportant. Compared to my current occupation, some of my own past interests might be considered shallow, too, I suppose, but most of my female contemporaries had seemed too content maintaining the status quo of their lives, and that was not for me. I preferred scandal to boredom. No wonder I had few friends.

Yet here I was with a niggling fear that Lucy Rose March would no longer tolerate my presence, would not raise a hand in smiling greeting when she saw me or huddle with me against the rain or share inconsequential gossip or wish me a safe trip when I departed, would not sit across the table from me, both of us clutching cups of hot coffee, struggling to talk about something, anything, not connected to the chaos and damage that surrounded us. If my worry hinted at friendship, it was a kind of friendship I never knew was possible, everything extraneous stripped away, just two women with a common experience talking and no need to impress or fear.

Since my nearly fatal experience, they had moved the whole clearing station a small distance to the southwest for safety's sake. Lucy had laughed a bit at that, a touch of uncharacteristic bitterness creeping into her words when she told me about the decision.

"A concession to safety, they said, as if there's safety anywhere."

"But it does make sense to keep back from the fighting if you can," my role suddenly that of the calm, sensible one.

"Oh, sense! That's a laugh, too! You know as well as I that there's no sense to anyone fighting now—if it ever did make sense. As soon as the Americans landed in France, someone should have declared an armistice. The Germans can't hold out against half a million fresh soldiers. They don't have the resources. Everybody knows it, but both sides still keep killing each other. It makes me so damned mad sometimes!"

Lucy March was usually careful enough about her speech that I knew the emotions she expressed ran deep. She wasn't a prude but she was proper in her own way.

"Foch and Haig and Pershing and Ludendorff are all interested in your opinion now, are they?" I tried for a light response.

She gave a laugh, the tinge of bitterness gone. "No one is interested in my opinion, Meg. Absolutely no one."

"Well, then, do what you do best and forget about everything else. What good does it do to think about what should be or what might be if nobody cares what you think?"

We were silent a while.

"Right. You're right, Meg. I'm sorry. That sounded a lot like self-pity just now, didn't it?"

I wanted to give her a reassuring pat on the hand but didn't. Not my style. "Nothing to be sorry about," I said instead, "and, yes, it did sound like self-pity, but you're allowed to be human like the rest of us once in a while."

She smiled at the end of our little exchange, her mood lightened, and before heading back to the surgery tent added, "I'm more human that you realize and often not proud of it, but thanks for the encouragement. If that's what it was. I can't always tell with you." Her smile broadened into a grin as she turned away.

For all my desire to remain solitary and aloof from human connections, I would be sorry to lose those shared moments with Lucy March, however brief and infrequent they were.

A while later, on a pleasant night illuminated by the intermittent bursts from the guns that flared in the distance like a string of campfires, then quenched and flared again, I tracked Lucy down to where she sat on a stool outside the flap entrance to the nurses' tent. She looked up at my arrival.

"I was looking for you," I said.

"Well, here I am." She sounded tired but not dejected or depressed. "Pull up a crate."

"Just getting off?" I asked as I sat down beside her.

"Yes. I worked with Dr. Clement all day and just had some really awful soup for supper. I don't feel like sleeping, but I don't have the initiative to do anything else." She paused and I heard her exhale, the soft sound something like a sigh. "It's a nice night."

"If it weren't for the guns and the war."

"Well, there is that," she agreed, "but you have to admit it's nice not to be rained on." I nodded and reached for a cigarette. "You can have Mary's cot, Meg. She drew nights this week." I lit my cigarette; it glowed in the darkness between us.

"I heard the Americans are gathering south, somewhere near Rheims." Lucy's voice was disembodied in the night; I couldn't see her features in the darkness.

"I heard that, too," I said. "How far is that from here?"

"Not quite a hundred miles, I think. A French soldier told me it was a pretty area. A land of old forests, he said."

"It won't be pretty for long if armies are gathering there."

"I suppose not."

We sat in the cooling evening, the distant guns replacing the natural sounds of a late spring night, creatures and birds of the darkness long displaced by man's violence.

"Have you seen Mac lately?" I stilled at Lucy's question. Was this some kind of trick on her part to gather more information about my relationship with the captain? She never appeared to have a devious bone in her body and yet I'd been surprised by something almost cunning about her on more than one occasion. I heard her chuckle. "No, Meg. It wasn't a question meant to trap you into anything. Just a question, is all. Accept it on face value."

I took a drag from my cigarette before answering, "No. He tends to show up when and where he's least expected."

"I thought when you picked up those sick doughboys you might have— Well, it doesn't matter. I just wondered."

It does matter, I thought, to you, anyway, and admitted to her, "I looked for him up by Cantigny, but he was nowhere around. I'm sure of it."

"I asked if I could be transferred south to the American Front, and they said yes. I guess my request hit at the right moment. Two additional nurses are en route here this week from St.Valery-en-Caux and with the A.E.F. looking to see some action, I guess the powers that be thought it made sense to have an experienced nurse there that speaks English."

"You're a noble woman." She knew me well enough not to take the words at face value.

"No, I'm not, but—"

She hesitated so long that I completed her sentence. "But you think you'll have a better chance finding Captain Chesney among the Americans."

"Yes." One of the things I appreciated about Lucy March was her forthright, candid nature, never a woman to dissemble.

"You're probably right." I dropped my cigarette and with the toe of my boot flattened the butt into the dirt. "Look, there's nothing really between Mac—"

"Not on your part," she interrupted, "but there is on his. I've known for a while. He lights up when you're around. Can't keep his eyes off you."

Same as you, I thought, when he's anywhere in the vicinity. The situation had its share of absurdity but I didn't find it especially laughable.

"I don't know whether I should be glad or broken-hearted that he cares more for you than you do for him." I was surprised by the note of humor in her voice. "Well, there's not much to be done about it right now, is there?"

"Lucy, he and I never— I mean, it's been—"

"Don't keep talking, Meg. I mean it. Stop. I'm not your keeper or his and I don't want to know any details. I mean *any*. Not a one. Right now Mac's crazy about you and we both know it, but there's no telling what the future holds or how we'll end up after the war when we're all back on home ground. Things could change when our lives get back to normal. It's not unheard of, and I'd like to have as little as possible that I need to pretend doesn't matter."

"Sometimes it's better knowing the facts," I said. "Imagination can be hell."

The volume of the guns suddenly swelled and exploding shells lit up the distance. I felt more than saw Lucy stand.

"But nothing that can't be borne," she said. "Not by comparison to this. War is hell, the barbed wire and the gas and the bayonets and the bombs, that's what hell is. I'm going to bed. I think I can sleep now. Are you coming?"

"In a while." Pause. "Lucy?"

"Yes?"

"What did Mac say that day? I couldn't hear anything just then." She didn't ask, *What day?*

"He said, 'Please God, don't take her. I need her here.'"

A prayer, then. The knowledge touched me deeply. There was no other person on earth for whom my presence was such an immediate necessity. I had left behind two people dear to me but had no doubt that they carried on perfectly well in my absence.

"I see. Thanks."

"You're welcome," her voice neutral. "Good night, Meg. Don't wake me up if I'm still asleep when you leave."

"Right," I said. After she was gone, I sat there a long time, staring at nothing, thinking, just thinking. What makes that woman tick, I wondered. Is she exactly what she seems, an honest, ingenuous, straightforward young woman? Or are there depths to her that she keeps hidden from my view? From that night on, I knew we had reached the closest we would ever be to friends. I knew, too, that it was not I who had drawn the line.

The rumors were right about the Americans showing up to the south, but it was along the Marne River. The Argonne Forest would come later. Major General Bundy and his Marines joined the French in the general area of Belleau Wood, a pretty, green, and dappled part of the French countryside. Or it would have been if the Americans, the French, and the Germans hadn't bombed the hell out of it.

The Americans tried to set up a hospital in Chateau-Thierry but the Huns overran it and before the A.E.F. was able to reclaim the city, the hospital was moved to a sixteenth-century house outside of a small town called Rebais. Before the war the two-story, white-washed house must have been a charming place with extensive gardens and its own vineyards, but its owners had fled and the place sat looking neglected and run down. It would do for the injured, however, who could be taken there from the front lines, patched up, and if they showed the potential for survival forwarded another forty miles to Paris.

Gerard and I shifted, too, making our ambulance runs between the clearing station set up along the Marne River and the hospital in Rebais. By the end of the first week of June, American casualties began to pour in, all of them looking like boys to me, a medley of the country I'd left behind, the long vowels of Boston, the soft consonants of the South, Texas twangs, that curious, flat Midwestern sound that I knew best of all: Ohio, Wisconsin, Minnesota, Indiana, Illinois. They came from everywhere, those valiant American boys. I might be standing at the edge of a forest in eastern France but suddenly I was home.

Lucy and I acknowledged each other's presence, shared a quick coffee now and then, but we were incredibly busy with no time for heartfelt talks. She was a cyclone of activity, moving from stretcher to stretcher, feeling for pulses, cutting away uniforms, beckoning the doctor when someone seemed especially needy. But somehow in the middle of the gore and the guts, she was able to smile at a soldier, offer him a cup of water, grab hold of his hand and say something in a low voice only the two of them could hear. I have my own gifts: can keep an ambulance on the road, can drive through crashing shells and avoid oncoming traffic with a steady hand and sheer bravado, but Lucy Rose March had the gift of kindness. Nothing I possessed could match that, and I knew it.

I wondered if every time she bent over a stretcher she expected—feared—to find Mac Chesney lying there. He survived the battle of Belleau Wood unscathed but his luck would not hold much longer.

One day, without warning or expectation, Mac materialized at a clearing station. Watching him from a distance, I felt such a rush of relief and, yes, happiness at the sight of him that for the moment I was almost light-headed. He was filthy with mud churned up by a sudden downpour and clearly fatigued, his face drawn, his eyes a little bleary. When he took off his helmet, his hair lay plastered against his head like a medieval skullcap, and still I thought him a beautiful sight. He stood talking to another man, discussing something serious by their expressions, but when he turned and saw me staring at him, his face changed. Lucy was right; he did "light up" at the sight of me. He loped over to where I stood and would have taken me in his arms if I hadn't backed away.

"God, I'm glad to see you," he said, "but I wish you weren't this close to the guns."

I laughed. "I had my moment of eternity and survived, remember?"

He didn't laugh in return. "I'll never forget it. I thought I'd lost you for good. Lost the pleasure of your company, I mean."

"As you can see, I'm still here, and I'm glad to see the same for you. Are we making progress?"

"It's the damnedest thing but I don't know. How can anyone tell? It's all woods and it's like a see-saw. We take some ground and the Germans take it back and then we take it again. It's nothing like any war I ever read about."

I watched him steadily as he talked, not really listening, and before I knew what he intended he stopped speaking, reached both hands to the sides of my face and leaned close enough to kiss me.

"There, that's better." He didn't pull back and neither did I.

"Glad I could be of help." He laughed, kissed me again, and would have pulled me into his arms except I finally found the will to detach myself from him. With some regret, I admit. "Gerard's waiting," I said. "I have to go. Have you seen Lucy?"

"Is she here?" That was a *no* without his having to say the word.

"Of course, right in the middle of the action."

"I'll find her later, then," his words dismissive but not uncaring. To me, in a completely different tone, he said, "Be careful, will you?"

"I'm always careful. Are you in the area for a while?"

He shook his head. "No, the general's on the move."

"So you are, too, then."

Mac just smiled in response. Something of the boy he must have been was in his smile, something unexpectedly endearing, and I couldn't help myself. I rested two fingers against his lips.

"Take a page from your own book," I said, "and you be careful, too." Then I turned away toward the waiting ambulance. I did not care for the man with any true and genuine depth, I told myself later. I had known men more handsome, men of greater charm and power and wealth and more significant reputation than Mac Chesney from the plains of South Dakota, but just the same, I would miss him if he weren't around. Perhaps the tables had been turned on me, perhaps despite my firmest intentions I had found a man that could make me light up, too. The idea was surprising and unwelcome and if it could not be eradicated, must certainly be ignored.

# *"~sowing for new Spring~"*

# Chapter 8

By July the Americans were a force to be reckoned with and everyone on both sides of the front lines knew it. They were fresh and eager and ready for action. No one would have guessed from the tough competence of the young men I saw that just two years before the United States hadn't had a standing army to talk about. I might tease Mac about his loyalty to Pershing but the general had done something right to turn hundreds of thousands of untested young men into battle ready soldiers.

All summer the Americans fought throughout northeastern France, sometimes beside their European allies and sometimes on their own. They fought at the Battle of Hamel, at the second Battle of the Marne, at Chateau-Thierry, and at Amiens. Americans were wounded there, too, lost their lungs from mustard gas, lost hands and arms and legs and feet, were burned and scarred and mutilated. Through it all, Lucy's clearing station for the wounded followed the lines of battle and my ambulance followed the clearing station. By late September we had shifted so far southeast that we were closer to the German border than we were to Paris. Surely those poor German boys, by that time so very near to their families and homes, longed for the war to be over as much as the rest of us did!

Equipment and nurses from the American Red Cross joined military doctors at a hospital set up in what was left of a schoolhouse just west of the Argonne Forest. Gerard and I stayed busy. Lucy and the rest of the medical staff at the clearing station stayed busier.

My unraveling, as I have come to call it, started innocently enough on a September afternoon, a day like all the others and no hint of the long shadows it would eventually cast over my life. The clearing station looked as it always did, the ambulatory wounded hunkered down to one side, heads bandaged, arms in slings, some with makeshift crutches, some, poor devils, staring out at nothing with glassy-eyed stares. All would eventually make it to the hospital, but it was the ones on stretchers that got first attention, the ones bleeding and shattered. There was always the murmur of requests for water among those poor men, or cries of pain or the rambling mutterings of the terribly injured or sometimes the raised voice of a man fighting his excruciating pain with loud profanity. Lucy followed a doctor as he moved from man to man, nodding at the orderlies to indicate which of the injured should be added to the lines waiting for an ambulance and which moved to the side to wait longer—and for most of those, ultimately to die. After so many months as a driver I was used to it all.

These were American wounded, however, and what I had feared from the beginning would happen finally did happen. Gerard and another orderly were loading the stretchers into our ambulance when one of the men reached out and grabbed me by the wrist with such a firm hold that Gerard had to halt.

"Margo?" I looked down at the man and felt my heart take a small but heavy flip in my chest. "It *is* you, isn't it?" The words were disjointed but it was a question nevertheless. "Margo?"

I tried to shake free from his grasp. "No, not Margo, it's Meg. Meg. You have me mixed up with somebody else, and no wonder with that hole in your shoulder. We'll get you to a doctor straightaway."

He was persistent, however, and still strong enough to raise his voice. "It's me, Bruce Stockard, Margo. I know you remember me. We shared some good times on the lake. You must remember me." He started to move restlessly, his voice loud and peevish from fever and injury. "We wondered where you disappeared to. God, wait til I tell them where I saw you. In the middle of a war of all places!"

Lucy appeared at my side, detached the man's grip from my arm, and laid her hand on his forehead.

"You, sir, need to lie still and let this driver get you to a hospital if you want to save that arm." She gave a quick nod to Gerard, who together with his helper moved the injured soldier away toward the ambulance.

For just a moment I could do nothing but stand immobile. The whole exchange start to finish hadn't lasted two minutes, and yet I felt that all his words still hung in the air right in front of me. Bruce Stockard. It seemed too incredible to believe.

And yet, when I turned my head, it was to find Lucy watching me with her head tilted to one side. I'd seen that look often before when she gave a matter serious thought, that turn of the head that resembled a small bird contemplating a worm. Her expression was thoughtful and grave. After a moment, she rested her hand very briefly on my shoulder—commiseration? comfort? understanding? I couldn't tell—and walked away without speaking a word.

Gerard's voice calling my name gave me a start and brought me back to the present. There was a task to be done and he was impatient to get started. So was I, for that matter. I had a great deal to think about but not at that particular time. Better to concentrate on transporting the men to the hospital. Driving would help clear my head and calm my nerves. There is nothing like confronting a present danger to temper fearing one's past.

We delivered our cargo safely to the American hospital, which had recently been infused with additional doctors and nurses, as had Lucy's clearing station. It was always *Lucy's* station, even with the addition of four nurses from the States and a doctor, newly inducted, who specialized in severe trauma. I left Bruce Stockard and the other injured soldiers in good hands and convinced myself that if he survived, Bruce would not recall his sight of me or if he did, would consider it a part of a delirium that had naturally resulted from injury and fever. If he did not survive, well, that would work best for me but I could not let myself wish for that. Bruce had a family to grieve him if he did not come home.

I waited a few days before making a casual inquiry about him on a subsequent trip to the hospital and was told he would almost certainly survive and that he had already been sent on to Paris, the first leg of a journey that would ultimately take him all the way back home. Home: Euclid Avenue, Cleveland, Ohio. What the only son of a prestigious family that lived on Millionaires' Avenue in a mansion designed by the famous Charles Schweinfurth was doing fighting in this horrific war I couldn't imagine. I wouldn't have expected it of the lighthearted Bruce I'd known years ago. Perhaps I wasn't the only person who had thought being in a war zone would be a lark, a bit of fun. I could see Bruce Stockard thinking exactly that. Well, he and I had both learned lessons in humility. His family must be sick with sorry.

Throughout that September I began to hear whispers of an armistice to end the war. Soldiers, citizens, and medical personnel began to speak in low voices about how the infusion of American energy into the war was driving the Huns to their knees. For several reasons, not all of them altruistic or compassionate, I hoped it was true. After my exchange with Bruce Stockard, I'd once again begun to give serious thought to pursuing anonymity. Personally, however, I never saw anything different that month than I'd seen all the months before. From my perspective, the results of German shells and bayonets and barbed wire and rifles and gas did not change. I don't suppose the Germans saw any difference, either. Men were as wounded as they'd always been; men were just as dead. Still, there was something, however ephemeral, in the wind. I couldn't see it but every once in a while I caught, in a smile or a glance, a teasing hint of hope.

The Day That Made All The Difference started out the same as any other, not a capital letter day, at all, but one deceptively routine. Gerard and I had experienced a relatively easy time of it for a while. The fighting had shifted east almost to the German border, and as a consequence we saw fewer wounded in our location. Every day I expected to hear that Lucy's clearing station would move east, too, and attach itself to another medical station already set up in the general area of Verdun, which two years before had been the scene of a ghastly battle that ultimately left hundreds of thousands of casualties on both sides. Now, in the useless and endless manner of the war, fighting had resumed there as if the earlier battle had never occurred. I had come to understand and share Aggie's disdain for the generals in charge of waging a war that fought for the same ground over and over again as if the first dead weren't enough and the blood must not be allowed to dry.

When we pulled into the ambulance waiting area, I saw Lucy right away. An American soldier was speaking to her—not Mac; he had Mac's height but this man's hair was the color of wheat—and something he said caused Lucy to stiffen in a way I'd never seen before. It was just a moment, infinitesimal really, but for that brief moment she could have been a statue. Nothing about her moved. She still leaned slightly toward the speaker, her head tilted, her right palm pressed against the base of her throat, seeming to concentrate deeply on the man's words, but I knew her well enough to realize that what appeared to be single-minded attentiveness was really shock. Something in her stance gave my stomach a queasy turn. Lucy March was not a woman to react to anything with immobile shock. She was motion personified, any action for her preferable to doing nothing, and yet there she stood as if frozen. Only a tiny moment in time but for me she might as well have been shrieking at the top of her lungs.

By the time I was out of the ambulance, hurrying in Lucy's direction, she and the soldier had disappeared around the corner of the nurses' tent, which backed against the edge of the forest. I followed and then stopped abruptly at the sight of Lucy on her knees beside a stretcher, every bit of her fearsome energy focused on the man lying there. Mac Chesney. I knew it without ever seeing his face, knew it by the intensity of Lucy's posture, her hands pulling apart his jacket with ruthless purpose, her voice barking out commands to the men that had carried the stretcher.

"What happened?" My voice surprised me by its shakiness. I didn't sound anything like me.

"Sniper," the fair man explained. "We were on reconnaissance. I'd have sworn there wasn't a German anywhere in the area. We thought they'd all moved east and then, just like that, he was down."

"Captain Chesney." I said his name just to be sure.

"Yes, the captain. He was out in front. Careful like he always was but neither of us too worried. He and I were just back from—well, that doesn't matter, but we were in the woods. It was shady. Protected. Safe enough, we thought. Then he was down. I didn't see anyone. I had to wait a while. Got to him as soon as I could." He spoke in short, jerky sentences. "Dragged him along until I ran into some Canadians. They helped me get him here."

"Still alive." Everything I said was for my own personal assurance.

"Yes, but he got hit in the throat and he bled a lot." The soldier stopped speaking and the two of us watched Lucy as she stood, gave a terse direction to the men waiting there, and led the way past me. I don't think she noticed me at all. Her face reminded me of the time she'd scrambled up and down the rope on board the *Ausonia*. Fierce in concentration. Intent on success.

I caught a glimpse of Mac's face in passing, still and pale and bloody. So much blood soaking through, I thought. How could he live after losing so much? The small procession disappeared in the direction of the surgery tent and my companion followed them, but I remained standing there, not quite knowing what to do or even think. I felt as if I stood outside a window looking in, felt suddenly bereft of something precious and dear. How will Lucy endure it, I asked myself, if Mac Chesney dies? And then, how will I endure it?

I waited outside the surgery tent, restless, smoking one cigarette after another, shooing Gerard away when he came to ask about the delay. If Mac died, then he died, but I needed to know before I got into the ambulance and made the drive to the hospital as if it were any other day. I knew Lucy would reappear when she could to let me know what happened. She was as aware as I, perhaps more so, of the unusual tie that bound the three of us together. How I had come to be one of the corners of the triangle, I didn't know. I'd neither intended nor planned it, just the opposite, in fact, but I wasn't fool enough to deny that an indistinct bond connected Lucy March, Mac Chesney, and me. How, when, where it happened I couldn't have said, but I had realized our unspoken connection with sudden clarity when I stared across at Lucy Rose March turned to stone over the prone figure of a soldier. Without a sound I'd known the whole story, without a word on anyone's part.

She appeared at my shoulder as I ground out a cigarette with my heel, something in her face making me say, "He's not dead, then."

"No, but he needs to get to the hospital. The bullet is lodged at the back of his neck by his spine, and Dr. Clement said he doesn't have the instruments for such a delicate removal.

I sent someone to get Gerard. There are two other patients you can take with Mac."

"All right." Breathing again, suddenly rejuvenated, I stumbled over my words. "Listen, Lucy, I'll be careful with him. I promise."

She gave a small but surprisingly mischievous smile. "Oh, I'm not leaving the two of you alone."

"What?"

"I'm coming, too."

"But—"

"I told Dr. Clement he may or may not see me again. You probably noticed that our numbers are down. The line's moved east, and the station is scheduled to move east, too. If anything, we're over-staffed right now, and I told him and the head nurse that I was taking a leave. Today. Now. It's my first request ever and neither of them made a fuss about it."

A wise decision, I thought, eyeing her expression. Today would not be a good day to pick a fuss with Lucy Rose March.

"By the time the patients are boarded, I'll be back. Don't leave without me." She was gone with a sudden pivot, as if she were a dragonfly flitting from one blossom to another, her movements abrupt and quick and intentional.

With Lucy in the back with the wounded, Gerard sat up beside me for the trip, which we made in good time and with as few bounces as I could manage. I had told her I'd be careful with Mac, after all, and Lucy would hold me to the promise.

I put out a hand to Lucy's arm as she passed me following Mac's stretcher into the hospital. "You'll let me know," I said.

"Yes." Her gaze met mine. "Fifty-fifty is my guess, but it will be a while. He'll be lined up for surgery, but I can't get him moved to the front of the line. He'll have to wait his turn like everyone else."

If it were I, I thought, I'd have him at the front of the line no matter what it took to get him there, but Lucy was made of different stuff. Sometimes the differences between us were startling, and my disapproval, perhaps even scorn, must have shown on my face.

"I know," she said softly, "but that's not how it works, Meg. Every one of them is loved by somebody somewhere. The surgeon will decide who goes first. It's not up to me or to you, either."

With a shrug, I turned away. "Sure," I said without bothering to hide my skepticism. I knew better than she that everything had a price, that everything could be bought, even a place in the surgery line, but Lucy would stand as Mac Chesney's guardian angel and not let her halo tilt even a little. Sometimes I found her integrity incredibly annoying. "I've got time to make another run," I told her. "I'll check with you when I get back."

We parted without any further conversation, Lucy hurrying into the hospital and I headed back to the ambulance where Gerard waited. With sudden urgency, I wanted to get back on the road, wanted to be anywhere but here waiting to find out if Mac Chesney lived or died.

He was still alive that evening when, ambulance parked for the day and Gerard poking around under it in search of an ominous growling sound that could be heard only immediately after the engine was turned off, I went in search of Lucy.

"They haven't done anything," Lucy told me. We nearly collided in a hallway, neither of us paying proper attention to our surroundings, and she spoke before I ever got a question out.

"Why not?"

"He's lost a lot of blood and they're afraid he's not strong enough to endure the surgery. There would be considerable probing for the bullet, too, and they're not sure he's up to it." Her tone was low-voiced but objective and calm. Lucy March, nurse, speaking, not Lucy March, woman in love. I thought she probably couldn't afford to let the latter role loose just then.

"Can I see him?"

"He's had a lot of morphine pumped into him so he won't know you're there."

"That's all right."

She eyed me for a long moment and then gave a kind, almost sweet, smile. "Of course, you can see him, Meg."

I could not make the tall, broad-chested man I knew as Mac Chesney fit the figure in the hospital bed, everything about it white from bandages to skin tone. A pale, thin, immobile stranger lay there, not the Mac I knew, the Mac that would rather run than walk and whose presence always seemed to fill whatever room he was in.

"He doesn't look good," I said and turned away from the bed. I found it unnerving to stand beside a man who had suddenly become a stranger to me, and there was nothing I could do for him, anyway. I never liked feeling helpless; it went against the grain.

"No." Lucy and I moved to the hallway outside the ward.

"What are you going to do?" I asked her.

"I'll stay here at the hospital. They can use me."

We shared a silence until I said, "If there's any change, let me know. I have a room in what's left standing of that old farmhouse across the way. All the drivers sleep there."

"I will, and it wouldn't hurt if you said some prayers for Mac. He could use them."

"I don't pray."

"Not any more, you mean. Well, maybe for Mac's sake you could put whatever argument you have with God aside for a while."

I shrugged. "I'm not positive that anybody's prayers would do Mac any good, but I'm absolutely sure that mine wouldn't." I changed the subject. "Several of us are driving southeast tomorrow to a new clearing station to pick up some American wounded. It's a new route for us and I don't know when I'll get back."

"We'll be here," Lucy assured me, but late the next evening when I finally made it back to the hospital, she and Mac weren't there. The doctors had decided to send Mac on for specialized surgery in Paris and Lucy, to no one's surprise, accompanied him. She left a note on my pillow.

> *Meg,*
>
> *I'm taking Mac to Paris. The doctors think the Paris staff can do more for him than if they tried to probe for the bullet here. I don't know if I agree, but it's not my decision. I'm going with him, of course. That won't surprise you.*
>
> *I'll get word to you when I have news. Any news. Good or bad. Mac would want me to. You know how he feels about you. I might have to leave word with your friend at the Hotel*

*Premier so be sure to check with her. Her
name's Aggie, I think.*
*Rumor has the war ending sometime in the next
month. Sooner rather than later, I hope. If not
in time for Mac, maybe someone's boy
somewhere will make it home safe and sound.*
*Take it easy on the roads.*
*Lucy*
*p.s. When the war is over, will you be able to
stop running? I hope so for your sake.*

I read the note twice, tore it into pieces that I threw into the mud, and went to bed. People come and go in your life, I told myself, and it doesn't pay to get too fond of any of them. True enough, but I'm not a fool and only self-delusional some of the time. I didn't expect either Mac or Lucy to return to the front lines and knew I'd miss them both. I hadn't expected, didn't want, and didn't plan to make friends on my trip to France, but I had. Sort of, anyway. Not friends in the way friends were usually pictured, but I thought that was probably because I'd known so few of them in my life. At the very least, Lucy and Mac were more than mere acquaintances. Was there a word that fit somewhere between *friend* and *acquaintance*? I couldn't think of one so maybe that meant they were friends, after all.

Lucy was a precise woman and her shared rumors about the end of the war were on target. Within six weeks, at eleven o'clock the morning of the eleventh day of the eleventh month of the year 1918, the war to end all wars ceased.

Later, Aggie would curse the date and time. "Those damned generals and diplomats! They could have stopped the fighting sooner but some jackass somewhere liked the idea of all those elevens. How many boys that died on the tenth would have had the chance to see their mothers again if there'd been an ounce of sense in any of those old men's brains?"

She was right, I think, but then nothing about that war reflected any sense from anyone at any time. Fighting a tug of war over a field that meant nothing to either side and yet leaving thousands of young men buried in the mud between them happened again and again. The waste of it! The great wave of emotion that swept through the world at news of the Armistice was not merely one of relief but also held powerful repercussions of grief and fury, disillusionment and vengeance. It was not an overstatement to say that nothing would ever be the same again for the world. An entire generation of young men had been wiped off the face of the earth and in exchange for what? No one knew the answer to that question as far as I could tell, so how *could* anything, even intangibles like trust and hope and justice, hold the same meaning for people that had endured years of futile carnage? In its way, the war was a vast, sweeping farewell to a way of life we would never see again

Gerard and I were at the Verdun clearing station when news of the peace came through. We carried the injured in such a steady stream that I didn't have time to dwell on Mac Chesney's living or dying. I had my share of dying all around me and that was all I could think about. There were Americans, British, French, and Australians fighting in that last great offensive around the Argonne Forest and we carried them all. In the end, I had one objective and it was to get the wounded men lying in the back of my ambulance, regardless of the color of their uniforms or the language they spoke, to the nearest hospital while they still breathed and would have done the same if I'd had a German boy bleeding in the back. By then, the only enemy I knew was death.

I remember the exact moment I heard the war was over. I was ready to pull away with my load when a young American came racing toward the ambulance, waving his hat in wild abandon and with a grin plastered on his face.

"Peace, ma'am!" was all he could get out as he caught his breath.

"What?" Was this some kind of wartime code, some new greeting between allies?

"Germany surrendered. The war's over!" he said, clearly elated by the news.

"It's not over for the men in the back of my ambulance," I snapped and accelerated past him onto the drive that led back to the road. But sometime during that trip, I don't know when exactly, the words took root and without plan or will, I began to cry with enough tears to blur the road in front of me. The war's over, I thought, thank God, thank God. And then, what do I do now?

What I ended up doing was returning to Paris. By the middle of December, the ambulance corps had carried the last of the wounded to military field hospitals and some of them on to Paris for additional treatment. The army had its own official drivers, however, all of them men, and with sincere but cursory expressions of gratitude, the A.E.F. quickly sent the women drivers on their way. We were the first civilian volunteers to be cut loose, and I was happy enough to go. The last month of the war had been so intense that it was all I could do to get up every morning and head for the ambulance. Gerard and I were both dead tired, inside and out.

He and I said our goodbyes at the Quimper supplies depot where we had first met. "What will you do now?" I asked.

His shrug was quintessentially Gallic. "I know motors. I'll find something." His original village home had been leveled early on; his mother died under a shell; his father and older brother disappeared into the millions of war dead. His shrug had been learned across years of fighting and grief and loss.

"Yes, you do know motors, I'll give you that." After a quiet moment, I added, "If there's anything I can do—"

"No. There's a local garage that can't find good help. They'll have me. I'll be all right."

Can't find any help at all, I guessed, with their local work force either injured or dead.

Gerard and I had not grown close in the way one might have expected of two people sharing months of life and death situations, but when I met his gaze, I recognized a look in his eyes that was also in mine when I stared into a mirror. We had seen the best and the worst of human nature and lived through it. There was nothing left to faze or surprise us. I thought what Gerard said was true enough: he would be all right.

I wanted suddenly to grab him into a tight bear hug and never let him go, but fortunately I resisted the impulse and instead gave him a light kiss on the cheek.

"We were a good team. Take care."

For a moment I almost thought I saw a sheen of tears in his eyes, but then he stepped into the shadows and it seemed I was mistaken. He had lost so many people already that one American woman was hardly worth crying over.

"Yes," he said. "We were the best. You take care, too." He shoved his hands into his pockets and walked away. I wanted to call him back, wanted the familiarity of his presence, wanted the ordinary routine again, but the moment passed. People come and go in your life, I reminded myself, and it doesn't pay to get too fond of any of them.

I hitched a ride to the Quimper train depot and headed for Paris. I hadn't heard a word from Lucy March and didn't know if Mac Chesney was alive or dead or in some injured state in between. Sometimes the two of them snuck into my dreams, but for the most part I had carefully locked Mac away in a corner of my brain and refused to let him out. With the rumble of the train giving rhythm to my thoughts, however, I realized I was inordinately anxious to get to the Hotel Premier. Lucy had said she might leave word for me there with Aggie, and I was eager to find out if she'd done so. Had Lucy eventually returned to serve in a clearing station not in my sector? Had Mac survived the bullet lodged with defiant menace along his spine? I lay my head back against the train seat and closed my eyes, remembering the last time I'd seen both of them. Remembering, too, the question I had asked myself when I first had word of the armistice and which I had asked myself many times since: *what do I do now?*

## "~a harvest home~"

# Chapter 9

The Paris to which I returned at the tail end of 1918 felt like a different city than the one I had left many months before. A palpable sense of energy and good cheer enveloped the city, despite the presence of wounded soldiers and bewildered refugees wherever I looked. Peace had infused the place with hope and a certain grim satisfaction at the penalties Germany must pay immediately and on through the years to come. I understood the desire of the French and their allies for exacting such fierce retribution from Germany but thought the world in this particular circumstance would be better served by a bit more mercy. Twenty years later I would be proved right but would feel no gratification at one of my few moments of prophetic accuracy. This *War to End All Wars* had been inaccurately named because within two decades Germany would wreak its own vengeance for the conditions of the 1918 armistice.

But that was all in the future. At the end of 1918, when Aggie and I sat in her apartment welcoming in the new year with a bottle of champagne she had personally traveled all the way to Reims to procure for the occasion, we raised our glasses to peace and did not think any further than the new year. We celebrated everything we had left behind and did not miss: impassable roads of rutted mud, trenches and front lines, barbed wire and shells and mustard gas, clearing stations and bayonets and gas masks and ambulances.

"Here's to a new year where not a single boy gets blown to bits," Aggie proposed in a voice that indicated she had already had more champagne than she would remember imbibing.

I lifted my glass in an unsteady arc, having had nearly as much champagne as Aggie, and took a deep swig. It was delightful stuff and I was feeling quite happy about everything. No doubt part of the reason was the peace and the champagne, but there was also the note from Lucy Rose that Aggie handed me when I appeared at her door.

> *Meg,*
>
> *Mac will live. That's what you'll want to know first. The doctors took out the bullet, sewed him up, and arranged for him to be sent home. He's getting stronger every day but still has significant healing to do. With the war drawing to a close he can't do any good here any more. He fussed about leaving but Pershing, the great man himself, ordered Mac to an American hospital in the U.S. and Mac would NEVER think to refuse an order from the general. I'm going, too. They're calling it a leave because I've never taken one day off since I stepped off the* Ausonia *and I'm due a leave, but I know I won't be back to France. Peace will probably be official before we dock at New York City. I'll hand Mac over to his waiting family and head for West Virginia to see my father. What happens after that I have no idea.*
>
> *I'm sure Mac will find a way to get in touch with you no matter where you run. You're not a woman easy to forget and he's a man that knows his own mind. Look me up sometime.*
>
> *Lucy*

I had no intention of looking up either one of them but even knowing that I wouldn't see them again, I felt a strong surge of happiness that Mac Chesney was alive. I'd never been to South Dakota but still managed to conjure up a mental image of Mac Chesney dressed like a cowboy in the moving pictures galloping wildly across the plains on his faithful horse. The idea fitted him, somehow, fitted his desire for adventure that I had sensed lay just below his affable surface. I had enough common sense to laugh at my vision, however. Were there cowboys in South Dakota and if there were, would they race across the prairie for no reason? I had no way of knowing from my limited experience and rather doubted the notion, and even if there were and they did, why in the world did I think Captain McDermott Alan Chesney, suddenly resembling the dashing actor Tom Mix wearing a big white hat, would be one of them? I knew I was being silly but it was the effect of an emotion with which I had little familiarity: happiness. Mac Chesney was alive and I was happy. Plain and simple. That's all there was to it.

The year 1919 started innocently enough. Aggie had decided to make Paris her permanent residence, having made her peace with Gertrude Stein and forming something as near to friendship with the writer as either woman could tolerate.

I had almost decided on a similar course when a telegram arrived that threw all my plans into disarray and started a string of events that would not be resolved—resolved in their own way, at least—for months into the future and on the American side of the ocean.

Aggie, still active at the A.F.F.W. depot boxing goods to be given to the French wounded, left one morning and promptly returned long enough to push open the apartment door and shout, "Delivery for you, Meg!" before leaving again. I, sitting at the kitchen table with a cigarette and a cup of coffee, thought I must not have heard her correctly and sat there a while longer until I realized I had not heard the door shut behind her. I wandered out of the kitchen and saw a young man standing in the hallway outside the still open door, patient and quiet.

"Je suis désolée," I said and pulled the sash of my robe more tightly around my waist as I hurried toward him.

He gave a rather charming shrug and smiled. "No matter, miss." He spoke in halting English, pronouncing the words slowly and carefully. "I have nowhere else to be right now." He extended his hand. "I have brought a message for you." I stared at the distinctive paper in his hand as if I'd never seen a telegram before.

"For me? You're sure?"

"You are Miss Margaret Pritchard?" My heart skipped a beat. *Margaret.*

"Yes."

"And this is the Hotel Premier, is it not?" Now he was teasing me.

"Last I looked," I said and took the paper from his hand. I was momentarily so flabbergasted by the idea that someone had sent me a telegram that I just stood there, immobile and mute. Then, when he remained standing, too, but with a resolute smile on his face, I came to my senses. "Wait, please." I fetched a generous number of French coins from my room and handed them to the young man.

"Thank you," I told him, trying to smile, trying to pretend that I was grateful for what he'd delivered.

"This is the first message I have ever delivered from America," he said before executing a small, snappy salute and turning toward the stairs. "I am—" he paused to search for the right word "—honored, miss. Yes, I am honored."

Once inside the apartment, I leaned against the closed door to catch my breath. It must be from Lucy March, I told myself, although I wouldn't have supposed she'd have addressed the telegram to *Margaret*. Of course, Meg was short for a more formal Margaret, so that would be a natural assumption on her part. Or, I thought, my heartbeat picking up a bit, maybe it was from Mac. Both he and Lucy knew the hotel where I stayed in Paris. Maybe he wanted to let me know in his own words that he was alive and healing. Lucy or Mac, trying to convince myself as I lifted the flap of the envelope that I had narrowed down the sender to the only two people possible. But I was wrong. Even without a sender's name at the bottom of the brief message, I knew the telegram was not from Lucy Rose March or Mac Chesney. No salutation, either, for that matter, just the terse words:

*Mother very ill /stop/ Not much time left /stop/*
*Asking for you /stop/ Come home now*

I blinked, read the words a second time, and never hesitated. Perhaps I had always expected such a summons. Perhaps I had even, in some secret, private part of me, longed to have a reason to return. Certainly, for all my thoughtful intentions to lose myself in the French countryside, I had never acted as if I really meant to do so. Always an excuse. Always something else to do first. Always intending to disappear tomorrow, never today. And now: Come home. I was not the same woman who had boarded the *Ausonia* over eighteen months before. Somewhere amid the mud and the blood and the broken bodies I had become someone else. I did not yet know that newly formed woman's mettle but realized that if I went back to the place I had expected never to see again, I would likely have the opportunity, whether I wanted it or not, to find out what Meg Pritchard was made of. It would be a difficult return, perhaps disastrous, but from the moment I read my brother's words, I knew exactly what I would do. How Scotty found me I didn't know—Bruce Stockard? Mrs. Lathrop at the A.F.F.W.? A confluence of events or people of which I wasn't even aware?—but the message was unmistakable. *Come home.* I had seen so much of death and knew how irrevocable it was, how it sent people into eternity without a care that words were left unsaid, regret stacked upon regret, hearts broken into a thousand pieces. Well, I would likely be the one with regrets when I stepped onto American soil, but from the moment I'd torn open the telegram, there had never been a doubt of what I would do. The command was clear: *Come home. Come home now*, and that's exactly what I did.

I took the train to the coastal town of Brest the next day with the intention of buying a ticket on the first ship headed for America. Aggie did not ask why or quiz me about the telegram's contents, and I volunteered only the basic information that a sick family member needed my attention. She has secrets, too, I thought, catching her eye across the table where we ate our final meal together, and knows enough not to ask. Everyone has secrets. One of the basic facts of life it had taken me an ocean voyage to uncover.

"It's been a different adventure than you expected, I'd wager," was Aggie's only observation.

I smiled at that but did not comment in return, remembering my earlier words. *Something of a lark*, I'd said to Lucy Rose. *A bit of fun*, I'd told Mac. Over time I'd come to regret those words deeply, regret the woman I'd been then, someone nursing invisible wounds she thought could not be mended. Until I saw the first soldier with both his legs blown off, the first man coughing up blood, the dazed mother wandering the road with her dead child in her arms, Lucy Rose March holding a man to her breast and singing a quiet lullaby in his ear as his blood soaked through her dress. As I looked down at the still body of Mac Chesney with a bullet through his throat. Sometime in the intervening months, I'd come to understand that there were many, many more wounded walking the earth than one Meg Pritchard.

Finally, I nodded and held up my glass. "Here's to future adventures."

Aggie lifted her glass and clinked it against mine. "I'll drink to that, though I won't mind if they hold off a while. I kind of like the quiet for a change."

When we waved good-bye at the train station, I was surprised by the small wrench of emotion I felt as her figure receded from view. It seemed that I had been without friends a long time, without authentic friends, anyway, people of shared experience and similar passions, people I enjoyed being around, and within a few months I'd found three people to whom I'd said good-bye but would probably miss in one degree or another for the rest of my life. I was going home but thought I had in some indefinable and paradoxical way left another kind of home behind in France.

At Brest I spent one night in a small seaside "pension" before catching a passenger steamer, older, more compact, and less comfortable than the *Ausonia* the following afternoon. It would bypass the United Kingdom and land in Boston. Better than New York, I thought, where I might be expected to disembark.

"It's got no luxuries," the captain told me as I lugged my bag up the gangplank toward him. He offered no assistance and I had a quick memory of standing at the bottom of the steps leading to Dover's Harbour House and Mac Chesney not waiting for a request but lifting my bag with his easy grace. The captain of the steamer could have taken a few lessons from my captain's agreeable kindness. *My captain.* I shook my head at that and banished the memory. Those days were part of my past as surely as Mac Chesney was part of the same past. I had much better spend time remembering why I was returning to the United States: my mother, dear and dying, part of my past, too, but perhaps, if the ship made good time and Mother held her own, with some time yet remaining in my present.

We docked in a bitterly cold Boston the last week of January. The wind snatched at my breath and drove snow against my face as I stepped onto the dock and grabbed a passing porter.

"A taxi to the train station," I told him. Once that was accomplished I spent nearly half a day in the women's waiting area of Boston's South Union Train Station, not nearly as unpleasant as one might think because the waiting area was larger than the lobby of the Hotel Premier, with roomy oak benches, kiosk confectioneries, and several bathrooms with all the amenities. I could not help but think of the shelled French villages and their homeless inhabitants adrift in a ruined countryside as I sat in such public comfort. Had I been irredeemably changed by my time in France? Would I always compare my present experience to what I had seen there? I rather thought I had been and that I would, and if it were true, the future might be filled with a great deal of soul searching, certainly more than I'd been used to. Which was none.

By the time I stepped off the train two days later at Cleveland's Union Depot, I was exhausted. Cleveland's cold was as bitter as Boston's but at least there was no snow stinging against my face, although several inches of it lay on the ground. Because I'd been in that station many, many times, I felt a level of comfort from the moment I picked up my bag. Not much had changed in two years, and I knew how and where to find a cab. The familiar streets might have engendered a level of comfort if I hadn't been too tired to figure out exactly how I felt. All I knew was that I needed to see my mother again, needed to tell her things I hadn't been brave enough to tell her before I stole away without a good-bye. Let her still be alive, I said under my breath, please, and then recalled that I'd told Lucy I didn't pray, which added the offense of bold-faced lying to everything else I bore on my conscience. Remembering Lucy's tart response, I had to smile a little. "Maybe for Mac's sake you could put whatever argument you have with God aside for a while," she'd told me with uncharacteristic impatience. Lucy March was not a woman to pull her punches.

The cab stopped in front of an imposing mansion on Euclid Avenue, a red-bricked, elegant home with arched windows on either side of an awning that led up porch steps to an imposing front door. To the side was an ivy-covered brick arch through which a drive led to the garage and the rear servants' entrances. Several huge chimneys could be seen from the street, proof of warm rooms despite the dead of winter. There was no black crepe on the door, I noticed as I walked up the front walk followed by the cab driver with my bag. That boded well. No wreath of funereal black hung on the gatepost, either, and I felt my heart lift even higher. The outward signs of a recent death in the family had still been in place for my stepfather when I left Cleveland. Surely Mother must live if the accoutrements of mourning were not displayed.

I paid the driver, pushed open one of the heavy front double doors, stepped into the broad foyer, and took a careful look around. Nothing looked different, from the paintings on the walls to the broad curving staircase in front of me.

A man's figure came down the long hallway toward me, momentarily hesitated at the sight of me standing inside the front door, and then picked up speed.

"Yes, miss?" he began and then when he got a good look at my face stopped, speechless and staring, in his tracks.

"Hello, Kenyon," I said. "Yes, it's me, the prodigal daughter home at last. How is Mother?" At my voice, the man resumed his approach.

"Miss Margo, I can't believe it. We had no idea—"

"Didn't Scotty tell you he wired me?"

"Scotty?" The tone of Kenyon's voice was somewhere between confused and mystified. "No, but your brother hasn't been home in a while. He's at school."

"At school? With Mother so ill?"

"Your mother is ill?" Honestly, the dialogue could have been lifted straight from some zany Broadway comedy.

I stopped myself from answering, took a deep breath, and said, "Kenyon, I received a telegram that I thought was from Scotty telling me that Mother was close to death and asking for me. Your present reaction to my appearance makes me doubt every bit of that."

Kenyon, too, slowed down. "Your mother's heart has never been strong, as you well know, but she is as well as she was when you left. Your brother has not been home since the Christmas holiday and while he may have sent you a telegram, I am not aware of it and very much doubt that Mrs. Tankard is, either. I certainly was not told to expect you today." Or any day in the near future, I knew he wanted to add but was too proper to voice the thought. "Nevertheless, your mother will be beside herself with happiness when she sees you. She speaks of you every day—misses you every day, if I may be so bold as to say. We have all missed you."

A silence followed his words as I tried to make sense of them. No ill mother and no deathbed summons. I could hardly complain about that, but very likely no telegram from my brother, then, either. No bright side to that fact. Here I stood in Cleveland, beckoned home after an absence of nearly two years because someone wanted me within arms' reach badly enough to fake a telegram and a crisis. Someone very definitely wanted me in Cleveland, Ohio. I had been tricked into returning home and knew without needing to put words to the question who had done so and why. The answers did not bode well.

*Magnificent Farewell*

I saw his round mouth's crimson deepen as it fell,
Like a sun, in his last deep hour;
Watched the magnificent recession of farewell,
Clouding, half gleam, half glower,
And a last splendour burn the heavens of his cheek.
And in his eyes
The cold stars lighting, very old and bleak,
In different skies

Wilfred Owen

# Part Two – 1919

# *"~half gleam, half glower~"*

# Chapter 10

I had lived in the house on Euclid Avenue, a broad boulevard often called Millionaires' Row by the admiring and the envious, since my mother married my stepfather. Just thirteen at the time, my years and my temperament had made me inclined to be rebellious, but my mother thought that with time and maturity I would grow accustomed to the huge rooms, echoing halls, grand furniture, and the presence of servants rustling throughout the house. I never got used to any of it. I missed the house of my childhood, a smaller, less ostentatious but equally as comfortable home in Akron, a smaller, less ostentatious but equally as comfortable community southeast of Cleveland. I know it cannot be so, not really, but it seems that I was always happy, that *we* were always happy, in Akron. Happy until my father died. Happy until Mother met the great George Tankard at a charity luncheon. Happy until they married and we moved to the house on Euclid Avenue. I was never truly happy after that. I missed my mother and my brother when I left for France but not my stepfather, not Cleveland, and not this house. Yet here I was, returned to a place I had not missed or expected to see again.

Kenyon directed me to my old room—"You'll find it the same. Mrs. Tankard wouldn't allow a thing to be changed."— and told me he would let me know as soon as my mother returned home. I had just enough time to wash my face, straighten my hair, change my shirtwaist, and look longingly at the bed before there was a knock on my door. Without waiting for an answer, my mother pushed it open and stood framed in the doorway, both hands pressed to her mouth and her eyes filling with tears.

"Margaret!"

We examined each other for a moment, and then she flew into the room and took me into her arms. She had always been a small, slender woman with a look about her of fine china, her skin as perfect as porcelain, her figure elegant but fragile, but I thought she had grown too frail. I could feel the small bones of her arms as they held me to her, saw that her face was pale beneath expertly applied face powder and her eyes tired and shadowed. She looked all her age and then some, and that had come only with the past months, because of my stepfather's death and, I feared, because I had disappeared from her life. I felt a pang of guilt and regret.

After a few moments, Mother pulled me to the settee in the corner and when we sat down, she turned to place a palm to the side of my face. "My dearest," she said, her voice wavering with strong emotion, "this is the most wonderful day of my life! You can't know how I've missed you! You look well but different somehow. We must wire Scotty right away and let him know you're home."

I felt curiously passive, unsure how much to tell her of the reason for my return, reluctant to worry her with my suspicions, and so I said nothing.

She dropped her hands into her lap and stared at me a long time as her smile faded and the look in her eyes became more intent. Neither of us spoke. Finally, she stood.

"You look exhausted, Margaret. Why don't you lie down and rest? I'll wake you for dinner and we'll talk then."

I could only sit and watch her dear face. She was different, too, I thought, part of her as expressive as ever and yet holding a part of herself back from me, reserved in a way she had never been before, not with me, not with anyone. My mother had always been as transparent as glass, a genuinely kind woman with no mystery about her. People were always attracted to her forthright goodness and many loved her for the same reason, but in the months I'd been gone it was as if she'd drawn a shutter across her heart. Hiding something, it seemed to me. Unbidden, the words I'd thought as I shared that last bistro meal with Aggie came to mind: *Everyone has secrets.*

"I am tired," I admitted. "It was a long trip." To her credit, Mother did not ask from where. Unless she had known where I was all along. The unexpected idea made me realize I was too fatigued for rational thought.

"Go to bed this instant, young lady." That was the indulgent tone I was accustomed to hearing from my mother.

"Yes, ma'am. Gladly."

She grinned back at me from the doorway. "I will appreciate your uncharacteristic obedience for the rare occurrence that it is." Then her smile faded. "But, oh, my dear, I am so very glad to have you home again!" She pulled the door shut quietly.

The word *home* floated in the room as I stripped off my outer clothes and slid under the soft woolen blankets of the bed, my last conscious thought the realization that while the house was not home to me, my mother certainly was.

In some respects, it was as if I had never left, never crawled under a truck to make a makeshift repair, never driven an ambulance filled with wounded soldiers, never been nearly blown to high heaven myself, never shared a cigarette with Lucy Rose March or a kiss with Mac Chesney.

At the first meal Mother and I shared, she asked where I had been these last months. When I replied France, she asked, "Something to do with the war?" and at my nod, she concluded the topic with a noncommittal, "I see." That was the end of the matter for a long time.

After my mother remarried and her new husband, George Tankard, became central to our lives, we both became proficient at not talking about anything crucial, at sweeping the significant under the proverbial rug. With the man now gone, we might be able to regain the easy sharing I recalled from my childhood. Letty Phelps had been a warm and expressive woman of laughter and love, Letty Tankard nothing like that at all. I knew my stepfather had been the reason for the change in her and hoped that now that he was dead, I might find the dear mother I'd lost, but that first night home I didn't notice much change in her. A soft, unspoken anxiety still rested in her eyes and worry dimmed her bright smile. I thought I knew the reason why but did not choose to burden the conversation my first night back with questions or explanations. There would be time later, so I thought, for that necessary conversation. I would insist on it.

The city of Cleveland had grown significantly in the time I was gone and boasted a new Museum of Art, City Hall, and orchestra, in addition to an impressive bridge named the

Detroit-Superior Bridge that linked the city to its west side across the Cuyahoga River. It was the grandest bridge of its time, more than three thousand feet of reinforced steel and concrete. The world had seen nothing like it and neither had I.

It was one of the many sites Mother and I visited in my first few days back, and through it all we seldom spoke of anything more important than the new shops at The Arcade. I did not know how to begin a conversation that needed to be said, and she did not seem to feel a need for it.

Once I looked up and caught her eyes on me as we sat together in the front parlor. "Mother," I began, and she shook her head.

"It will be all right, Margaret," she said. "Everything will be all right. I guarantee it." She placed the book she was reading down on the table next to her and rose, stopping briefly as she passed me to rest her hand on my shoulder. "I'm so happy you're home. So very happy." My first few days back were, in fact, happy for me, too, but everything changed—as I knew it must—on the first Friday of February, changed with perverse contradiction, for the better and then for the worse.

The *better* part of the day saw my brother standing at the foot of the staircase calling my name. No one had bothered to tell me he was coming so the sound of his voice was a delightful and complete surprise. I had to stop midway down the stairs to take him in because I hadn't seen him in twenty-one months and nearly two years can make a big difference in a young man. I'd left behind a youth of sixteen and now stared at a young man, tall and fair and the image of our father. Were I a weepy type of woman, Scotty's sudden appearance would have brought me to tears, so dear was he to me, but as it was, his grin and open arms broke the emotion of the moment. And I'm not a weepy woman even in the worst of times, which this definitely was not.

"You scamp!" I cried and hopped from the second step directly into his hug. "You could have warned me!"

"What? And miss the chance to make you speechless? Not on your life! The opportunity doesn't happen often enough as it is."

Mother came to the hall doorway of the study where she'd been writing letters, watched us a moment, and then said,

"Hello, darling. Did you take a cab home? I didn't expect you for another hour at least."

Scotty went to Mother and gave her a quick peck on the cheek. "I got away earlier than I thought, and you know there's a train every hour from Columbus."

I closed the door gently behind us as we entered the study. It wasn't likely there would be any sudden family revelations and I thought Kenyon was more trustworthy than most family members, but there was no use tempting fate.

"You look different," my brother said, eyeing me with a critical look.

"Age," I said, "has a habit of changing a person. Look at you."

I was a different person than the Margo Phelps who had boarded the *Ausonia* in the late spring of 1917, and as I examined Scotty, I realized it was the same for him. There was nothing hesitant about him now or gawky, as there had been at our last meeting. Except for his eyeglasses, everything about him seemed different.

"How long before I see your first skyscraper?" I asked.

"Oh, an eternity. I don't even have two years under my belt yet."

"That's a relief. I need time to get used to the idea that you'll be building things with materials other than blocks."

"Ha ha." Scotty made a face at me and I returned the look by sticking out my tongue. How lovely it was to be with my brother again!

We talked a long time, I sharing more about my ambulance adventures in France and Scotty talking about life at the Ohio State University. My mother simply sat and listened, glowing a little because both her children were home where they belonged.

After luncheon, Scotty said, "Grab your coat. Let's take a walk." He wants to talk, I thought, and was conscious of my relief at the prospect, feeling a sudden need to get beyond the surface interests of our lives.

One could stroll Millionaires' Row, aka Euclid Avenue, in the spring and summer—at least, it had been fashionable to do so before I left—but pedestrians were at a premium in February, even a mild, blue-skied February day as that one was. We both jammed our hands into our pockets and set off down the walk side-by-side.

"How has she been?" I asked. "Really."

"Worried about you, but how do you ever know with her?"

"Her health?"

"Not strong. She's seemed frailer to me ever since the murder."

*The murder.* The words hung in the air between us with such tangible clarity they could have been frozen by the frigid February air. Neither of us spoke for a long while.

"And no progress there?" I finally asked.

Scotty shook his head. "None. At first the police were here every week but then I went away to school and Mother started going about her regular day and when they asked about you, we couldn't tell them anything, so after a while it appeared the investigation was at a standstill. That suited me just fine. I thought maybe everything would simply fade away."

"Murders aren't generally allowed to fade away," I said in my best big sister's voice.

"No," he agreed, "not even when the victim deserved what happened to him and then some. Not even when everybody's glad he's gone."

"Not even then," I said and paused. "Which brings me to the telegram."

"I heard about it. I didn't send it, Margo."

"I know."

Scotty stopped and turned to face me. "Who, then?"

"Someone that wanted me back on American soil. Who's left, after all, since Mother and you are accounted for?" His gaze locked on mine.

"Lots of people are left, Margo. No one liked and many people loathed George Francis Tankard."

"True, but I think I'm the only person on record who publicly declared that she hated him and wanted to kill him." I smiled. "Not my wisest strategy." The tense moment broken, we started walking again.

"You were always an awful poker player," Scotty said. "No restraint at all and going way too fast most of the time. I'm surprised anyone trusted you behind the wheel of an ambulance loaded with injured soldiers."

"They thought I was someone else."

"Ah." A pause, then, "I thought it was something like that. Who? And how? Spill. I want to know the whole story."

"I wrote a letter to a Mrs. Lathrop. I'd read in the paper about the work she was doing in France with an organization called the American Fund for French Wounded. From what I read in the article I thought it had to be the same Lathrop that did some business with Father years ago; I remember Father saying what a good man Mr. Lathrop was. That's why it stuck in my mind, I guess. Anyway, if I had the wrong Lathrop, what would I lose?"

Scotty turned his face to me with an expression that said he wasn't following my narrative. "But—"

"I wrote the letter over Mother's name, hoping Mrs. Lathrop would remember her, which she did, and I recommended a young woman of good family named Meg Pritchard, who would arrive in Paris in the near future."

"Oh." Silence as he put it all together. "Oh, I see. You took Mother's maiden name and recommended yourself. Very smart, sister."

"Yes, wasn't it? My initials were embossed on my luggage so it worked out nicely."

"And off you went to France, just like that."

"Just like that," I agreed.

"But why? Why did you go?"

"You know why."

"But you didn't kill him, did you?"

"God knows I wanted to often enough."

"So did I, for that matter."

"Yes, but you and Mother were together at the time of the murder. I, unfortunately, was alone, walking along the lake front in the blustery February wind with nary a witness. It was inevitable that the police would make me their top suspect."

"There were other suspects," Scotty pointed out. "He was hated by a number of people and made a lot of enemies along the way."

"I know, but the last time I talked to the police, it was clear that they had moved me to the top of the list."

"Your running away didn't help, Margo. It just made you look guiltier. You should have stayed here."

I wanted to distract them from Mother and you, I thought. Don't you see how questionable it was that each of you provided an alibi for the other, two people who knew George Tankard better than anyone else and might wish him gone from their lives?

Aloud I said, "Yes, I see that now, but it's too late. And I don't regret the months I spent in France. I learned a lot about life. I made some friends. It wasn't a complete waste of time."

We walked in silence, crossed the quiet avenue, and started back on the other side of the street.

"I swear I didn't send that telegram," Scotty said. "How could I? I didn't have any idea where you were."

"I know."

"Then who—?"

I left the question unanswered until our house was within sight and then said, "I think we're about to find out."

Scotty looked first at me and then followed my gaze to the black coupe waiting at the curb outside our house.

"No."

"Yes," I said with as much gentleness as I could muster. "It's time, Scotty."

"Time for what?" There was the hint of a quaver in his voice, and I heard once more the little boy who'd been afraid of the dark, the little boy trying his best to be brave.

"To face the music I tried to run away from, the music I refused to hear. Time to get it all behind us." I felt more than saw my brother stiffen and knew again a fierce desire to protect him. My younger brother, dearer to me than gold, dearer than life. I tucked my hand under Scotty's arm and pulled him closer as we walked the last distance to the big mansion on Euclid Avenue and the police that had waited almost two years for exactly this moment.

Once inside, Kenyon met us at the door. "You're wanted in the parlor, Miss Margo."

"I'm sure I am," I said, trying to put the man at ease. He'd been with us from the time we moved into the house and was devoted to Mother. Of course, everyone who knew my mother with any intimacy was devoted to her. That was the kind of woman she was. "You don't need to come," I said to Scotty. "I'm the one they've been waiting for."

He didn't bother with a reply, just gave me a look of deep disgust and followed me through the double doors, which Kenyon had pulled open for us. I might have been the queen of England by his expansive gesture and half expected to have him announce me. Not that it would have been necessary.

Detective McGuire, a fierce, short, ruddy Irishman who had established himself as my nemesis from the very beginning of the investigation, stood at my entrance.

I strode forward, hand outstretched. "Mr. McGuire. Why am I not in the least surprised to find you in our front parlor?"

He took my hand in his and gave it a cordial squeeze. "Ah, Miss Phelps, you're looking very fine, considering."

"Considering?"

"You're recent sojourn in a war-ravaged country. My admiration for you knows no bounds."

I wanted to respond with a hearty and disdainful "Ha!" but instead smoothed my skirts and sat, which allowed everyone else in the room to do the same, Mother, Scotty, Detective McGuire, and another policeman.

After a long pause, McGuire said in a brogue too thick to be genuine, "And where are my manners now?" He indicated the other policeman. "This is Sergeant Meier." The sergeant nodded in my general direction impassively.

After another long pause, I asked, "How may I help you, Mr. McGuire?" As if I didn't know.

"I've been holding on to some questions that I never had a chance to ask you, Miss Phelps."

"Really? I don't see how that could possibly be. As I recall, you spent a great deal of time asking me a great many questions. And now you have even more?"

"I do. You disappeared so suddenly two years ago that I never had the chance to use up all my questions."

For all the lightness of his tone, I knew what a danger the man was, recognized the threat behind his words, understood exactly what he believed, and feared the gleam in his dark eyes. Here was a man who could not be charmed or bought, a tough, shrewd, and experienced man, who had believed I was a murderess in 1917 when he first started investigating my stepfather's death and clearly still thought so two years later. There was something chilling about such relentless pursuit, but I was not going to let him see any touch of fear in my demeanor or hear it in my voice.

"I had to answer the urgent call to aid our French allies."

"A sudden call, as well, it appears. Everyone, including your own mother, seemed surprised to find you gone."

"Not surprised, exactly," my mother's quiet voice. "Even as a child, Margaret felt deeply for the afflicted."

"Did she now?" McGuire fairly twinkled at my mother. "She's a grand girl, no doubt. Still, I have a few more questions for her, though I'm sorry to spoil the homecoming." He turned to me. "When exactly did you arrive back in Cleveland, Miss Phelps?"

"Surely you were watching for me, Mr. McGuire."

He had the nerve to grin at me. "Now, Miss Phelps, how would I have known to expect you when your own family had no knowledge of your arrival?"

Because, I wanted to say, recognizing the self-satisfied triumph in his grin, you heard around town—probably from talk originated by Bruce Stockard after he was shipped home—that I was in northern France and from there it would have taken only a few telegrams to French authorities to track down a young, blonde American woman driving an ambulance. Child's play for the man in front of me, a man with the tenacity of a bulldog. Fire off a final, unsigned telegram to the Hotel Premier with the news that Mother was dying and wait for me to show up at her front door. Really, if I didn't loathe the man so thoroughly, I could almost have admired such a devious plan.

I contented myself with, "How, indeed?" and waited.

"Well, however it happened, here you are, and I hope you haven't made any further plans for the day. The sergeant and I need you to join us at the courthouse for a while."

I raised my brows at the statement—the words not a request by any stretch of the imagination—but left it to my mother to say with indignation, "Really, Detective, that is the outside of enough! My daughter is home after many grueling months caring for the injured and now without reason or explanation you demand that she accompany you as if she were a common criminal!"

"I apologize, Mrs. Tankard, if I've given the impression that I think your daughter is a *common* criminal. Far from it, ma'am. Far from it indeed." He stood and turned to me. "You'll come with me, Miss Phelps."

Mother and Scotty spoke their outrage at the command simultaneously, but I knew the detective better than they and saw from his expression that he had no intention of being placated or bullied into changing his mind. I doubted there was a person on the planet, in fact, who could bully Detective Frank McGuire into changing his mind once he'd set it on a specific course.

I rose and with some drama held out my wrists. The gesture silenced all the talk in the room.

McGuire placed his hand, the one that held his hat, over his heart. "No, no, no, Miss Phelps! No, indeed! I'm not arresting you." The word *yet* hovered between us.

"That's a relief, Mr. McGuire. I must have misunderstood your intentions. I'll get my coat and join you."

"Sergeant Meier and I will come right along with you, save us all some time."

"Good idea," I said, turning my back to him and heading for the door to the hallway. "In case I'm overcome by another urgent call to aid the downtrodden."

He was close on my heels and I heard his chuckle. "That wouldn't do at all, would it, Miss Phelps? No sudden disappearances for you for a while, I think." A moment of quiet, then, "That would be too much for your poor, dear mother, I should say." Damn the man.

At the door, Mother kissed me on the cheek and said in a very low voice meant only for my ears, "I'll call Herbert. He'll know what to do. Be careful." I thought that her concern was real, but that she was neither surprised nor shaken by the turn of events. Had she, like I, expected this confrontation? I had always thought her a woman fragile in body and sensitive in temperament, but perhaps in my absence she had changed as much as I.

"I will," I told her in return. "Don't worry."

"Rest assured, Mr. McGuire," Mother said in her haughtiest voice, "that I will be in immediate touch with Mayor Davis and with Chief Smith about your disgraceful conduct."

McGuire, replacing his hat as he stood just outside the front door, looked at her and answered in a cordial and surprisingly gentle voice, "I sincerely regret the intrusion, Mrs. Tankard, and understand your reaction. I would probably feel the same were I you. Good day."

We rode in the coupe, the sergeant driving and McGuire seated next to me in the back, without a word being spoken. I was deep in thought about the next few hours and McGuire— well, I might speculate but only the future would truly tell what the man had in mind. All I knew with any certainty was that whatever it was would not benefit me.

The County Court House had opened for business seven years ago and on its opening day citizens were allowed inside to tour its halls and marvel at the grandeur. Diana Cummings, my best friend at the time, and I had managed to evade our parents' inquiries and ignore their prohibitions and had joined the crowds touring the new court house, oohing and ahing with them over marble staircases and mezzanine murals. It had been a grand building then and was still grand, large enough to house most of the county offices: sheriff, commissioner, treasurer, auditor, recorder, surveyor, and other sundry officials in addition to several courtrooms and most importantly to my present situation, the county prosecutor's office.

To my surprise, the person awaiting my arrival in the prosecutor's office was a woman: Assistant Prosecutor Florence Allen. Under other circumstances, I would have been proud of Cleveland's progressive inclinations. A woman in the prosecutor's office had been unheard of when I left the city and here I stood before someone who in just a few years would become the first woman to serve on Ohio's Supreme Court, would, in fact, be the first woman in the United States to serve on any state supreme court. She gave a first impression of innocuous femininity: soft brown hair, a round face, ivory complexion, a mild smile, and small wire-rimmed glasses resting on the bridge of a pert nose. But with her first words of greeting, it was impossible to miss the sharp intelligence that lurked behind those spectacles or the shrewd skepticism that colored her speech. She sounded all polite innocence but I realized she was anything but. The only time I caught a glimpse of the woman behind the office was when I answered her few initial questions. Where had I been the last months, she asked me, and what had I been doing.

When I told her I'd been driving an ambulance on the Western Front in France, her expression softened. "American boys?" she asked.

"Yes." I was determined to say as little as possible during the interview.

"Many were very young to fight."

"Yes, and very young to die, too. It was my job to make sure they had a chance to get to someone who could keep them alive."

She stared at me a long while, measuring me against a standard I wouldn't understand until later when I found out she had lost two brothers in the war. If McGuire, not liking the direction the conversation was going, hadn't cleared his throat with an ostentatious growl at that moment, Miss Allen and I might have formed a bond, however tenuous, that would have served me well in the future. But McGuire's impatience was hard to ignore and Allen was only an assistant prosecutor and new to the position at that, so she brought the conversation back to the death of my stepfather with one incisive question.

"Are you sorry Mr. Tankard is dead, Miss Phelps?"

It would do no good to lie to this woman any more than was necessary and I said, "No."

"Why is that?"

"He was a brute."

"How do you mean, exactly?"

"Brute. An animal-like and cruelly violent person. I think that's close to the dictionary definition of the word."

"Was he violent to you?"

"Only once."

"Tell me about that." McGuire stilled in his chair and Allen's eyes stayed fixed on my face.

"I told the authorities about it already, quite soon after my stepfather's death, as I recall. In fact, I think it was Mr. McGuire who first asked me about the incident."

"Yes, but I wasn't present, Miss Phelps, and I'd like to hear what happened from you instead of reading about it on paper."

I held her gaze during the telling. "We were at home. Tankard was berating my brother in his usual abrasive and cruel way, calling him names, castigating him for some minor infraction of the barrage of rules he had laid down in our home and he struck Scotty full in the face with his fist. Knocked him unconscious and then kicked him for good measure. My stepfather did not have good parlor manners at any time, but when he was drinking, he was beyond reason. When I grabbed hold of his arm and tried to pull him away from my brother, the man turned on me and hit me with his fist, too, but I was more nimble than Scotty and he only grazed my cheek. He was a bull of a man, easily as strong as my brother and I together and I feared for my life. I went to his desk and pulled out the derringer he kept in the top drawer—George Tankard as you undoubtedly discovered had a great many enemies—pointed it at him, and told him I'd kill him if he ever laid a hand on my brother again. He didn't like it, of course, but my words had a very calming effect on the conversation."

"Was that the derringer that was ultimately used to kill him?"

"I wouldn't know," I said. "I didn't kill him with it that day and that's the last I ever saw of the derringer."

"Did you know the entire altercation was overheard by some of your servants and by a deliveryman standing just inside the kitchen?"

I shrugged. "Not at the time but then I wasn't thinking about being secretive. I was trying to protect my brother and myself."

"Did Mr. Tankard raise his hand to your mother?"

Inhale. Exhale. Answer. "Yes."

"Often?"

"Once is often enough, Miss Allen. If you're asking me if my stepfather struck my mother more than once, the answer is yes. I know of a few occasions she could not go out in public until the bruises healed."

"I would have been furious." I preferred to believe that the assistant prosecutor was being frank with me and not formulating a trap.

"I was."

"And in such a fury, killing the man that beat your mother would be quite understandable."

I had to smile. Did she think she could placate me into a confession?

"I hated George Tankard from the moment my mother married him and I have never pretended that I was sorry he was dead, but he was ruthless in business and amassed a fortune by ruining a number of people. I was not the only person that hated him and rejoiced at his death, and I surely cannot be your only suspect."

With a gentle tone, Florence Allen said, "You are, however, the only suspect seen and identified by two witnesses as being on the premises of the Hotel Winton the same night Mr. Tankard was murdered there."

Speechless for a moment, I finally said, "Impossible."

McGuire was unable to stay silent. "Not impossible at all, Miss Phelps. No, indeed." He paused, then asked with feigned innocence, "But surely the knowledge that we found witnesses that put you in the vicinity of your stepfather's murder isn't a surprise to you," I refused to respond to his teasing tone and he went on, "because we found them on one day and you were gone the next, the very next day, Miss Phelps. What was I to think?"

"Coincidence," I suggested.

"Ah, coincidence, the stuff of novels, perhaps, but not a part of good police work." He smiled at me. "You were seen on the hotel premises around the time of the murder, and yet where had you told us you were at that time? Let's see now if I recall—ah, that's right. You said you were taking a walk, enjoying a solitary constitutional on a frigid February night. Your story always beggared belief, Miss Phelps, a young society woman like yourself out for a walk on a dark winter night."

"I like to walk," I said.

"Well, 'twill be a while, I fear, before you're able to be out on another walk. Quite a while, I'd say. Don't you agree, Miss Allen?"

I thought I detected a touch of sadness in the woman's response, but perhaps it was only wishful thinking on my part.

"I can hardly speak to that, Detective McGuire. Innocent until proven guilty is a touchstone of our legal system." Then she nodded over at him, sending a message he understood and welcomed, because without bothering to hide his satisfaction, he came to stand beside.

"Margaret Phelps, I am arresting you for the premeditated murder of George Francis Tankard on the night of February twenty-third, 1917."

I felt relief at his words more than anything else. The time of running *from* was over. I did not regret my months at the Front, treasured my friendship, if that was what it had been, with Lucy Rose March, felt a stirring of warmth and something that might have been regret at the memory of Mac Chesney, but that was part of the past. *Face your fears and get them behind you,* Lucy had said in one of our first meetings. I hoped she had that right because it's exactly what I intended to do.

# "*~a last splendour~*"

# Chapter 11

We met Herbert Schmal, my mother's longtime attorney, in the hallway outside Miss Allen's office.

"Margo?" Schmal was a slender, almost effeminate man of daunting intelligence. He'd handled our family's affairs as long as I could remember, had managed our way through my father's death and had had the foresight to settle inheritances on Scotty and me in such a way that Tankard could not get his greedy claws on any of our money. Mother, as Tankard's wife, had not been so fortunate, but since all of her husband's fortune came to her at his death, I thought she had received her own back and then some. Nothing could make up for the misery she'd lived through under that man's thumb, but his enormous wealth now settled without dispute in her name might offer some slight solace.

From his clear, savvy gaze and the way his mouth tightened at the corners, I didn't need to explain the present situation to Mr. Schmal. He said to McGuire, "Where are you taking her?"

"The Women's Detention Home."

To me, Schmal said, "It's less than ideal, of course, but it will be bearable for you until the hearing. I'll get to the judge today yet and I should think you'll be home tomorrow."

"The judge might be afraid of losing Miss Phelps again. She has a way of appearing and disappearing when you least expect it."

We ignored McGuire's facetious comment and I said, "I'll be fine, Herbert. I was on the Front for over a year, remember. I'm used to trenches and mud and barbed wire." The lawyer smiled at that, a charming smile for a man with such an austere exterior.

"It's nothing comparable, I assure you, Margo. The facility is new, not even two years old, and has the necessary amenities.

However, the company you meet may not be quite what you're used to."

I laughed at that. "You'd be surprised at the variety of people I've had the opportunity to meet the last two years. Tell Mother not to worry." I patted his arm, I doing the comforting when he had most likely anticipated the need to console me, but there would be no need for anyone to comfort or console me. I was engaged for battle and prepared for whatever happened. How could I remember Lucy singing to a dying man and think that my troubles were insurmountable?

Herbert Schmal was right to say that the Women's Detention Home, also known as Sterling House, was bearable. Whether I'd have considered it so prior to my months in France, I don't know, but it was a large building with indoor plumbing and wards of clean, dry beds for the residents, and considering my experience with mud-clogged clearing stations, makeshift hospitals, and bloody ambulances, the place seemed perfectly acceptable. Mrs. Marshall, the warden, separated me adeptly from Mr. McGuire and before I knew it I had handed over my coat and bag and been led to a large room where a contingent of about twenty women sat in silence.

"We eat promptly at seven and then you are all escorted to your rooms for the night. There is a wardrobe for the clothes you have on. Night clothes are provided. There is no talking allowed after nine o'clock. If you need to use the facilities at the end of the hall, you must ask permission of the attendant stationed outside your ward's door. She will accompany you. You are not allowed out of your ward for any other reason until the morning bell rings signifying it is time to rise and dress. Have I been clear, Miss Phelps?"

"Yes. Very." She reminded me of every hospital matron I'd met in France, articulate and organized and indisputable, yet with a slight tinge of compassion. I felt surprisingly at home.

I experienced the well-organized routine of Sterling House for only one night. Supper was simple, the bed was utilitarian but clean, and there was little conversation among the women, who were accused of everything from fraud to outright thievery to prostitution. As far as I could tell, except for one woman awaiting sentencing for seriously wounding her husband with a knife ("Deserved it, he did. At least where I'm going I won't have to look at his ugly mug across the table.") I was the only woman there accused of a violent crime. I could have been wrong, however, because there was little talk before nine o'clock and none at all after. We were a cooperative group.

A police wagon took me back to the Court House late the following morning and Herbert Schmal met me just inside the entrance.

"Was everything all right?" he asked.

"Yes, Herbert. I have no complaints." We sat down on a bench under the watchful eye of a bailiff.

"I've had conversations with both the County Prosecutor and Judge Kohler, Margo. They are agreeable to remanding you to my authority and allowing you to be at home through the upcoming trial."

"Really? With my history of unaccountable wanderlust? Herbert, what exactly did you have to promise to make that arrangement?"

His gaze did not waver from my face. "I had to call in some markers, it's true, but more importantly, I assured them on my honor that you had no intention of disappearing and gave them my word you would be available for the trial." He did not follow up with the obvious question.

"Well, then," I said, "that's that. Thank you. I promise not to mortify you in front of your colleagues."

McGuire was at the hearing, as was Florence Allen. The detective was clearly annoyed by the decision to let me go home and after the judge's lecture to me about my obligation to be available to the authorities at all times, I saw McGuire whisper something to Miss Allen. Perhaps he wanted her to contest the judge's decision, I couldn't tell, but she merely gave an abrupt shake of her head in response to him, gathered up her papers, and exited the court room. McGuire departed more slowly, jamming on his hat with more force than was called for. He may truly have feared I would immediately escape, but I think it was more that the Irishman simply did not like me and hated that anyone had been at all generous with me about anything. He would be happy only when I was a convicted murderess.

In the week that followed, ensconced once more in the mansion on Euclid Avenue, I was surprised and not especially pleased to discover that I was the center of what promised to be (promised by both the *Cleveland Press* and *Plain Dealer*) "The Trial of the Decade." It took only one shopping trip to discover that the members of the press were fixated on me and my family. Against my advice, Scotty had put his schooling on hold and waited at home with Mother and me for whatever the future held. The first time I entered a room and saw my brother hastily fold the newspaper he was reading and shove it behind a chair cushion, I marched over to him and held out my hand with wordless imperative.

"Well," I said after a few moments spent reading, "I rather like *Mad Margo*. What do you think?"

"It fits you," Scotty trying to match my light comment, "but I'm not sure how the public will take to it."

"I'm not worried about the public, just the men in the jury box."

In one of the many meetings Herbert Schmal and I had had during the past week he had mentioned with typical aplomb that he felt relieved it would be only men on the jury. I must have looked indignant at the comment because he said, "I am all in favor of women at the ballot box and in the jury box, Margo, but you will make a better impression on men than women. Not all women would approve of you."

"Not all men approve of me, either."

"True, but you are an attractive young woman and men will like that, whether they approve of you or not."

It was that kind of comment that always made me wonder whether Herbert Schmal thought I was guilty or innocent of the murder of my stepfather. The few times I tried to broach the subject with him he reacted with a shrug.

"The law considers you innocent until proven guilty, Margo, and that's how I view you," an ambiguous statement at best. I could hardly blame him if he thought I had pulled the deadly trigger. The two witnesses at the Hotel Winton, one a middle-aged chambermaid and the other the lift operator of the hotel's elevator, were dogged in their insistence that I was the woman they had seen in the hotel the night of the shooting. I might declare that was impossible a hundred times over, it was naturally difficult to believe my words in the face of such stubborn evidence from two people with nothing to gain from their testimony except inconvenience and enough notoriety that they could lose their jobs because of it. The Hotel Winton was elegant, expensive, and discreet; and there was also the factor that the mother of the accused maintained a financial interest in the property. How the witness-employees found the nerve to come forward was a mystery on its own, but I thought it had a great deal to do with Detective McGuire and his unflagging insistence on my guilt.

My lawyer and his assistants were focused and methodical; my brother was worried but determined not to show it; and my mother—well, my mother was almost cheerful in her confidence of an acquittal. Always an optimistic woman even in the face of the most trying circumstances: the death of a dearly loved husband, for example, and life with a man that abused her—she was even more so in the face of my imminent trial.

"We have used up our full share of heartache," she told me, "and I refuse to allow any more grief in our home. If this comes to trial, and I can hardly believe such a ludicrous accusation will get that far, you will be found innocent. I know it. What jury would believe otherwise? You're Owen Phelps's daughter, Margaret. You'd be hard pressed to find a finer man than your father, and you're more like him than you realize. And look at your service in France. Who will believe that a woman that saved lives would take one? Someone else killed George. He had his share of enemies, after all. Even I recognize that fact."

She hesitated at the mention of her second husband, a man as different from my father as night is from day, and for the first time in our lives I asked, "Why did you marry him?" We stood an arm's length apart, and I saw that the question, which might have startled her in its abruptness, only gave her pause for thought. "Not love, surely," I added.

Mother shook her head slowly. "No, not love. Your father held all the love I would ever need from a man." She searched through her thoughts. "It was for you and Scotty."

"What?!" I found it deeply repugnant that she included me in her reason.

She saw the look on my face and said quickly, "No, that's not the way I meant it, Margaret, don't look so outraged, but try to understand. Your own father was gone and I knew I wasn't strong. My heart was already troubling me. I didn't know how long I had left and I thought, wrongly as it turned out, that

George would have the wealth and influence to pave your way through life if I wasn't with you. I was weak and tired at the time, both physically and spiritually, and I allowed him to make the decision. He was a forceful man, as you well know, and I could not find the energy to resist him. It was a mistake I regretted almost immediately, but what was done was done. I soon realized that I was simply another trophy for his hunting collection, the wife of his rival, the respected Owen Phelps, to be hung on the wall next to his bears and lions and elk," no bitterness in my mother's tone but a surprised sadness, as if the realization still came as a complete shock. She lifted her gaze to my face and said with quiet dignity, "I didn't see him for what he was until it was too late and I am so very sorry. I'm the one to blame for the predicament in which you now find yourself. Can you ever forgive me?"

Would it have helped if we'd have had this conversation years ago, I wondered. Would it have made a difference to the woman I became? Would it have changed anything?

"There's nothing to forgive," I said. "George Tankard's death lies wholly on his own shoulders, regardless of who pulled the trigger, and I have no intention of taking the blame for it. Mr. McGuire can go to hell." Mother, a woman who abhorred profanity, grinned and tucked her hand under my arm to lead me out of the library toward a cooling supper.

"My sentiments exactly, Margaret. He's such a dreadful little man that he'll be right at home there." Her dry tone, as if she were commenting on the amenities of life in Akron, made me laugh. McGuire, having earned the irreverent scorn of Letitia Phelps Tankard, had better be on his guard.

My restlessness grew in proportion to the proximity of the trial date. I would not run away, not this time, but I found life to be suffocating within the confines of our home. Mother did not hesitate to go out and about in public, chin up and wearing a generic, noncommittal smile, but I found the attentions of journalists annoying and the forced charade of acquaintances who acted as if they had not heard a word about any trial tiresome. Often during those days I surprised myself by longing for the action of the Front, for the challenge of keeping the ambulance on the road, for the heady feeling of being part of something that was life and death and really mattered. So it was as if I conjured her up from memory.

"You have a visitor waiting in the front room," Kenyon announced one afternoon, ignoring the fact that I was smoking in the library, ordinarily a mortal sin in the man's catechism.

I crushed out the cigarette in a piece of fine Austrian porcelain, undoubtedly for Kenyon an even greater sin, and stood. "If you let a journalist in, I'll have your head."

"She says she's a friend."

"Ha!" I threw back at him over my shoulder as I exited. "I have no friends and you know it!" Forced seclusion had taken a serious toll on my temper.

But Lucy Rose March waited for me in the front room, as close to a friend as I'd had in many years, certainly since Diana, my partner in adventures of much earlier times, had married and moved away.

Lucy rose when I pushed open the door and we each stood and stared at the other without a word.

Finally, Lucy said, "Hello, Meg," then paused and asked, "Do I still call you *Meg*?"

I laughed and went forward, surprised by my pleasure at the sight of her. "Meg is fine. My brother calls me Margo, my mother Margaret, and the legal system Miss Phelps. Frankly, I answer to almost anything right now. My present situation doesn't allow me to stand on much ceremony. What in the world are you doing here, Lucy?" I stretched out a hand toward her, but she brushed by it and gave me a hug instead.

"I saw a picture of you in the newspaper. You're famous, you know."

"Infamous, more like. Let me ring for something to drink." She raised an eyebrow at the words and I said, "We live in a mansion and we have servants. That's how we get their attention. Is tea all right?" Lucy nodded, sat down, and waited for me to join her.

"So did you come to watch the show?" I asked. "I can get you front row tickets in the courtroom if you like." Lucy Rose March had had a disquieting influence on me from the first moment we met on board the *Ausonia*, had forced me to think about things I didn't want to think about and to say what I didn't want to say. That effect had not changed any more than her reaction to my poking at her seriousness.

"I came to see if there was anything I could do to help." She wore a plain traveling suit with a less than becoming hat that tried valiantly but unsuccessfully to keep her hair in order. The same slim woman of boyish figure, grave, dark eyes, too many freckles for fashion, a smile like sunshine, and a way of caring about people that lit her from within. If she was my friend, I realized I was damned lucky to have her. For all her common appearance, her offer of help was not ridiculous in the least. It could never hurt to have Lucy March on your side.

Kenyon rolled in a tray with refreshments just then and it wasn't until Lucy and I had settled ourselves around tea and cakes and little sandwiches with the crusts removed—another raised eyebrow on Lucy's part at that practice and I couldn't blame her, as if eating a crust would somehow ruin one's teeth or digestion—that I replied to her words.

"I don't know what there is for you to do. I'm accused of a terrible crime and it doesn't look good, so I'd much rather talk about you. I haven't heard from you since Christmas and that wasn't much of a note. What have you been doing? Did you go home to West Virginia?"

She shook her head. "Not really. I spent a little time with my family, but then I took a job at a hospital in Pittsburgh where I've been working these past months." She paused, adding, "I was recently accepted to the Perelman School of Medicine and I start in a few weeks, so I left the hospital a little earlier than I originally planned and came here."

"You'll be *Doctor* March, then, Lucy?"

"Yes."

"You'll be a good doctor. You're more suited for it than most of the male doctors I know."

"Thank you." Another pause, then, "Mac's well. He's healed and healthy and back home in South Dakota."

"Good. You keep in touch, then."

"Of course, I do, Meg. Did you think I kept him alive all the way back to the U.S. just to let him go as soon as we got back home?" The touch of impishness in her tone made me smile.

"Sorry. I didn't think before I asked the question."

She smiled in return and said, "Mac writes faithfully, actually, and we met in Chicago a month ago. Just to catch up. He feels grateful to me."

"He should feel grateful."

"He asks about you often, Meg, and I don't think that's because he feels grateful to you for anything. Or does he?" There was more to the question than the words indicated.

"No. We were good friends in France, but there's certainly no reason for him to be grateful to me for anything. Is he well enough to work?"

"Yes. In fact, he recently took a position with the Prosecutor's Office of Pennington County. The work suits him. Mac has a flair for the law and believes in maintaining an orderly, peaceful society. People say he could be governor some day."

"I'd vote for him."

"Me, too," Lucy said, and we both smiled at the idea. Then, "Meg, I want to help you."

"By doing what?"

"I don't know. By being your friend, maybe. My dad always says you can never have too many friends. You said the situation doesn't look good. Can you tell me about it?"

She had unpinned her hat and handed it along with her overcoat to Kenyon and now sat back in a posture I remembered from earlier days: hands in her lap, eyes fixed on me, head tilted just a bit, giving the impression that every bit of her energy was intent on the words being spoken. It felt suddenly as if someone had opened a door in front of me, freeing me from the deep and strangling isolation I'd experienced ever since my arrest and subsequent confinement at home.

"Yes," I said. "I'd love to tell you about it," and did so in detail. By the time I finished, daylight was replaced by early evening dusk creeping through the windows.

Through all my telling Lucy had not spoken a word, had just listened until I stopped talking. Then her only comment was, "You've given me a lot to think about." She roused herself and stood. "I have to go, Meg."

"Join us for dinner, at least. You can meet my mother and brother. Where are you staying? We have plenty of room here."

I paused. "Of course, staying at the home of an accused murderess isn't everyone's idea of amenable lodgings."

"Thank you. I'd love to stay for dinner and meet your family, but I'm staying at the YWCA and" —she held up a hand to my protest— "that suits me just fine so don't make me regret my visit by arguing about it."

"Far be it from me to tell Dr. March what to do. My mother and brother are probably waiting for us in the dining room now so I'll show you the wash room and give you a chance to do whatever you must while I tell Mother you're joining us." I pulled back when we reached the door to the hall. "You never asked," I said.

"Asked what?" She was puzzled.

"Whether I killed him or not. Whether I'm guilty of the crime as charged."

Lucy Rose March shrugged. "Oh, that. I don't have to ask you about that, Meg. I worked with you long enough to know the answer without needing to ask," and with that assured response, really no more illuminating than my own attorney's words had been, Lucy preceded me out of the room.

Following dinner, we sent Lucy to the YWCA in a cab over the protestations of my mother, who took to Lucy from the start and wanted her to stay with us.

"I like her," Mother told me when I came back to the library after seeing Lucy off, "but I admit that in ordinary times, I would never have expected the two of you to have anything in common."

"I'm not sure we do," I said but thought of Mac Chesney and placed him at the top of a list made up of just the one item. I looked at Mother and smiled slightly. "But Lucy March is, in her own way, a woman to be reckoned with. I have seen her do the most extraordinary things."

"That's something you have in common, then," Scotty said, "because the same could definitely be said about you." He yawned and rose from the chair where he sat. "I'm going to bed."

I was tired, too, tired of doing nothing, tired of waiting, tired of strategy meetings with Herbert Schmal, tired of the same walls every moment of every day. Lucy had been a welcome diversion.

"Miss March mentioned a Mac in passing. Is he her sweetheart?" Mother asked.

"He's a good friend, someone we met in France, an American captain in the Marines."

"Ah. If not her sweetheart, yours then?"

I caught her look of curiosity and smiled. "Mother, dear, you should know by now that I don't have sweethearts. I passed that stage a long time ago."

"Lover, then." She surprised me with her calm. Perhaps she understood more about me than I realized.

"No, neither sweetheart nor lover. Just a man." I remembered sitting across from Mac at a café, remembered the laughter in his voice and the look in his eyes that promised something we never found the time for. I wish I had that memory, too, I thought. With little effort and more time, I might have had an altogether more pleasurable recollection of Mac Chesney. I should have handled him differently, but then I wished that about more people than Mac Chesney so what was the use of thinking about all the might-have-beens in my life?

"She's certainly nothing like Diana." Diana Cummings, my best friend of many years ago.

"No," I agreed. "Diana was a good friend, though. We enjoyed some entertaining times together."

"Until she married, as I recall. Do you ever hear from her?"

"No. I lost track of Diana a few years ago. I think she and her husband moved out of the country."

"Yes, to Argentina. I believe her husband teaches at the national university there. I always thought him a rather exotic match for Diana."

"Oh, I don't know. Diana was not exactly the innocent sweet thing she appeared. That's why we got on so well."

Mother laughed. "Do you think I didn't know that? There was the incident at the lake that scandalized the yachting club."

"Oh, that." I laughed at the memory, too, of Diana and me parading around in our revealing bathing costumes, daring anyone to say a word to us.

"Her poor parents." Mother's memories had shifted; her tone became somber. "I always thought she was never the same after that terrible boating accident."

"She lost everything."

"Whoever would have guessed that her father was at the edge of financial ruin? The Cummings family always appeared so prosperous."

"Looks can be deceiving," I said, remembering ambiguous comments Diana had made at the time that a less self-absorbed friend might have questioned. "Was it an accident, do you think?"

My mother sent me a sharp look. "Of course, it was. Edward Cummings might have taken his own life in a moment of despair, but he would not have endangered his wife, too."

"Maybe you're right."

"There's no maybe about it."

I wondered if Mother was right. Diana had had a streak of her father in her, had been quick-tempered and arrogant as he had been. Whatever the truth, Diana had turned reclusive and had stopped welcoming most of her friends after her parents' deaths. With her attorney's assistance, she had sold her grand home and then without warning had married Carlos Alcorta in a modest ceremony where I was her only attendant. As a visiting professor of the classics at John Carroll University, her new husband was both a foreigner and a Catholic and thus was unknown in our social circles, but he was also intelligent, sophisticated, and darkly handsome. Once I met him, I couldn't fault Diana's selection of a husband. There was something latently passionate about the man which made him very alluring. Like Mac Chesney, who was equally as alluring in his own way, Carlos possessed a depth of emotion I found intriguing.

"I wonder what Diana's doing now," I said.

"She's a mother and lives in Buenos Aires. They had a little boy."

"How in the world would you know that," I stared at my mother, "when I didn't even know where she was?"

"People talk sometimes and I listen. She was your friend, Margaret, one of the few friends you were close to, so if her name was mentioned, my ears picked up." Mother paused. "I heard their son was born with an illness, something in the blood. Too sad."

Try as I might, I could not picture the Diana Cummings I'd known years ago as a tender mother. She had been nearly as wild as I, extravagantly beautiful, willful, and self-centered. Nothing at all like Lucy Rose March and yet I considered both to be my friends. Perhaps it was that Diana had been Margo Phelps's friend and Lucy Meg Pritchard's, and perhaps that said more about me than them. Thinking about the past was not something I chose to do for very long and I stood and stretched.

"Too much introspection for me," I said. "Too much nostalgia. I'm going to bed. What about you?"

"I'll stay up a while yet. I have some letters to write."

"At this hour?" When she did not respond, I went to her and kissed her on the cheek. "You're an awfully good sport," I said.

"For a mother, you mean." Her smile was warm.

"For a mother or anyone."

"Well, thank you. I do try." She wore an expression I couldn't quite read. Not exactly satisfied with herself but close to it, a woman who had finally arrived at a conclusion to an issue that had caused her several sleepless nights. God knew she'd had her share of sleepless nights in her life and I was only adding to their number. Poor woman.

I wished her good night and went upstairs, dressed for bed and then lay awake for a long time thinking about the friends and lovers I'd known in my life and the consequences of actions I'd taken with both, wondering if it were ever possible to make up for the hurt one caused, even if it was done because one was herself hurting and in need of comfort or retribution or both.

"I'm spending way too much time with attorneys," I said aloud and finally fell asleep.

Lucy and I bundled up the next day, a winter day that held the promise of spring in its late morning sunshine, and because I was not in the mood to scurry past the journalists that always managed to find me, we went out the back door to take some exercise in our rear yard. I was glad for the company and had been pleased out of proportion to the event when she stepped through the front door that morning. Lucy had said she would return and I knew her well enough to know that she did not make idle promises, but I held a notoriety that might make an ordinary person hesitate. Not that I ever thought of Lucy Rose March as ordinary.

We passed the kitchen garden, circled and eventually entered the carriage house that had at one time stabled horses but now acted as garage for the Oldsmobile Touring Car my stepfather had owned but which we seldom used. When Tankard died, Mother had dismissed his chauffeur, and Louis, our family driver from earlier times, had moved away years ago.

Lucy took a look at the imposing vehicle and asked, "Do you take it out?"

'I have but not recently."

"Do you miss it sometimes?" I didn't need an explanation; she wasn't asking only about driving but about driving an ambulance and the whole wartime experience.

"Yes, a lot. The energy of it, the unexpectedness of each day, the importance of what we were doing. I miss all that. Do you?"

"Not the way you do. I'm still doing important work at the hospital, and each day holds its own unexpectedness. I'm not like you, Meg. I don't crave adventure and I'm not easily bored. In fact, I find a degree of comfort in routine." I lit a cigarette and offered it to her, but she shook her head. "I gave it up. I don't see how smoking can be good for you."

"Most things that are good for you don't taste or feel good," I pointed out after I inhaled deeply.

"True enough." Lucy's agreement was surprisingly cheerful, "but I'm content to experience adventure vicariously through you." She made me laugh with that.

"I'm glad I can give you that pleasure but don't count on that continuing much longer. I believe that once I make it through this particular adventure I'll have had enough." We were outside again, headed back to the rear door that led into the kitchen.

Lucy started to laugh, a surprisingly deep and robust sound for such a slim person. "Oh, lord, Meg, sometimes you just tickle me!"

"What?" I found not knowing what I'd said to cause that eruption of laughter irritating in the extreme and the abrupt word reflected my annoyance. Lucy caught the exasperation in my tone and swallowed her next laugh before it had a chance to escape.

"You could never have enough adventure in your life, enough drama, enough change, enough excitement. You're all about adventure. Don't you know yourself well enough to realize that? You weren't made for this." She swung one arm out toward the paneled hallway with its chandelier and luxury carpets. "There's something in you that thrives on a dare." She didn't wait for a response. "I'm not going to stay for luncheon but please thank your mother for the invitation. I'll see you tomorrow afternoon. Will you be home?"

"I'm always home, but I think Mr. Schmal and his associates will be here most of the day working on my defense. Such as it is."

Lucy sobered immediately. "Don't you trust your attorney?"

"He's a good man and he's doing the best he can, but we can't seem to get past those two witnesses from the hotel. They refuse to consider that they might be mistaken. I can tell Herbert thinks they'll make a good impression on the jury, and he's worried."

"We'll think of something." Lucy's tone was confident. "You said it was impossible they could have seen you and that's what the jury needs to believe." She had refused my offer of a cab, preferring, she said, the exercise to the nearest corner where she could find a street car. I watched her as she stepped off the porch and down the walk, wishing suddenly that I was going with her, heading off for crowds and stores and sidewalks, but that wouldn't have been wise.

"Stay out of the public eye," Herbert had directed early on, and I knew that any kind of publicity, either good or bad, was forbidden. The public was still too interested in murderous *Mad Margo* and I was just frustrated enough to end up on the front page of all the local newspapers in a melee of fisticuffs. I hoped Lucy wouldn't be harassed by anyone in the press but had enough experience with her to know she could handle herself in a difficult situation with anyone, even a reporter from the most prominent newspaper in the city.

As anticipated, most of the following day was spent going over my testimony and exploring ways to deflect and disprove the prosecutor's allegations. On my better days I was able to sit through those meetings with reasonable patience because I realized what was at stake. For all my disdain of notoriety and enjoyment of novelty, I had no desire to be the first woman sent to the electric chair in the state of Ohio, the first woman executed by the state by any method, as far as I knew.

On days that were not so good, I paced and sulked and acted only a fraction of my age. To Herbert Schmal's credit, he never lost patience with me or my restlessness, but not all the associates in his law practice had his forbearance. I knew I deserved their lowered brows and exasperated glances and I made myself endure them without responding with curses or threats. Audible curses and threats, anyway. By the end of the afternoon, we had all had more than enough of each other and said our good-byes with poorly concealed relief.

When Kenyon said my name from the doorway of the study we used for legal consultations, I thought he was bringing the brandy I'd requested, but he was announcing a visitor instead.

Lucy, I thought with relief, a new face and a new voice, a welcome contrast to the pedantic legal questions I'd had to sit through the past few hours, but it wasn't Lucy waiting for me.

"Hello, Meg," he said and then exactly like Lucy: "Do I still call you *Meg*?"

I remember that moment as the first and only time in my life that I felt happiness actually wash over me. I might have been standing in the ocean on the hottest summer day and had a refreshing wave splash me head to toe, it was that tangible. Mac Chesney had made me feel a lot of emotions, but this was the first time it was an overwhelming wave of pure joy.

"Yes," I said. "Meg is fine." I stopped in the doorway and examined him with undisguised care. Thinner than the first time I'd seen him at the foot of the steps of Dover's Harbour House, and somewhat paler, too, but well, nevertheless, with wind-reddened cheeks and clear eyes. Not quite fully recuperated from that dreadful wound, perhaps, but not far removed from the vigorous, broad-shouldered man I had sat across from at an Arras café and contemplated taking as a lover. Would anything have been different if that had occurred? Not for me, I feared, but definitely for him. It was how the man was made. He would have wanted more than the passionate release of wartime emotions and I would not have been able to give it. Maybe the old cliché of everything turning out for the best had a basis in fact, after all.

I stepped into the room and turned to pull the doors shut behind me, needing time to calm my racing heart and rearrange my expression.

Finally turning back to face Mac, I smiled, went forward, and held out my hand. "You look a thousand times better than the last time I saw you."

"I feel a thousand times better." He took my hand in both of his and the gesture displayed the tip of a puckered scar that disappeared under his shirt collar. He caught my glance and said, "The doctors say I can expect a full recovery. I'm one of the lucky ones."

I felt lucky, too, but didn't say so. Instead, I withdrew my hand from his warm grasp and motioned him to sit as I did the same. Putting more distance between us was a strategic choice on my part.

"I'm glad about that, and I'm glad to see you, Mac, truly, but I have to ask what you're doing here. Aren't you supposed to be starting a new job somewhere out west?"

"I did start but as the resident war hero, when I asked for a couple of weeks off in order to help a friend from the war who was in trouble, I was given carte blanche. 'Take all the time you need,' they said. So here I am."

"Don't tell me I made headlines all the way to South Dakota! You do *have* newspapers in South Dakota, don't you?"

He grinned. "Indeed, we do. You'd be surprised how civilized we South Dakotans are, but no, you didn't make any newspaper I saw."

"Lucy Rose, then."

"Yes, Lucy Rose." I looked for a reaction from him at the mention of her name and was rewarded with a smile that almost made me jealous despite myself because of the affection I saw behind it. "She wired me the news and said she was coming to Cleveland. How could I ignore the challenge?" He sobered. "You're in trouble so, of course, I came."

"You don't owe me anything. It was Lucy that saved your life," I reminded him.

"Mostly," he agreed, "but she didn't drive the ambulance that got me to the hospital."

"Where they couldn't do a thing for you, as I recall. Lucy's the one who made sure you got to Paris for the care you needed."

"You're right. That was definitely Luce. She can be a force of nature when she puts her mind to it." *Luce.* I heard casual intimacy in the nickname.

"She can, can't she?"

After a pause, he said, "What can I do to help? Do you have a good attorney?"

"The best." I eyed him. "And I don't need another prosecutor, thank you. One is more than enough."

"I know how prosecutors think, Meg, and I might be able to offer some insight to your lawyer. What's his name?"

"Herbert Schmal. He's known me forever."

"Good, then he won't have any doubts about your innocence." It was the first time anyone had credited me with being innocent, which was not at all the same thing as not guilty.

"You don't know the facts of the case against me, Mac, not the damning testimony of credible witnesses or the motive I'm said to have or my lack of an alibi."

"Doesn't matter. I know you. I know how dedicated you were to saving lives. I saw how you acted with the wounded and how personally you took it when someone in the back of your ambulance didn't make it alive to the hospital. That was a woman who cherished life, not a woman to take it."

He hadn't known Margo Phelps, I thought, only Meg Pritchard, and they were worlds apart, but his words still touched me.

"Thank you."

After a silence, Mac stood. "I didn't mean to barge in like this, but I couldn't keep myself from stopping to see you first thing."

"Did you take the train here?"

"No. That's my roadster at the curb." He grinned. "And before you ask, yes, we have automobiles in South Dakota, too." His hazel eyes were laughing at me. I hadn't realized how much I had missed his self-deprecating, almost mocking humor, hadn't realized how much I had missed *him*. "Lucy's expecting me," he added.

"Look," I said, "why don't you get her and the both of you come back for dinner? My mother, brother, and I are so sick of each other's company we've been tempted to invite strangers in off the street."

"Lucy and I are a step above strangers, then. That's good to know."

I had to laugh. "I think so but we'll have to wait and see what the other members of my family decide. Do you know how to get to the YWCA?"

He patted the breast pocket of his suit coat. "Right here. Lucy leaves nothing to chance."

"Come back at seven, then."

"Are you sure? I don't want to become an obligation and something else you have to think about when you don't want to."

"I never think about things I don't want to," I retorted, directing him out into the hallway where Kenyon, in his usual perceptive way, had disappeared after hanging Mac's overcoat and hat on the ornate coat tree that stood in the corner of the hallway. "It's my motto in life."

"One of your mottos, maybe."

"I have others?"

Mac took time to put on his coat. Holding his hat he turned back to face me, smiling. "Oh, I think so."

I couldn't help myself. "And they would be—"

"Never show fear and always keep them guessing." He reached for the handle of the front door. "Barring my getting hopelessly lost on the streets of Cleveland, I'll be back with Lucy in tow in a couple of hours."

"If you get to a big body of water with ice at its edges, you've missed the YWCA," I said as I stood in the doorway and watched him depart.

He stopped at the top porch step and turned toward me enough so I could see him touch the brim of his hat with two fingers in a mocking salute and give a slight grin before he continued down the steps toward the dark roadster at the curb. Something by Mitchell Motors, I thought, so nothing luxurious but fashionable enough for a soldier just back from the war and an attorney just starting his career.

"I'm glad I get to meet this Mac that is apparently no one's sweetheart," Mother said when I informed her we needed to set two more places for dinner. "Will I like him?"

"Everyone likes him."

"We'll see," she said, but later, after we'd enjoyed an enjoyable supper, good conversation, unexpected laughter, and Mac's impeccable manners, and after Mac and Lucy had departed taking most of the good mood with them, Mother said with a thoughtful tone, "I can see why everyone likes him." After a pause she added, "But it seemed to me that for Miss March it's passed the liking stage."

"I think she fell for Mac from their first introduction." I relayed the story of their meeting as I'd observed it all those months ago when I was seated with Lucy at an outdoor café and Mac Chesney had appeared out of nowhere, casting a shadow across our little table. "From that moment on, Mac replaced the sun for Lucy," I concluded, "and I'll never scoff at the idea of love at first sight again."

"I've heard it said that in any relationship one person always loves more than the other."

Not quite the non sequitur it sounded, I realized, and nodded. "Maybe that's true here, I don't know, but it seemed to me that tonight Mac acted differently toward Lucy than he did in France. Over there it was as if she were his kid sister, but I didn't get that same impression tonight. Did you?"

"I hardly know either of them, Margaret."

"But still," I persisted, "what did you think about them together, as a couple?"

If my mother was curious about my insistent probing, she didn't let on. "There was nothing lover-like about his attention to her," she said finally.

"True, but I thought they seemed affectionate together and intimate in a way, as if they shared something no one else was privy to."

"And that's agreeable to you?"

I sent her a sharp look. "Of course, it's agreeable. I like Lucy March and I have no designs on Mac Chesney." Scotty, listening, gave a snort and said good-night without additional comment.

My mother met my look with an innocent one of her own and repeated, "But I've heard it said that in any relationship, one person always loves more than the other." My sharp look turned into a glare and she laughed. "He's a very nice young man, Margaret, and I think his idea of offering Herbert his assistance is sound. Herbert's no fool. Maybe he'll ask Mr. Chesney to wear his uniform and sit at the defense table. I think that would make a favorable impression on the jury, don't you?" When I didn't respond, she rose and kissed me lightly on the cheek. "You worry more than you want anyone to know, but you don't need to. After tonight, I feel very encouraged that this whole distasteful business will be behind us very soon, and you will be able to find a measure of happiness."

The placid, hopeful certainty of her tone touched me. I never for a moment doubted that my mother loved my brother and me, but for the first time I could recall her words and tone were raw with the emotion. I only hoped that she was not trying to build a future that included Mac Chesney and me. She was right that he had not acted lover-like toward Lucy, but love or something very close to it had lingered between them, nevertheless, and a tentative awareness of each other that had been lacking in France. I wanted to be happy for Lucy but thought I would have to work on that particular charitable emotion. While I knew I didn't desire Mac Chesney for anything permanent and long-term, it seemed I didn't want anyone else to have him either. It was a good thing I had very few illusions about myself left or I might have felt almost ashamed.

Late the following afternoon, Kenyon summoned me to a meeting with Herbert Schmal and Mac in the library.

"Margo," said Herbert after a perfunctory greeting, "please give Mr. Chesney a dollar."

"Coin or note?"

"Whatever is quicker."

I went out into the hallway to a side table where we kept a wooden box filled with small monies for newspapers and stamps, returned with a paper note, and walked over to Mac. He took it from my hand with a smile.

"I am now officially your attorney," he said.

I looked over at Herbert, who nodded. "Yes. Mr. Chesney just joined your defense in a consulting capacity. Going forward, whatever you tell him in his role as your attorney is privileged information, the same as I."

"With all due respect to Mr. Chesney," I replied, "we're one week away from the trial. Isn't it somewhat late in the day to bring on a man that doesn't know anything about the case?"

"I'm a quick study," Mac looked as near to annoyed as I'd ever seen him, "and Herbert has given me complete access to all his files. I won't disappoint either of you."

Ignoring Mac, I asked Herbert, "What function will Mr. Chesney serve? You know he's a prosecutor by trade."

Still annoyed, Mac didn't wait for Herbert to answer. "I am going to investigate the two witnesses who place you at the hotel."

"I believe they've already been investigated quite extensively."

"Not by someone who spent two years working under Colonel Conger." My expression must have shown that the name meant nothing to me because Mac added, "Our country's chief intelligence officer during the war."

I let the information sink in a moment before saying, "So I was right. That's why you always showed up unexpectedly at places you shouldn't have been long before any other Americans arrived. You were G-2 during the war."

"I was."

I clicked that fact into the puzzle that had been Captain Mac Chesney, a man who more often than not arrived quietly and in solitude and disappeared in similar style. It was gratifying to have validated what I'd often suspected.

"You could have said something."

"No, I couldn't. Secrecy was part of the job."

"I suppose it would have to be."

We both had had secrets, then, I thought. How odd to think that the clear-eyed American with his unpretentious smile and engaging accent that reflected the open, unencumbered plains of the American West should have been a spy!

"I can't quite picture you as a spy," I said.

The words made him grin. "Not a spy, exactly. Just an information gatherer."

"Wearing a Marine uniform."

"I didn't usually wear my uniform when I was on the road, Meg."

"Of course not. Sorry. I can see that wouldn't have been very smart. And now you're going to bring the full force of your experience in military intelligence against two hotel employees adamantly mistaken in their testimony about me."

"Mistaken may be too kind. I'll find that out."

Herbert Schmal had listened to Mac's and my exchange with patience but finally felt compelled to intervene. "That's part of the assistance I believe Mr. Chesney can offer us." He pulled his pocket watch from his vest pocket and gave it a quick glance. "I have another appointment. Margo, good afternoon. Please greet your mother on my behalf. Mr. Chesney, I will see you back at the office this evening."

"Yes, sir," Mac, ever the military man. After Herbert's departure, Mac said, "Come for a ride with me, Meg."

"I don't go out. I risk getting my face on the front page of the newspaper when I do."

"But you'll be with me, and I'm your attorney. All perfectly above board, and it's not like we're doing anything suspicious or notorious like going to a speakeasy for a slug of demon rum."

"More's the pity. A slug of demon rum has a certain appeal at the moment."

Mac grinned and motioned me toward the door. "Grab your hat and coat and come for a ride. You need to get out of this house."

He was right. I hurried up to my room for my coat and hat and said to Kenyon as I passed him on the stairs, "I'm off with Mr. Chesney for some fresh air. I doubt we'll be very long, but please let Mother know and don't wait dinner for me," and then I was out the front door and down the porch steps with Mac right behind me and glorious freedom in the form of a Mitchell Club Roadster just ahead.

I navigated as Mac drove, which was a feat in itself because we had no itinerary and I had no idea where we were going. A few turns on city streets and we were headed west, and without any predetermined plan ended up at the Cleveland Yachting Club. We pulled into an open area in which a few other automobiles were parked, but it was much too early for there to be any great surfeit of people at the club despite the fact that it was one of the largest yachting clubs in the country. Mac turned off the motor and for a moment we were both silent, viewing the club that overlooked Lake Erie. The building was illumined by late afternoon sun and looked splendid. The lake glistened with the warm colors of sunset.

Mac finally spoke. "You probably don't remember that I once told you I had a landlocked childhood."

"I do remember. A landlocked heritage, you called it. You said your familiarity with bodies of water went only as far as full bathtubs on Saturday night."

He turned in the driver's seat to look at me. "You do remember."

"More than you think," I said, "more than you know," and reached for the door. "Let's go for a walk."

We strode toward the lake side-by-side without touching, hands thrust into coat pockets. The wind across the water was sharply cold and stinging enough to bring tears to my eyes, but the late winter, choppy, ice-edged water still seemed beautiful to me, churning gray and blue and frothed with white.

"I love the lake," I said and took a deep breath of the damp air. We stood on a small ridge overlooking the water. "It's so untamed, so out of anyone's control."

"Do you come here often?"

I sent Mac a quick glance. "Yes, but Detective McGuire thinks the idea that I'd take a lake walk on a cold night the height of absurdity."

"More fool McGuire. It's exactly the kind of thing you would do." I smiled over at him.

"Thank you for that, but you have to admit it's not much of an alibi."

Mac shrugged. "We'll get to the bottom of it."

"Those poor witnesses don't know what they're up against. Do you have a plan for confronting them?"

"I always have a plan, Meg. It's how I'm made."

"Everything by the book, you mean?"

"I like order and I like rules, and I value the law because it brings order and rules to a chaotic society so yes, for the most part, I tend to do things by the book."

"The law doesn't favor women, so perhaps that's why I'm not as much of a proponent of it as you."

"Lady Justice is blind for a reason, Meg."

"Yes, so she doesn't have to view the inequities of the society over which she presides." Both Mac and I heard the bitter edge to my words. "Sorry. I just get so damned angry about everything."

"The trial, you mean?"

"More than that. About the way my stepfather was allowed to treat my mother, about how he so badly wanted the money my father left me and how he used the law to try to get it, about his camaraderie with judges and politicians that allowed him to take advantage of us and so many others. The law should have protected the vulnerable but it was no friend to any of us."

Without prompting, we started to walk along the rough path that ran along the ridge toward a set of steps that descended to the lakeshore.

"It's people that were flawed, not the law, but I'm sorry."

"It's not your fault. Maybe South Dakota doesn't breed men like George Tankard so you can't appreciate what a bastard he was."

"Bastards aren't exclusive to Ohio." A pause. "You did hate your stepfather, then?"

"*Hate* is too mild. I loathed and despised him, and I was delighted beyond words when he was dead." I think my words and the feeling behind them startled Mac because he stopped and turned to face me.

"Meg—"

"I won't dissemble with you, Mac. You're my attorney, and I don't have to. George Tankard was a disgusting excuse for a man and whoever killed him did the world a big favor and our family an even bigger one. There. I've shocked you."

Mac put both palms to the side of my face. "No, I'm not shocked, just sorry for what you had to live with. I wish I'd known you then; I wish I could have done something to help you." He ran a thumb over my lips. "I want to help you now, Meg, in any way I can. I'd like to play a small role in making you happy." He leaned very close so that his breath warmed my cheek. "Making you happy is important to me." He kissed me slowly, possessing one lip and then another, moving his hands to my shoulders and running them down my arms until he shifted them to my waist and pulled me to him almost roughly. What started out slow suddenly took fire and we were both caught up in the moment, our mouths and hands searching and hungry, our arms wrapped around each other as tightly as chains, our bodies so close we might, for just that moment, have been only one person. I loved the feel and smell and sound of Mac Chesney, his faint spicy scent, his insistent mouth, the low sound in his throat that balanced somewhere between a growl and a groan, his warm breath that tickled my ear, and I could have stood there wrapped against him for a long time. It was Mac who finally pulled away.

"It's pretty public here. I'm sorry. I know you don't want to draw attention to yourself."

"Right," I said but kept my hands on his arms as he backed up a step. "Still, just this once probably won't hurt."

He backed farther away. "Meg—"

"It's all right, Mac. You didn't step over any lines. I can see you think you did."

"I'm your attorney, for God's sake. That kind of behavior with a client isn't acceptable."

"Consulting attorney," I said, "and it was just a moment in time, a single moment in time, that's all." I gave him a small smile.

"It's almost dark," Mac said. "I'll take you home."

As if we had never touched and kissed, as if our hands had not explored or our breath mingled, we began to walk back to the waiting roadster, hands again thrust into pockets.

Once seated inside, I waited for Mac to start the vehicle and slide into the driver's seat.

"You still look troubled," I said, glancing over at his set expression. "I wish you wouldn't. We're both adults and no harm was done. We shared as much in France, too, and we're neither the worse for it."

"I know, but—" He hesitated, looking for the right words, "this isn't France and it's different now."

"Different? Not that much. Of course, there's no war, but—"

"There's Lucy," Mac said abruptly. He looked at me. The words made my heart stop.

"You mean you and Lucy—?"

Mac shook his head. "No. Yes. Not exactly. Not exactly what you mean, anyway, but I care for her, Meg, and you're her friend."

"Do you love her?"

He puzzled over the words as if he were translating them into another language and then repeated, "Love her," in a thoughtful tone. "She saved my life. She never left my side. She was always there for me, protecting me, holding me, singing to me, praying over me. Little Lucy March turned into someone else right in front of me, someone strong and splendid. There were times I thought she was the most beautiful thing I'd ever seen. I don't know if that's love, but I care for her and"—he repeated the three words that seemed to be the important ones for him—"you're her friend."

For just a moment I felt a hot and unbecoming flicker of jealousy followed by a kind of haughty superiority. I believed I could have Mac Chesney, have him as anything I chose him to be in my life. My belief did not come from any personal conceit or pride but from experience and practice. Men might think they ruled the world, but they were easy to read and Mac's emotions during our time together on the crest overlooking the lake had not been hard to interpret.

Yet when all was said and done, Mac was right. *There's Lucy.* Would I want Mac at Lucy's expense? I put my head back against the seat. Where had this sudden conscience come from? It was totally unlike me; I blamed the pressures of the trial.

"Let's go home," I said. "Can you find your way back or do I need to navigate us to Euclid Avenue?"

"I'm good with directions."

The drive home was quiet, as was our trek up the walk and onto the porch. When I reached for the front door, Mac said my name. I stopped with my hand on the knob but did not look back at him.

"I don't know whether to say thank you or I'm sorry."

"It's not necessary to say anything. Doesn't Herbert expect you back at the office?"

Mac fumbled at his coat sleeve for his wristlet watch and peered at the time in the dim porch light. "Yes."

"Then you'd better go. Do you know the way?" adding, "Of course, you do; you're good with directions. Good night, Mac."

"Good night, Meg," and taking his cue from my cool tone, he didn't say another word, just walked back to the roadster. I stepped into the house and closed the door so quickly I didn't hear the automobile accelerate away.

A sound on the stairs made me look up to see my mother descend from the first landing to the foot of the staircase.

"Good," she said. "You're home in time for dinner. I wondered if you and Mr. Chesney might make a longer night of it, do something fun."

"No. He has a meeting with Herbert this evening."

"Too bad."

"Yes." I shook off the memory of Mac Chesney and started up the stairs. "I'm hungry. Let me freshen up and I'll join you in a minute. Anything good?"

"Pork chops with spiced apples. One of your favorites. Mrs. Litton asked about your favorite foods. She said you deserved to have exactly what you liked."

Exactly what I liked would be Mac Chesney not driving away but I supposed that for the time being I'd have to make do with pork chops and spiced apples, a meager but still tasty consolation.

Somehow the week before the trial passed, each day filled with meetings and legal instructions until I thought I couldn't stand it another moment. But I made myself stand it, made myself listen and nod and answer the same questions again and again. Herbert had initially enlisted the aid of the famous defense attorney Earl Rogers, a lawyer known nationwide for his creativity and fearlessness, to supplement my defense.

"He's lost only three trials over the course of his career," Herbert told my mother and me. "We can't do better," and despite the exorbitant charges we would have had Rogers guiding the defense, but at the last minute Mr. Rogers had to withdraw because of poor health—within three years he would die at a relatively young age because of illness—and Herbert brought on a pair of Cleveland defense attorneys instead. It was an intimidating team even without Earl Rogers, the best Cleveland defense money could buy, but I never felt that any of them had the same measure of confidence in my innocence that Mac Chesney had, who never wavered in his belief that I was wrongly accused and as much a victim as George Tankard.

Mac and I didn't speak about our time together on the ridge overlooking Lake Erie; it might never have happened. He came with Lucy once for dinner at our home in the following days, and our interaction was friendly but bland.

Lucy was a daily visitor, pleasant, cheerful, encouraging, funny, frank, everything a friend should be. In retrospect, I believe I would never have survived the tension and the isolation of that time without her presence. I was used to being on my own but would have found it unbearable without Lucy's company that final week before the trial. Facing not just imprisonment for a very long time but also the threat of death in the electric chair cluttered up my thoughts despite my best intentions not to dwell on the future, and Lucy was the respite and the distraction I needed.

Mac spent hours and hours tracking down the backgrounds of the hotel witnesses, but there was nothing in their histories to suggest why they would lie with such firm impunity. They had seen me, they told Mac, in the hotel the night of the murder and recognized me from other times I'd been there.

"Were you at the hotel often?" Mac asked, raising his eyes from his written report to look at me. We were alone at the time in Herbert's side office going over the statements.

"No, not often."

"But you had been there before?"

"Yes. The Winton has a first-rate restaurant and it was a popular place for charity events and dinner dances."

"Had you ever been in the suite of rooms your stepfather kept there?" I hesitated an infinitesimal moment, but Mac didn't miss the pause. "Meg?"

After a long moment, I said, "My stepfather had majority ownership of the Winton and commandeered its best suite of rooms for his own use. He made no secret of it and Mother, Scotty, and I all knew about it. Supposedly, he used the suite for out-of-town customers and colleagues and anyone he wanted to impress, and he may have used it for that a time or two, I don't really know, but that was never the primary reason he kept those expensive rooms."

Mac set down his pen and asked, "What was the primary reason?" But he already knew. He must have if he'd spent the last days talking to the staff at the hotel.

"George Tankard was a man of coarse appetites. He liked women, especially paid women, and he entertained them there often. If he didn't come home at night, I knew that he had other plans, that he had hired a woman or two for the night."

Mac's expression did not change. "Was that general knowledge?"

"It wasn't a secret among his social peers and he wasn't the only man to do so, if that's what you mean." I met his gaze directly. "Does that shock your South Dakota morals?"

He smiled slightly. "People are people regardless of the state, Meg."

"Men are men, you mean."

He sobered at that. "Yes, I'm afraid that's true, too." Then he added, "And you say you had been in that very suite of rooms?"

"Not exactly in, but almost. One night I made up my mind to confront Tankard. He wasn't home and I assumed he'd be at the Winton. I simply couldn't stand it any more, his unkindness and disrespect toward my mother, the way he expected all of us to conduct ourselves in a way that was unremarkable and yet he could act as immorally as he pleased with people of the lowest standards. The hypocrisy of the man made me furious, and I planned to have it out with him. I can be rather – uninhibited – when I'm angry and I thought it best to approach him at the hotel so I wouldn't have to worry about Mother or Scotty or our servants overhearing the conversation."

"What happened?"

I remembered the night, how prepared I was to do battle, how ready to confront him. "He wasn't there. I went up to the room and knocked. Loudly. I called his name. Loudly. I think I might even have kicked at the door. I tend to do that kind of thing when I'm in a temper, but there wasn't an answer. He'd gone out earlier, the desk clerk told me later when I stomped downstairs." I looked at Mac. "I'm sure the desk clerk recognized me and would remember the occasion. I was in a terrible temper. Perhaps the witnesses have that night confused with the night of the murder."

"Perhaps." Mac made some notes and asked a few more questions until Herbert appeared and took us to another topic.

"I want you to wear something demure," Herbert said.

I repeated the adjective blankly and looked at him. "What do you mean?"

"Something simple, dark-colored, and elegant without being ostentatious. A prim collar would be a nice touch."

"I think we gave all my grandmother's clothes away when she died," I said with acerbity, but neither he nor Mac smiled.

"Simple. Elegant. Dark. Dignified." Herbert said. "Nothing showy. You're a young woman who saved soldiers' lives in the war. You sacrificed your own comfort. You respect life."

I looked at him and then at Mac and finally shrugged. "If that's what it takes."

"That's what it takes, Margo," Herbert said in a firm tone that would not be disputed.

The trial was in its own way a game, I thought, a drama played out in a courtroom with the audience seated in the jury box, and I would play the game because the stakes were so very high.

"All right," I said. "Whatever you say," and was surprised to discover that threats of imprisonment and the electric chair could make me uncharacteristically docile.

## *"~in his eyes The cold stars~"*

# Chapter 12

The attorney assigned to prosecute my case was not Florence Allen but a colleague of hers in the Prosecutor's Office named Aloysius Chaloupka. When one of the attorneys in Herbert's practice expressed regret that Miss Allen was not leading the prosecution because he thought a woman would be less ruthless and forceful than a man on the attack, both Mac and I rounded on the speaker.

"Ridiculous!" I snapped. "Watch a mother defend her child and then tell me a female can't be as merciless and uncompromising as a man."

"Nonsense," said Mac almost simultaneously with my words. He let me finish speaking before he fixed a cool gaze on the speaker. "Our client is innocent of the charge brought against her and we will prove it. We don't need charity from the Prosecutor's office to do so," a noble sentiment, but privately I thought that a little weakness on the prosecution's part wouldn't be entirely unwelcome.

Unfortunately, there was nothing weak or charitable in Mr. Chaloupka or his case against me. He painted me as a spoiled, immoral, and ungrateful young woman, who resented anyone, including George Tankard, that did not give her what she wanted. I had not made it a secret among my set that I loathed the man. I had mocked his pomposity and hinted at his cruelty. I had argued with him at home and been overheard by the house staff. Tankard did not come off well in the witnesses' relating of events, but I came off equally as unattractive. I might sit at the defense table in a high-necked dress and do my best to appear helpless and incapable of enough violence to swat a fly, but that vision could not hold up against the recounting of words I had spoken in fury and hatred. Well, I could not argue with the past or with the fact that I was spoiled. I had been adored by my father, missed him beyond words when he died, and never imagined that anyone would treat me and those I loved any differently than he had treated us. I hadn't imagined that men like George Tankard existed. I think even my mother, for all her years, had been shocked at the man behind the mask, not that she ever voiced a word against him, always glossing over his tempers and his dictates and his violence, always the peacemaker. My nature as a younger woman had been even more intemperate than it currently was, and as the years passed I had hated my stepfather with a passion that consumed me. He had deserved that hatred; my only regret was that I had not been more discreet with my feelings. Everything the prosecution's witnesses reported from the stand was true, but how to explain that the young woman about whom they spoke was not the same woman now seated before them? Maturity had come hard to me, and the war had been a significant part of that maturity; its death and its bombs and the relentless trudge of the homeless and dispossessed had shown me another part of life I hadn't imagined. I had found other equally despicable targets for my fury, had discovered other enemies. So much of my younger years had been wasted on that dreadful man! I felt no shame as I remembered my angry words and pointless threats, only a profound regret that I could not turn back the clock.

Detective McGuire explained his actions and how he had believed I acted in a guilty manner from the beginning. He barely managed to conceal his scorn at the idea that I would take a walk on a February night and he repeated the coincidence of discovering two eyewitnesses to my presence at the hotel at the same time he discovered I had disappeared and no one knew to where. I could not fault the man for doing his job and doing it rather well, but I could fault him for the quality of his voice whenever he said my name. His dislike for me was always close to the surface and his confidence in my guilt was transparent in every word, tone, and expression.

The really damaging witnesses, however, were the chambermaid and the elevator operator, the former a gray-haired woman with the round face of a cherub and the latter a pimply-faced youth who couldn't have been older than eighteen. They were simply unimpeachable, two people common in speech and appearance determined to tell the truth despite the fact that they spoke against the family that owned a portion of the hotel at which they were employed. Their livelihoods might be at risk but they were going to tell the truth come hell or high water. That's certainly the impression they gave and that the jury saw. I glanced at Mac during their testimonies. He stared at them intently, eyes narrowed. I could almost hear his thoughts: *What's their game? What did I miss about them?*

In the end, when all the prosecution's witnesses had come and gone and Chaloupka rested his case with firm voice and satisfied expression, I thought that if I had been on the jury, I wouldn't have had a doubt that I was guilty as sin. Why even bother with the defense?

When I said as much to Lucy that evening after dinner, the two of us seated in front of the library fire, she said with a brisk tone, "Don't feel sorry for yourself, Meg. It's not a becoming quality in you."

She had sat faithfully through all the days of testimony but despite her loyalty, I turned and glared at her. "Thank you for your sympathy. I hadn't pegged you for a Job's comforter."

Lucy's voice had an impatient edge to it. "You don't have the luxury of losing hope or feeling guilty about your youthful follies. The jury will pick up on it. Yes, you hated your stepfather, you shouted at him, you defamed him to your acquaintances, you even threatened to kill him. You did all those things, but so what? I can guarantee that the men on the jury have said things in anger that they didn't mean, too." She paused. "The only real problem we've got are the two people that place you at the hotel that night. They were such perfect witnesses." She gave the word *perfect* a slightly disdainful twist.

"You don't think they were believable?"

"I didn't say that."

"So you do believe them?"

"I didn't say that, either. I said I found them perfect. That's all I said."

I waited for more from Lucy and when no additional words came, I put my head back against the chair, shut my eyes, and said, "Well, I for one find that perfect people are generally boring."

"I agree. Except for you, of course." I didn't have to look at her to hear the laugh in her voice.

I gave a little snort of laughter, too. "I didn't think you fully appreciated the extent of my perfection."

"More than you realize, Meg." After a moment, she added, "Mac believes in you, and he won't let anything happen to you. He'll figure everything out."

I opened my eyes and turned my head toward her. "You think he's perfect, don't you?"

"Good heavens, no. Mac's no more perfect than you or I, but he's very—" she searched for the word "— honorable. He's the most honorable man I know."

"Is that what you love about him?" I had never put her feelings into words before. In response, Lucy Rose March gave me an open smile that was neither shy nor sly.

"I love his heart, Meg, and his sense of fairness, and yes, that sense of honor he carries with him. Well, I love everything about him, I guess, the good and the not so good. That's how love works."

"Is it? I wouldn't know."

Lucy stood and stretched. "Does the offer of a ride to the YWCA still stand?"

I stood, too, went into the hallway, found Kenyon, and asked him to call a ride for Lucy. Kenyon brought her coat and held it for her as she pulled it on, then went to stand by the entryway and watch for the cab.

The hall light illumined Lucy's hair from behind, turning her wild curls into something like a halo, and I had the passing thought that the two hotel witnesses weren't the only ones that seemed perfect.

"Your defense starts tomorrow, Meg, and you've got good people on your side who know what they're doing." At the door Kenyon gave a small cough.

"The ride's here," I said, recognizing the signal.

"I know." She pulled on her gloves and then looked up at me. "Say good-night to your mother for me. She's a remarkable woman, isn't she?"

"Yes."

"Well, the apple doesn't fall far from that tree. Good night."

I stood behind Kenyon and through the partially opened door watched Lucy March's small figure, swaddled in a coat just a bit too large for her, descend the porch steps and the front walk. Just before she ducked into the taxi and the driver closed her door after her, she turned and gave me a quick wave, an innocent gesture that made me think once more that Lucy Rose March possessed a kind of childlike perfection, or if not perfection, at least, goodness. From the beginning, she had been the one who had pursued friendship and I had tried to keep my distance at every opportunity. Now, seeing her go, I felt a curious emptiness and realized how the tables had turned. I would have kept her longer in conversation, would have used her as a defense against the dark night and the dark thoughts that accompanied it, and Lucy was the one choosing to put herself at a distance.

"Good night, Kenyon," I said, after he closed and locked the door.

"Good night, Miss Margo."

He set about his final check of doors and windows and I walked slowly up the stairs. I passed Mother's room, where no light showed under the door, and went to my room. Mother had sat with stoic imperturbability through all the days of testimony, but although I could not see it on her face, I thought doing so must have taken a toll. Earlier in the evening, Scotty had taken off for the billiards room and Mother had wished Lucy and me a very early good night. Lucy was right: my mother was a remarkable woman, hopeful, calm, and ever certain of my acquittal. How did she do that? How could she be so sure? I wished I had her same confidence but since I didn't, I settled for hoping my attorneys would be able to change the impression of me that the prosecution had left with the jury. God knew that would be work enough.

The first thing I noticed when I arrived at Herbert Schmal's office early the next morning was Mac's absence. A small thing on an important day, the day that would see the start of my public legal defense, but I had grown used to Mac always being present at the early pre-trial meeting Herbert held every morning. Scotty chauffeured me to the office at an ungodly hour so I could arrive at the courthouse phalanxed by my attorneys, who kept the journalists at a distance and shielded me from the bright pops of newspaper cameras. Mac always brought up the rear of the group and made sure I made it safely inside the courthouse unaccosted.

"Mr. Chesney sent a note to say he received a message from someone that claimed to have helpful information about the night of the murder," Herbert explained. His expression mirrored my own curiosity.

"What exactly?"

"I don't know exactly," the terse response a rare sign of impatience. "He said he was to meet with the man privately at a park. I don't know any more about it. Now we should talk about how we will present you to the jury."

"I've tried to look as demure and timid as I could."

"I know, Margo." Herbert's tone softened. "It's not your fault that there's nothing demure or timid about you. That's not what I meant. I meant that while it would be useless to try to say that there was any love between you and Tankard, we want to be sure the jury sees that the same could be said of many others. You are just one of several people that had reason to hate him, and we plan to parade those people one by one in front of the jury. We need to plant reasonable doubt of your guilt in their minds, and we will spend the next few days doing exactly that."

"Reasonable doubt might be more probable if it weren't for the chambermaid and the lift operator, wouldn't you say?"

Herbert shook his head at my pessimistic tone. "One step at a time, Margo, and you might add hopeful to your repertoire of expressions. Bemused innocence would help, too." I didn't miss the chiding note in his voice.

"I know. Someone else told me that same thing last night. I'll do my best."

He patted me on the shoulder. "This is hard, I know, but it's not hopeless, and maybe the lead Mr. Chesney is following up will turn out to be what we need to discredit the key witnesses against you."

I thought Herbert's words were just syllables spoken to lift my spirits and did not take them to heart, but I should have because Mac showed up at the noon break with information that would turn the whole case around.

From my point of view the morning went well. The jury had had the opportunity to meet Richard Stanley, a former business partner of my stepfather's who had dealt with George

Tankard on a handshake—always a mistake with my stepfather—and had ended up losing every cent he owned.

Even after two decades, Stanley's resentment was palpable when he spoke about the ruined relationship and his subsequent ruined finances. "Had to sell our home to pay the debts Tankard left me with. My boys couldn't finish college. My wife died from the shame of it. We lost everything to a man that claimed to be my friend." The words might have come off as melodramatic except for their underlying despair and grief. Clearly, Stanley was a man that had never forgotten the injury George Tankard had done him, and even better, the man had no firm alibi for the night of the murder. Hearing him almost made it possible for me to look hopeful and bemusedly innocent.

When we returned to Herbert's offices at noon for a light luncheon, Mac was waiting. He did not look at me and didn't wear even a hint of a smile, but there was something about him, nothing specific that I could identify in his expression or tone but still *something*, that made all of us in the room stare at him.

Still not looking at me, he said to Herbert, "I'd like to talk to you privately," and the two men sequestered themselves in an inner office until it was time to return to the courtroom for the afternoon session. Mac had disappeared again and while I think the afternoon went even better than the morning, detailing as it did George Tankard's carnal relationship with a married woman and offering the jury a jealous husband as suspect, most of the time I sat trying to look shocked at the salacious testimony I was really considering what Mac Chesney had uncovered to give him that odd air of excitement tinged with a vague sense of something almost embarrassing. He had not met my eyes in a direct gaze during his brief earlier visit.

At the end of the day, when I would ordinarily have been chauffeured home, Herbert asked me to join him and Mac at the office. "Mr. Chesney has new information, Margo, a new witness, really, and we should talk about it." He sent everyone away except for Mac and me and pulled three chairs around a low, small table placed in front of his desk. We sat and at first nothing happened. Herbert looked at me, I looked at Mac, and Mac stared down at the open note pad in his lap.

Finally, unable to stand the silence, I said, "It's clear something happened but I'm not going to play *Twenty Questions* to find out what. Just tell me if it's good or bad."

At that Mac raised his head and almost smiled. "Good, I think, Meg. Good for this trial, anyway." He glanced at Herbert, who nodded, and Mac asked, "Do you know a man named Carlos Alcorta?"

Oddly, the first thing that came to mind was that my mother and I had recently discussed that very man. I had not heard his name for literally years and now twice in a few weeks? I heard an inner whisper of warning and said with careful accuracy, "Yes." Both men waited for me to expand on the word and I added, "He married a friend of mine. I've lost touch with them both."

"That friend was Diana Cummings." Mac said. "Was she a good friend?"

"For many years she was my best friend. We did everything together."

"When is the last time you were in touch with her?"

"Oh, years. She moved with her husband to Argentina, his home country."

"So you knew her husband, too?"

"Of course, I knew him. I was an attendant at their wedding, and I was a guest at their home a few times when they were still in Cleveland. Carlos was a guest professor at John Carroll University but that was years ago."

Mac repeated the name once more for emphasis: "Carlos Alcorta."

I was growing tired of the conversation and my feelings showed in my voice. "Yes, Carlos Alcorta. I've had a long day and I'm not in the mood for this, Mac. You're not a prosecutor right now, remember? So tell me what it is you think you know."

He didn't smile this time, only nodded. "Sorry. Two nights ago I received a message from Carlos Alcorta saying he was in Cleveland and that he had information that would help you. *Exonerate* is the word he used in the note. Of course, that got my attention. He's not the first person to offer us information, but he is the first one that didn't ask for anything in return for testimony. We met this morning at a park along the lake." I waited, silent. "Mr. Alcorta lives with his wife and son in Buenos Aires, where he teaches at the national university, but he maintains his relationship with John Carroll and returns to Cleveland periodically as a guest lecturer."

"Is that why he's in Cleveland now?"

"He says so. He says he only recently arrived and read about the trial in the newspaper. He would have spoken sooner, he said, but he was unaware of all that had taken place."

"Spoken sooner about what?"

"About the night your stepfather was killed, Meg, about why two witnesses can place you at the Winton Hotel that same night."

"What did Carlos Alcorta tell you?"

"Perhaps it would be better if you told us."

"No," my tone brusque. "You're telling the story, not me."

With something close to a sigh, Mac closed the notebook that lay on his lap and looked directly at me. "He said you and he were lovers and that he met you early in the evening of February 23, 1917, at the Hotel Winton. He said the two of you spent the entire night together, that you were never out of his sight and you never left the room. He said he knows it's his duty to testify to that fact, even though the two of you had promised you would keep the assignation a secret. However, Mr. Alcorta rightly understands that because of the seriousness of the situation, he has no choice but to speak, even if by doing so he jeopardizes his relationship with the university and with his wife." Nothing admiring in Mac's tone but nothing condemnatory, either, just a lawyer relating a story.

All the time Mac spoke, I was thinking: about my friend Diana Cummings and how the terrible loss of the parents she loved had changed her, about the woman I had once been, about my mother knowing the whereabouts of the Alcortas.

"My motives are my own business, but I'll never admit it's true, not on the stand," I said.

"You'd rather go to prison than admit an indiscretion?" By the incredulous tone of Herbert's voice, I knew he considered my words the height of folly.

"I'll never admit it's true," I repeated.

"You won't have to," Mac said. "Alcorta will swear to it. He says that he probably won't be remembered at the desk that night because it was cold and he was dressed in a dark coat and dark hat and was, of course, anxious not to be recognized."

"His name won't be on the register," I said, "if the register from two years ago even exists."

"It does exist and you know his real name won't be on the register. He told me in advance that he signed in as Gustav Bolshov and there's a scrawl that could possibly be that name in the register for that night. I just came from the hotel and saw it myself."

I didn't speak and finally Herbert said, quite gently, "The information will save your life, Margo."

"And ruin others," I retorted.

"Everyone will survive," Herbert responded. "Mr. Alcorta will give his testimony and return to Buenos Aires. His wife may never find out, if that matters to you."

"You don't think it does?"

Herbert Schmal looked at me a long time before speaking. "I don't know, Margo. I don't know if it did then or if it does now, but we need to put Mr. Alcorta on the stand tomorrow morning. The prosecution will have their chance to pick apart his testimony but from what Mr. Chesney says, there isn't much chance of that."

"Could I stop you from doing so?" I asked.

"Do you really want to?"

I thought about the question, pictured my mother's face, imagined life in prison, remembered how damaged Diana had been when her parents died, and said, "No. I want this to be behind me. I want a future. And right now I want to go home. I'm tired."

Herbert stood and exited the office. I heard the murmur of his voice as he spoke to someone there. Mac and I sat without speaking, without looking at each other.

"There's a car waiting for you outside the front entrance," Herbert said when he returned, "and someone to walk with you downstairs. Go home and talk to your mother. She should know about Mr. Alcorta before she hears his testimony with everyone else in the courtroom tomorrow. Mr. Chesney and I need to talk about the approach we should take. I'm especially glad right now that we have a prosecutor on our side."

I stood and went over to where Herbert waited with my coat. Mac stood, too. I picked up my gloves and bag and shrugged into the sleeves of my coat.

"Well," I said from the doorway, "I guess I should thank you both. What Mr. Alcorta says on the stand will dovetail nicely with everything the prosecution already said about me. No one will be surprised."

But later as I was driven home through the night I mentally rephrased my comment. No one except Mac Chesney would be surprised. His opinion of me must certainly have changed in the past twenty-four hours. Still not guilty, but no longer innocent. He should have known better. I had tried to tell him more than once that I was never the woman he thought, that I was always the kind of woman who would seduce her best friend's husband, but Mac was a man of order and decency and had never been able to see me as I was. He saw what, exactly? Woman of mystery? Rescuer of wounded men? Daring ambulance driver? Now he knew different. Now he saw not the woman he'd created but the woman I really was. I imagine he thought there would be no more surprises for him, not about me, anyway (although that assumption would eventually be proven wrong, too) but a surprise did remain for me. I discovered that I missed the girl I had never been, the girl Mac Chesney had created, missed the woman of mystery and daring ambulance driver. There was no going back, however; Meg Pritchard was gone for good.

Once home, Kenyon opened the door and let me in, took my coat and hat and said, "Your mother is waiting for you in the library."

She had taken to waiting up for me every afternoon in the library before dinner. Sometimes we discussed the day's courtroom proceedings, but most of the time we moved to the commonplace as a respite from the pressures of the trial. That night she looked up from her book when I entered the room, then placed a bookmark between the pages and closed the book with deliberate care.

"You're very late," she said. "What's happened?"

I looked at her. For some reason she seemed shockingly fragile with her skin drawn tightly over the fine bones of her face and her eyes dark and sunken. She was more ill than I realized.

"There's been a development that I think you and I need to talk about," I said, taking a seat across from her and reaching for one of her hands.

"I'm always here for you, Margaret. I hope you know can tell me anything," she said. "There must never be secrets or surprises between us."

She meant the words with all her heart and I knew of all the people in the world, my mother would always be the one who understood me best and loved me most. It was right that there never be secrets or surprises between us.

"Thank you," I said and began to speak. We talked into the night until everything that needed to be said was said and everything that needed to be known was known, a necessary catharsis for us both. When we finally went to bed, we were at peace.

## *"~the heavens of his cheek~"*

# Chapter 13

Carlos Alcorta was called as the first witness for the defense the next morning. Despite the time since I had last seen him, he did not appear to have changed much, if at all. He'd been a sophisticated, slim, dark-eyed, handsome man with thick black hair and he remained the same, emanating an aura of warmth and energy and passion that I recalled from Diana's wedding day. Only a touch of silver just beginning to show at his temples indicated he had aged at all. Carlos never once looked in my direction, not for the entire time he was in the courtroom but always kept his attention firmly fixed on his questioner, whether Herbert or Aloysius Chaloupka, when it was the prosecutor's turn. Carlos might be of Latin blood and temperament but he was never anything but cool and self-possessed when he spoke. I had to admire his nerve.

After he stated his name, his residence, and his profession, Herbert led Carlos through the story that would eventually find its way to the front page headlines of newspapers, all in bold capital letters, and would do lethal damage to my reputation for months to come. The story would be the reason I was set free, however, so read no complaint in my words. Everything has a cost.

"Are you acquainted with Margaret Phelps, who is known as Margo to most of her acquaintances?"

"Yes, sir."

"How do you know her?"

"She is—was—a close friend of my wife's. They were good friends for many years."

"When and where did you first meet Miss Phelps?"

A slight hesitation as Carlos thought. "As far as I recall, Diana, my wife, introduced us at the Cleveland Yachting Club. That was before we were married and just before my wife's parents died in a boating accident. The Club was holding a gala of some kind, I don't recall exactly what, and Miss Phelps was there with an escort."

"What did you think of Miss Phelps?"

"I admired her. I thought she was very beautiful and intelligent. She was exciting to be around, a woman that took risks and wasn't afraid of a dare. I liked that about her."

"No doubt. So you were friends with Miss Phelps and engaged to be married to Diana Cummings, correct?"

"That is correct."

"When were you married?"

"The Sunday after Easter, April 11, 1915."

"And what did you and your wife do then?"

"I finished out the last weeks of my teaching at John Carroll University and we returned to my home in Buenos Aires."

"Did you have any communication with Miss Phelps in those final weeks before you returned to Argentina?"

"My wife had not recovered from the shock of her parents' deaths and she did not welcome any company except Miss Phelps's, so she visited our home on at least two occasions that I recall."

"And did you still find Miss Phelps to be a beautiful and intelligent and exciting woman?"

"Yes."

"Did you develop an intimate relationship with Miss Phelps at that time?"

"No."

"But you and Miss Phelps were eventually intimate, were you not?"

"Yes."

"Just not then?"

"That's correct. Not then."

"Would you please tell us how your relationship with Miss Phelps moved from one of friendship to one of sexual intimacy?"

"In the fall of 1916 I returned to Cleveland following a teaching invitation from the University, and I met Miss Phelps by chance one evening at the theater."

"Did your wife accompany you on this trip?"

"No. She was expecting our first child and was not strong enough to travel. She stayed behind in Buenos Aires."

"So you met Miss Phelps at the theater and renewed your friendship in the fall of 1916."

"Yes."

"When did your friendship become something more than mere friendship?"

Carlos paused for thought again. "We met for dinner once or twice. We attended a lecture together. It was innocent at first. Nothing more. I recall that we often talked about Diana and how much she looked forward to the baby."

"But eventually your friendship became something more, isn't that correct?"

"Yes."

"Eventually you and Miss Phelps enjoyed a physical relationship, also. Isn't that correct?"

"Yes. Eventually. One thing led to another."

"How often did you meet Miss Phelps for carnal relations, Mr. Alcorta?"

"Just one time."

"When and where did that meeting take place?"

"At the Winton Hotel the night of February 23, 1917."

The people seated in the courtroom had been very still during Herbert's questions and very attentive, no doubt wondering where the inquiry was headed, and now the rustle of voices and stir of bodies indicated they understood the importance of the queries and the answers.

Mr. Chaloupka rose from his seat at the prosecution's table as if he had been shot from a cannon, but for all his protests and requests to the judge for a recess, he was told to sit down and be quiet.

"You will have your chance to question the witness, Mr. Chaloupka," the judge told him. "Wait your turn like a gentleman."

Mr. Chaloupka did wait his turn, but not with an attitude that by any stretch of the imagination could be called gentlemanly, and when his turn finally came, he was not able to find a crack in Carlos Alcorta's story, try as he might.

How had I managed to enter the hotel without being seen? Carlos understood that I had entered through a back tradesman's entrance.

Was there a moment that I might have slipped out of the room that night, gone to the suite at the top of the hotel, and murdered George Tankard? Carlos said with prim discretion that he and I had been fully occupied all night, that he was always conscious of my presence, and that we were never out of the other's sight.

Why was his name not on the hotel register for the night of February 23, 1917? Because, Carlos explained, he had registered under another name. "One cannot," he said as if instructing one of his classes, "be too careful under such circumstances."

What alias did he use? When Carlos gave the name Gustav Bolshov, Chaloupka, frustrated, snapped, "Only a blind man would think your surname could possibly be Bolshov." The judge had to give the prosecutor a mild rebuke for the scornful comment.

I risked a glance at the slowly reddening face of Detective McGuire and would have been hard pressed to say whether he or the prosecutor was the more frustrated as they saw the case against me slipping away on the words of an Argentinian adulterer.

Years later, when Aloysius Chaloupka looked back on his career, which was if not stellar certainly competent, I often wondered if he considered my case to be the one he most regretted. If he had dropped the charges against me based on Carlos Alcorta's testimony, he would have retained the opportunity to recharge me at a later date if new evidence arose or old evidence proved false. As it was, however, after Herbert's defense was complete, Mr. Chaloupka charged at Carlos as a bull might charge a red flag, but despite his contempt for the situation in general, for Latin men and for Carlos Alcorta in particular (apparently a true American man was never, never, never unfaithful to his wife; even some members of the jury squirmed when Chaloupka implied that fantasy) Carlos Alcorta remained cool in his demeanor and consistent in his words. Nothing shook him, not even Chaloupka's expressed pity for the poor young wife left at home to darn socks and sew baby buntings while her husband cavorted hundreds of miles away in sumptuous hotel suites with wild women doing what should only have been done with said wife. The judge had to intervene again to chastise Chaloupka for turning his questions into a frustrated and scathing diatribe against not only Carlos's morals but the morals of all South American men, who were undoubtedly led by their passionate natures to be unfaithful to their wives willy-nilly, the inference being that Cleveland's cold climate encouraged men not to stray. The aggravated Chaloupka knew his case against me was dissolving and did not apologize.

The jury neither liked nor approved of me—it was, after all, generally understood that while men might be expected to fornicate pleasurably it was completely unnatural for a woman to do so—but when all the questions and counter questions and summaries were completed and the men eventually trudged out of the courtroom to deliberate, there was never a doubt about what verdict they would bring back. Carlos Alcorta's morals might be questionable but his testimony in words and demeanor was not.

"Not guilty," the jury foreman read aloud, and suddenly the whole circus was over. Herbert smiled at me and squeezed my hand and my mother and Scotty came to stand next to where I sat. I could hear the murmur of voices and the shuffling of feet as the people exited behind me. On to the next nine days' wonder, I thought, and stood.

My mother put her arms around me and pulled me close, saying softly in my ear, "It's time to go home, Margaret. We're done here."

"Yes," I said, reached for my gloves and asked Scotty to go in search of my coat. To Herbert, I said, "Thank you."

He did not seem to have been affected by my iniquitous alibi at all. Did that mean he had always believed me dissipated beyond redemption? It didn't matter. He had been my father's friend and to the best of his ability my mother's champion as long as I could remember.

"You're welcome, Margo, but you owe as much to Mr. Chesney's resolute action on your behalf." He saw me look around for Mac. "He left to take Mr. Alcorta to the train station."

I slipped into my coat and as Herbert adjusted his hat before departing and Scotty disappeared down a side aisle to get the family sedan, I wondered if I would ever see Mac Chesney again. I wouldn't have been surprised if I was sunk beyond reproach in his eyes. Did he think me a loathsome hypocrite for condemning in my stepfather the very behavior that made up my alibi? I had never pretended to be anything other than I was when in Mac's company and yet I had grown somewhat used to the admiration I saw in his eyes, despite knowing all along that the image was a sham and there was little to admire in me. For a while I had even wondered if I could somehow be the woman Mac thought I was, but seeing myself reflected in Carlos Alcorta's words had firmly ended that speculation.

Lucy stood waiting patiently at the rear of the courtroom. "I'm so glad it's over for you," she told me. She had attended every day of the trial and remained resolutely cheerful throughout. That afternoon she flashed me a broad grin after she spoke.

"Let's hope the public has a short memory," I said. "*Mad Margo* was bearable if unflattering but if news of the trial lingers, I dread to think what new name the newspapers will give me."

Lucy shrugged. "What difference does it make? A month from now it will be someone else on the front page. I'm just happy you can put all this behind you." Looking at Lucy's face, I could not doubt her words. She truly looked happy, with a sparkle to her eyes and a flush of emotion on her cheeks. It had taken me a while to learn to take Lucy Rose March at face value and accept that she tended to speak her thoughts without apology. I remembered our walk aboard the deck of the *Ausonia* when Lucy had said with casual accuracy that I wanted to disappear. I had thought her remarkable then and thought the same thing today. There was something remarkable about her, something implacable and staunch and admirable and in its own way frightening, too because those same qualities would make her a formidable foe. The thought made me suddenly wonder if Lucy's happiness had more to do with Mac's probable distaste for my behavior than it did with my release. Well, if that were the truth, I could hardly blame her, and I found a measure of satisfaction in thinking Lucy March was not so saintly, after all.

Mother, standing beside me, reached across to Lucy and took both her hands between her own hands. "Come with us now, Lucy. I've planned a quiet celebration at home and would love to have you join us. What a good friend you've been to Margaret!" The color on Lucy's cheeks deepened at my mother's warm touch and words. She shook her head.

"I told Mac I'd wait for him here."

"Well, then, when he comes, both of you should plan on joining us for dinner."

"I can't speak for Mac," Lucy said quickly.

Smart girl, I thought, because Mac Chesney might have decided he could no longer match my friend-betraying image with his ideal of the all-American girl. The comparison must have been difficult for him at times, but now the fit was impossible. If I ever had been, I doubted I remained in his mind as the kind of girl a man took home to meet his mother and sisters.

"But," Lucy continued, giving lie to the words she'd just spoken, "I'm sure he'd be happy to come."

"Good. We'll look forward to it. We owe both of you a debt of gratitude."

Mother and I went into the courtroom hallway and slipped out a side door to the curb where Scotty waited. None of us spoke on the ride to Euclid Avenue, but as the automobile pulled away, mother reached for my hand and kept it in her warm grasp all the way home.

When all was said and done, only Lucy took advantage of my mother's dinner invitation. "Mac wasn't able to come. He said to tell you how much he appreciated the invitation, but Mr. Schmal wanted to meet with him and since Mac's returning to South Dakota tomorrow, their meeting had to be tonight."

Most of what Lucy related was old news for me because a messenger had delivered a note from Mac earlier:

> *I'm sorry I can't make dinner. Herbert wants to meet this evening to tie up some loose ends, but I'd like to see you. If you're agreeable, I'll show up in the Mitchell tomorrow morning at 11:00. Will you let me take you for a drive? Don't say no, just be waiting at the front door.*

*Please thank your mother for the invitation.*
*Mac*

I acted surprised at Lucy's words to spare her feelings; she didn't appear to know he had sent the same information in a personal note.

Dinner was relaxed, conversation subdued. I felt exhausted in a queer way, my brain unable to hold any thought for an extended period of time, my mouth stumbling over ordinary words. Mother seemed withdrawn; fatigue darkened her eyes. Scotty and Lucy did their best to keep up a reasonable conversation, but eventually even they were silent. I, contemplating the dessert plate in front of me as if I'd never seen chocolate torte before, looked up to find my three dining companions watching me. The sight made me smile.

"I'm sorry. I guess I'm more tired than I thought."

Mother put down her napkin and pushed her chair away from the table. "That makes two of us, and no wonder. I believe I'll go to bed. Forgive me for the early hour. Lucy, will we see you tomorrow?" We had all risen when Mother stood.

Lucy shook her head. "I'm afraid not. My train leaves in the morning."

"You're leaving?" Of course, Lucy March had a home and a plan for the future, and she'd told me she would soon start medical school so why did I feel so surprised? And, truth be told, more than surprised. Disheartened, even dismayed. At her nod, I said quickly, "Well, of course, you're leaving. I wasn't thinking. Sorry, *Doctor* March. But you'll join me for a brandy before you go, won't you? For old times' sake?"

"I'd like that." She turned to my mother. "I enjoyed getting to know you, Mrs. Tankard. You're a remarkable woman, just like your daughter." There was an odd, quiet moment as each met the other's eyes with a gaze that seemed too serious for the occasion, and then my mother smiled.

"Thank you, Lucy, but you're the remarkable one and such a faithful friend! I can't thank you enough for your—" Mother paused to search for a word and finally concluded with, "—understanding." I thought it an odd choice, expecting her to say *support* or *encouragement,* but Lucy nodded in agreement as if she recognized an unspoken message. I hadn't the energy to think further about their exchange and wondered why it even mattered. I was more tired than I imagined and hoped that tomorrow I would be able to think clearly again.

Scotty spoke a charming farewell to Lucy before heading for his room. "I have significant studying to do if I hope to catch up when I head back to school. Tonight would be a good time to get back into the habit of cracking the books," my kind-hearted brother offering Lucy and me the chance to say our own private farewells to each other.

That evening, the last evening I would ever speak with or see Lucy Rose March, she and I sat in the dimly lit library in wing-backed chairs that faced the fire. April was just a spring breeze away, but someone had forgotten to tell Cleveland; the city still shivered. I knew from experience that even the memory of winter had the power to lower the temperature several degrees. A smiling Kenyon set a tray with two crystal snifters and a decanter of brandy between us.

"Good night, Miss Margo, Miss March." We murmured simultaneous good-nights in return and waited for him to pull the library door closed before I reached for the decanter and the glasses.

"Here's to the future," I said, and we reached across the space between us to clink glasses.

"Yes, the future."

The liquor gave a pleasant burn down my throat, relaxing, comforting.

After a moment, Lucy asked, "What will you do now, Meg?"

I did not turn toward her at the question but sat staring at the fire, thinking about my future and how tied it would always be to my past.

"I don't know," I finally said. "I haven't thought that far."

"No, I suppose not. It's one hurdle at a time for you, one moment at a time. I'm the planner."

Something in her voice made me turn my head. Lucy was looking at me with thoughtful gravity. In the golden light of the room she seemed to eye me as if I were a new specimen of human she'd only just discovered, as if I were a stranger. At the moment, she seemed a stranger to me, as well.

"What?" I asked.

She turned quickly to look at the fire. "Nothing."

"Are you surprised at what you heard in court about me, Lucy? Disappointed and disapproving of my lack of morals? Shocked that while a friend of mine sat at home pining for her husband, keeping the home fires lit, knitting baby clothes and— well, I honestly have no idea what domesticated women do with their time all day but you get the picture—her husband and I were enjoying a roll in the hay? Are you going to say that you expected better of me?"

She smiled faintly. "No, I can't say that or that I was surprised by Mr. Alcorta's titillating testimony."

Despite myself, I felt a small pang of something—was it my own disappointment at her frank response?—and said, too quickly, "Well, you're in the minority, then."

"In fact," she went on, "having met your mother and having spent considerable time in her company, I expected something unexpected. That doesn't sound quite right but you know what I mean."

"No, I don't."

"Oh, Meg." Lucy shook her head and I was once more walking beside her on the deck of the *Ausonia* with all my secrets exposed. "The thing is," she said, not looking at me, "I understand why your mother did what she did and I don't blame her, not at all. If I were she, I believe I'd have done the same."

The room seemed to tilt at her words in much the same way the deck of a ship would shift in rough waters and then righted itself once again.

"But, you see," Lucy continued, "Mac would never understand."

"What does Mac have to do with anything?" I was sitting upright again, all my comfortable lethargy gone, clenching the brandy snifter in a too-tight grasp.

"For me, everything. You know that." She gave a deep sigh. "Everything. Sometimes I wish I could change that, but I can't. For me, it's Mac Chesney or nobody at all."

"Well, don't let me get in the way." I heard the flippant chill in my voice, as did Lucy, who grimaced at my tone.

"I'm sorry. I'm not doing this very well."

"Doing what?"

"Begging." My face must have reflected my total lack of comprehension because she said, "I should have come at this differently but I've never been very tactful and I'm used to saying what I think."

"Not much of a bedside manner," I pointed out, "for a physician."

"I know." She breathed in deeply once more and turned herself in her chair so that she faced me. "Mac loves the law and the rules of civilized society. That's what the war was all about for him. Maintaining security and safety. Decency between people. Social integrity. He has real principles, not just words in a law book. He's a wonderful attorney, Meg. People are drawn to him because they see how deeply entrenched his values are, how he won't compromise justice. People trust him to do what's right and in return he trusts them. He can't help it."

"And you think I did compromise justice."

"Yes, at least the justice Mac believes in. I don't know how your mother arranged everything or how she convinced Mr. Alcorta to say what he did, but in the end, to Mac's way of thinking, what happened would be unforgiveable and insurmountable, especially since he was a part of it. The fact that it was all unknowing on his part wouldn't matter." At my continued silence, she added, "He and I talked a lot during his recuperation, shared a lot."

I said, "I'm not sure I'm following any of this, Lucy, but I don't really understand what the point of the conversation is, anyway. I don't have designs on Mac Chesney."

For the first time, I saw uncertainty in her expression. "I know I sound like a know-it-all, someone that expects everything to suit her, and I'm sorry, Meg. I've been thinking about you and Mac a long time, and it's true that I don't know exactly how he feels about you. I know he loves me because he once told me so, and I believed him. Even if there was a lot of gratitude mixed with that love, I don't care. But I know he feels something for you, too, and I'm not sure what that is, if it's love or something else."

"I doubt it's love, Lucy," as if I were an expert on the emotion.

"I can't tell that for sure, Meg. Maybe I just don't want to accept it, but I am sure of one thing and that's that he could never make you happy."

"Lucille Rose March, loyal to a fault, compassionate and brave—a woman of so very many exemplary virtues! And now a prophet, as well! I never would have guessed. What other unexpected sterling qualities have you kept hidden away?"

Even in the dim room, I could see color creep up her face. My mocking words must have stung.

"It's your sterling qualities I'm thinking about."

"Please, Lucy, spare me. I'm not you, a selfless compassionate do-gooder, and after today everyone will know that I don't possess a single sterling quality, not a single one."

Lucy shook her head. "What the common crowd believes about you isn't important. The problem is that the very qualities that made you such a formidable woman at The Front would make life hell for those around you in ordinary times, and on some level people see that. Isn't that what finally happened with your stepfather?" I didn't answer, just kept my eyes fixed on Lucy's face as she talked. "You're impatient and competitive and fearless and scornful of the odds. You can be ruthless when it's called for and you never let sentiment get in the way of action. There's no way you'd ever be satisfied being the wife of a small-town lawyer on the plains of South Dakota. It's not for you. There's something else in your future, something better."

"Prophetic again?"

"Only enough to see that if Mac ever discovers how he was used, whether tomorrow or ten years from now, he'll never forgive you or himself. You need to free him by telling him first before he discovers it on his own. It would be the lesser hurt."

I set my empty glass down on the tray with a noticeable clatter and stood abruptly. "I don't *need* to do anything, Lucy."

She ignored my comment. "You need to free yourself, too, Meg. Cut the strings and leave the past behind. It's all over now. You can do and be anything you want."

"Except Mrs. Mac Chesney if it were up to you."

Lucy placed her glass with unhurried care next to mine before she stood, too. "I know you don't like being told what to do. That's why I said I was begging. Please think about what I said, Meg. Please."

I went to the library door and opened it. "I'm awfully tired, Lucy. Aren't you? Keeping secrets can be so exhausting. I wouldn't be surprised if Mother didn't ask Kenyon to have a ride waiting for you at the curb. You should take advantage of it." Lucy followed me out into the foyer and slowly took her coat from its hook. I opened the front door and said, "Yes, there's a cab waiting for you. It's the kind of thing Mother would do. She thinks you and I are friends."

"Oh, Meg, you and I shared a war. Of course, we're friends!" I heard protest and a kind of anguish in her voice. "Don't you realize that? Your mother does." In the hallway light Lucy looked as tired as I felt.

"We don't see things the same way, Lucy. You and I, I mean. You're a hard woman to have as a friend."

For all the gravity of the evening's conversation, she still laughed out loud at that. "O, lord, Meg, it takes one to know one." She pulled a cloche hat down tightly on her head, trying to crush all her unruly curls under its wool dome. "I admire you and I like you and whatever you think, we are friends." She paused and finally said, "Good night."

I stepped to the side. "Good-bye," I said.

We stood looking at each other for one more moment before Lucy shrugged and said, "Yes, good-bye." She went down the porch steps, descended the walk, and climbed into the automobile, all without a backward glance. The driver closed her door and walked to the other side. I did not bother to watch the vehicle depart but closed the front door and turned toward the staircase. I had never felt more exhausted, even with a dozen consecutive ambulance runs behind me over the most treacherous roads northern France had to offer. My mind was filled to overflowing with everything Lucy had said and everything she had implied. For a moment I had to clutch the banister of the staircase to keep myself from sinking onto the steps. So much done and behind me and yet so much ahead, so much to think about! Mac Chesney would be here in twelve hours and at that particular moment I had no idea what I would say and what I would do when he showed up at the front door.

# *"~the magnificent recession of farewell~"*

# Chapter 14

**A** good night's sleep made all the difference in the world. I was soundly asleep almost before my head hit the pillow despite the intensity of my departing conversation with Lucy, and I awoke alert and clear-headed. No courtroom today, I thought, no stoic reactions, no demure clothes, no being talked about as if I weren't present, no feeling exposed to the curiosity of strangers, no pretense, no trial. No trial. Thank God.

By the time I finally made it downstairs, Scotty had gone out and only Mother sat at the breakfast table.

"Did Lucy say what time her train departed this morning?" she asked.

"No."

My curt tone made her set down her toast and give me a searching look. "Did you have an amicable good-bye?"

"No," I said again and after a moment added, "Lucy Rose March doesn't miss much."

"No." It was my mother's turn at the syllable. "I recognized that right away, but I think she's your friend, no matter what passed between you last night. Did it have something to do with Mac Chesney?"

"Good God," I said, "am I allowed to have any privacy in this house at all?"

"Lucy cares for him a great deal, Margaret." I might as well not have spoken. "She reminded me of myself when I first met your father. Head over heels. Lost to reason." She smiled to herself at the memory.

"Did you know Father was the one from your first meeting?" I recalled the suddenly enrapt expression on Lucy's face the moment she looked up from that café table in Paris and caught her first sight of Mac Chesney. From the start she'd seen more than a handsome man in uniform. I might not understand exactly how that phenomenon worked, but there was no doubt that Lucy had loved Mac from that moment in time to the present.

Mother gave a quiet laugh. "I knew he was the one, but it took him a lot longer to realize he couldn't live without me. He was courting another girl at the time, and he had plans to start his own business, besides. His head was full of everything except me."

I'd never heard that before. "Not love at first sight for him?"

"Oh, my goodness, no, but I never gave up. I always knew somehow that I was what he needed to feel complete and happy. That sounds awfully smug, doesn't it? But sometimes a woman just knows."

"And you were right, weren't you?"

Mother looked at me across the table with a soft expression that took twenty years from her age. For a moment she was lost in the past. "Yes," she said slowly. "From the start we were a well-matched team and I was a patient woman. In time, and not that long of a time really, he came to love me wholeheartedly. He was worth the wait. We were very happy." I watched her return to the present with a little regret still lingering in her eyes. "I'm sorry you and Lucy parted on uncomfortable terms."

"I am, too. Apparently, I'm quite without conscience when it comes to my women friends." I smiled to take away any reproach she might hear in the words, but she flushed slightly, anyway. I pushed away from the table. "I expect Mac this morning."

"Oh? Should I tell Kenyon to add a place for luncheon?"

"No. It won't be a long visit," I said. "Just another good-bye. I'm getting quite practiced at them."

My mother shook her head, the sudden color faded from her cheeks, her eyes shadowed once more. "Oh, that's just begun for you, Margaret. Good-byes are the stuff of life and you should get used to them. You'll see."

By the time Mac's knock sounded on the front door, it had begun to rain, a cool, gray rain from cool, gray clouds with no sign of stopping in the near future. Kenyon shook the water from Mac's coat when he took it.

"Leave it in the hall to dry," I told Kenyon and led Mac into the library where Lucy and I had sat some twelve hours earlier.

"I'm not in the mood for a drive," I said. "Do you mind? Sit down, Mac."

He did so without speaking, not taking his eyes from my face. I remembered how Mac had not looked at me the first time he related Carlos Alcorta's story about being with me the night of the murder and how little he had spoken to me since. His presence told me that he had arrived at some kind of personal acceptance of my behavior, or if not acceptance, at least tolerance.

"How are you, Meg?"

"I'm fine. Relieved, of course. Happy it's over." I pushed on. "I should ask how you are. I imagine Carlos's testimony must have been something of a shock for you."

Mac blinked, not expecting my blunt words, and then recovered enough to say, "I was shocked, but not in the way you think. I couldn't believe that all the while you could account for your whereabouts at the time of the murder and chose not to do so. For a long time I couldn't make sense of it."

"Ah, but you sound like you've come to some kind of understanding now." He gave me the full force of his warm gaze and warmer smile, an attractive man oblivious to his appeal and made all the more attractive because of it.

"Who am I to speculate about your motives?"

"Rhetorical question, I assume."

Mac nodded. "I'm afraid so. I've been considering your motives since the first day we met and not with much success, either, but this—this really threw me. Why would you risk your life when a few words would set you free?"

"Maybe I just didn't want the contempt of society heaped on my shoulders."

"Right, like going to prison for murder is something society finds completely routine and acceptable, and when have you ever cared what other people think, anyway? No, I think it had to do with wanting to protect your friend and maybe to appease whatever guilt you felt for betraying her in the first place."

"Does that sound like me?" I asked, truly curious. What did Mac Chesney think he saw in me? What kind of woman had he created?

"It sounds like Meg Pritchard."

I looked at Mac a long time before I finally said, "But there is no Meg Pritchard, Mac. There never was. The woman you knew in France was always Margo Phelps behind the mask." When he didn't respond, I asked gently, "Why are you here today? Did you come to say good-bye?"

Mac nodded. "Yes, but I wanted you to know that I care about you and I admire you," an echo of Lucy's parting words.

"I don't deserve your admiration, and frankly, I don't want it," my response calm and slightly amused.

"I can't help that. When I look at you, I see a woman who lost her father too young, a strong-willed woman who had to watch her mother being abused and felt helpless to do a thing about it. I don't know who killed your stepfather, and if the killer's ever identified, he should be prosecuted because murder is a terrible offense against a civilized society. But George Tankard's death wasn't your fault or your offense. You were a young woman looking for answers, looking for safety, maybe, I don't know, but whatever it was you were looking for, you thought you found it in Alcorta and he certainly did nothing to convince you otherwise! Why would he? I don't blame you for any of it, Meg."

As he spoke, I heard Lucy's voice: *Mac loves the law and the rules of civilized society. That's what the war was all about for him. Maintaining security and safety. Decency between people. Social integrity. He has real principles, not just words in a law book.* She was right. Lucy March was always right, dammit. Mac Chesney and I were polar regions apart in every way that mattered. Even if we wanted the same thing in the end, we would arrive at that end from two opposing directions using completely contradictory means. Mac would consider me unethical at best and to me Mac's insistence on the rule of law would seem sluggish and ultimately ineffective. He would always want to do the right thing in the right way and I—well, I was willing to do whatever it took to get what I wanted, regardless if anyone but me considered it to be the "right thing."

I realized Mac had stopped speaking and was waiting for me to respond in some way. I didn't love him, not the way Lucy did, but I loved him in my own way and regretted what I was going to do. *The lesser hurt*, Lucy had called it, and time to get it over with, but it was the hardest thing I ever had to do in my life. Harder than running away from home. Harder than sitting in a courtroom hearing myself portrayed as a spoiled, selfish, wanton murderer. Harder by far.

I rose and Mac did the same. We stood an arm's length apart. That close I saw how easy it would be to get lost in his eyes, how alluring it would be to have his arms around me, to be held and loved by a man that would remain faithful even in hard times. It was how he was made. The passion and the security that were inherent in this man were incredibly seductive just then. I would never know what it was like to have Mac Chesney's hands on me in any way that mattered, and I felt the loss.

I stepped closer to him and rested a palm against his cheek. "My dear," I said in a low voice, looking directly into his eyes, "what a fantasy you've created! Of course, I killed George Tankard. I hated the man. I stepped into the room, took the little gun from my purse, and without saying a single word I shot him dead. He deserved to die, and I'd do it again without a moment's hesitation." I said it all gently and with great tenderness.

Mac went completely still, staring at me with such fierce concentration that there was almost a tangible force linking us. I knew the moment he believed my words because he recoiled from my touch, stepped away and put another arm's length between us.

"What do you mean?" Nothing tender in his voice, just a prosecutor that wanted answers. I felt overwhelmed with a kind of piercing pity for him.

"I mean exactly what I said. You don't need details and I wouldn't give them, anyway. I was found not guilty and I know my rights. Our constitution doesn't allow double jeopardy so I can't be tried again, not that I plan to go around crowing about how I escaped the electric chair. I'm no fool. Carlos Alcorta is back in Argentina to stay. I may have to endure society's scorn for a while but that will pass, and I don't give a damn if it doesn't. It's all over now and I'm moving on." Mac was only partially listening as he processed my confession.

"But how—?" he began. I noticed that he never said *I don't believe you,* an omission humbling in its own right.

"Go back home, Mac. There's nothing for you here." I could tell there were a hundred questions trembling on his lips, but he was smart enough to realize I would have no answers for him. I meant it: I really was moving on, but I had yet to figure out to where and what purpose. That would all come in good time.

"I see that," he said. My words might have been a surprise, but one would never have guessed that by his even tone. "You used me. I was a fool, wasn't I?"

"No," I said. I felt an ache inside at his words. Was that love? "You're not a fool. You're a good man with a good, trusting heart. Don't lose that, and don't blame yourself. Nothing was your fault." I went to the library door and held it open, much as I'd done the night before with Lucy. "Good-bye, Mac."

He walked past me, took his hat and coat from the hall hooks and with his coat thrown over one arm opened the front door. The rain had stopped and been replaced by unexpectedly brilliant sunshine, the former gray clouds blown away and replaced by small puffs of white. Mac stopped in the doorway and put on his hat, then turned to me. He almost smiled. Maybe my words hadn't been such a surprise, or a hurt, after all.

"Well," he said. "It looks like spring is finally here." He gave me a small nod and something that might almost have been a smile. "Good-bye, Margo," he said very, very quietly and pulled the door shut after him. *Good-byes are the stuff of life.*

Luncheon was quiet, just Mother and Scotty and I, all of us lost in our own private thoughts until Scotty announced that he would be returning to the university the following week.

"Now that it's all over." He looked at me. "It is all over, right?"

"Yes." Mother and I answered simultaneously and then we both laughed.

"Count on it," I said to my brother and rose to give him a quick kiss on the cheek. "You were a good brother to stand by my side but now I think I hear a skyscraper calling your name."

"Margaret, stay for a moment." My mother sat at the table holding a delicate teacup in hands that seemed equally as delicate. She sent a glance to Scotty.

"I get it. Time for girl talk. That's something I don't miss when I'm at school." Prescient in his own way, he closed the door firmly when he left. I sat down at the table again.

My mother, for a while fascinated by the dregs of tea in her cup, finally looked up and over at me.

"So they're both gone, Lucy and Mac?"

"Yes."

"I liked them."

"Me, too."

"How much do they know, Margaret?"

"With Lucy, almost everything, I'd guess. She didn't believe Carlos's story, said it had something to do with getting to know you. And, of course, she knew me very well and what I was capable of. Lucy March didn't find it at all farfetched to think that I might shoot someone."

"She's very perceptive, that girl. And Mac?"

"I had to tell him that I wasn't the innocent he thought I was."

"I'm sorry. He's a good man."

"Yes."

"But not for you."

"No, not for me."

Mother set her cup down in its saucer and clasped her hands on the table in front of her. "Do you understand why I did what I did?" she asked.

"I think so. You love me."

"Yes, more than you know, but I had to make it right. It was love, but it was duty, too, because it was my fault you were driven to do what you did. I'm so sorry."

"Sorry you kept me out of prison or worse?"

"Of course not, but I do regret that I had to expose you to people's scorn and disapproval in order to do so."

I shrugged. "That will pass." After a moment's thought, I said, "I have to admit, Mother, that I had no idea you could be so Machiavellian. Even now, knowing what I do, I can't quite figure out how you came up with such a plan and managed it so discreetly. "

Her turn to shrug. "I've always known the truth about that night, Margaret. You're my daughter. So when Mr. McGuire showed up with the news that he had eye witnesses to your presence at the Winton, I knew I had to have something in place to protect you if worse came to worse, a reason you'd be at the hotel that everyone would understand, and a rendezvous with a man came to mind. I inherited part ownership in the hotel so my asking to look at the books, including the registration records, wasn't too extraordinary. I noted the names of men registered that night and picked an illegible name from as far away as I could find, a man from Moscow, of all places."

"An alias for Carlos Alcorta to use but still a risk, Moscow or not."

"Yes, but the original desk clerk from that night was long gone and really, everything was a risk. At the time, I didn't know how or if I'd use the name. The details of the plan came later, when I heard that Carlos and Diana's son had been born with a serious illness that needed rare and advanced treatment. Luncheon gossip. I wrote to express my concern and suggested to Carlos that if he returned to Cleveland, he should contact me because I might be able to assist the child in some small way. Carlos arrived post haste. He loves the boy very much." Mother looked over at me. "I understood what a parent would do for a child, and I'm afraid I took advantage of the Alcortas' desperation. The treatment for the child's illness is very expensive, and the Alcortas don't have the money, so I manipulated their situation for our gain." I saw that she was troubled by her decision to offer money in exchange for false testimony.

"No one lost, Mother. The child has a chance at a healthy life and I'm home scot-free. I think everyone got what they deserved, including my stepfather." She said nothing. "You married a man behind a mask," I went on and at the words was suddenly struck by the similarity to me, to Margo Phelps hiding behind the mask of Meg Pritchard. The idea that I shared any similarity with George Tankard was sobering. "I can't say I'm sorry for what I did, but I'm sorry I caused you so much trouble. Can we leave it at that?"

"We both have regrets, don't we? But here you sit in front of me, and Mr. Alcorta is safely back in Argentina, and I understand the child showed improvement after the first medical treatment with a hopeful prognosis. I've done what I can for you and for them, and while I'm not proud of what I did and I think your father would have been horrified by my actions, I'd still do it all again. Can we both put our regrets aside and not talk about the subject again? I for one am done with it." She lifted her tea cup as if raising a toast, and I did the same.

"Yes," I said, "I'm done with it, too. It's time to bid a long overdue farewell to the past and concentrate on the future," and through the years that followed, neither of us reneged on that breakfast agreement.

# *"~In different skies~"*

# Epilogue

Now, decades later, I remember The Great War as the determining factor of my life, the dividing line that separated my past from my future. I didn't consider it so immediately after the trial but felt adrift throughout the summer of 1919, felt lethargic and irresolute. If people talked about me, I didn't know it and wouldn't have cared, anyway. My thoughts turned often to Mac and Lucy, both friends in their own unique ways, and I was pleased to hear from Lucy that she had begun her medical studies. Her letter was brisk but pleasant, filled with the day-to-day routines that filled her student life. At the very end of the letter, she had added with casual importance, *Mac is back in South Dakota. He's invited me to meet his family, but I can't get free until Christmas.* Nothing more than that but I thought it a precursor of happier news to come. Lucy Rose March was a woman who knew what she wanted and was smart and patient enough to wait for it. She and I have corresponded sporadically for the last forty years, but I never heard a word from Mac after he walked out of the front door of the house on Euclid Avenue all those years ago. Lucy was right about him, I know now. A man of such deeply seated, intractable principles would have made an uncomfortable companion for me, and I don't believe it took him long to realize that fact once he left Cleveland. It was Lucy who was right for him all along; she knew it, and so, somewhat later, did I. He was the slow one. From Lucy's letters, Mac is still trying to keep up with her. I wish him luck with that. I wish them both happiness, too, but it sounds—on paper, at least—that they have had that for a long time.

The most surprising event of the months following the trial was my mother's marriage to Herbert Schmal. I may have had other things on my mind in the spring of 1919, but I'm still disappointed with myself that I missed the warmth between them. They were content together for the short time she had left. I owe my mother everything and miss her to this day.

In 1920, I moved to Paris, took an apartment there, and resumed my friendship with Aggie Beechum. With Mother settled and Scotty at school, I was bored and restless in Cleveland, so when Aggie wrote to suggest she had "just the thing" for me, I couldn't resist the lure. There was nothing else on my horizon and frankly, the eighteenth amendment to America's constitution prohibiting the consumption of alcohol generally made life miserable. Why not France, with all that lovely champagne and no one breathing down my neck telling me what I could and could not drink?

I found a measure of satisfaction working with Aggie and the Red Cross to assist the vast number of displaced immigrants that roamed France and Belgium for years following The Great War. The memory of that gray-faced line of lost souls I saw in Paris in 1917 never left me, and it was almost a relief to be able to throw myself into resettlement projects. I discovered I had a knack for bringing order from chaos. That natural talent combined with a scornful disregard for the feelings of the complacently self-righteous and a ruthless energy to get what I wanted at any cost made me an unqualified success at the tasks I took on.

For Scotty's and his family's sakes, I go back now and then to the country of my birth. I have nieces and nephews planted from Chicago to Boston and I enjoy being with them, whichever side of the Atlantic I'm on, but as with most families, I'm happy to visit and happy to leave.

I spent World War Two in London as a refugee myself, survived the Blitz of 1940, helped as much as I could (which wasn't very much) with the Allied war effort, and because I had acquired a little fame from my efforts twenty years earlier, returned to France with authority from Harry Truman himself to take a leadership role on behalf of the United States for the refugee problem that engulfed Europe. Aggie was gone by then, but she was always with me in spirit. To this day, I remember her with a smile whenever I shift my car into reverse.

That second world war brought about the greatest shift in population in the world's recorded history. Between the Nazis' concentration camps and their intention to repopulate Europe according to their own vile master plan, millions of people were left displaced and homeless. When peace was declared, I took the first boat I could find and landed in Calais. Had I possessed a tendency for maudlin nostalgia, I might have recalled landing there almost thirty years before, sharing an apple tart with Mac Chesney, and sleeping against his shoulder on the train all the way to Paris. I remembered it, yes, but it was as if it had happened to someone else, and in a way, I suppose it had—to Meg Pritchard, whatever and whoever she was. She disappeared many years ago and I, Margo Phelps, was the woman who crossed the Channel in 1945 and eventually stepped off the train in Paris, relishing the idea of battling bureaucracy and strategizing ways to bring a million people home. In doing so, I discovered a home of my own, as well.

Sometimes I have a moment—a very brief moment—of contrition for my past, for words said and actions taken that cannot be revoked, for lovers taken, too, and discarded along the way. But the moment quickly passes. Lucy Rose saves lives and heals the sick in South Dakota as she loves her husband and her family and makes a home for them there. I admire that about her, but it's not who I was or am or could have been. I would never have been content there and in the end I might have damaged a lot of hearts, my own—such as it is—included. Somehow Lucy knew that and was wise to plead for a *lesser hurt*. Mac and I both benefited. Over the years, Lucy's foresight has become so clear to me that I'm slightly mystified I didn't see it then.

A lifetime ago Lucy March Chesney faced me in a fire lit library and told me, *There's something else in your future, something better*, and she had been right. Lucy knew how important it was to look forward not back, had understood long before I ever had a glimpse of the idea that if we worked to make a difference in our own individual corners of the world, that simple act of trying might hold the appeal of home and the power to satisfy, at times might even offer an elusive happiness.

I should have believed that woman. When was she ever wrong? Well, to my credit, I had been right in my own way, too, because exactly as I guessed, Lucy Rose had possessed the gift of prophecy all along.

If you enjoyed *Magnificent Farewell*, don't stop here. Karen J. Hasley's books are all available at Amazon.com and in the Kindle Store, and you're sure to find more to enjoy. Her writing has been described as "satisfying" and her research as "flawless"* so there's no way you can go wrong.

**The Laramie Series** by Karen J. Hasley
*Lily's Sister*
*Waiting for Hope*
*Where Home Is*
*Circled Heart*
*Gold Mountain*
*Smiling at Heaven*

**The Penwarrens** by Karen J. Hasley
*Claire, After All*
*Listening to Abby*
*Jubilee Rose*

**Stand-alone novel** by Karen J. Hasley
*The Dangerous Thaw of Etta Capstone*

~ Remarkable Women. Unforgettable Love Stories. ~
All in Historical Settings

*Akron Beacon Journal, 2010

CPSIA information can be obtained
at www.ICGtesting.com
Printed in the USA
BVHW082118160123
656373BV00004B/146

9 781517 796464